D0191207

Acclaim for Ronica Black's Fiction

"*In Too Deep* is more than a story of forbidden romance, dangerous liaisons, and perilous passions. It's…a high speed thrill ride that keeps you guessing from one hair pin turn to another. As soon as you think you know where she's heading, Black gives you another subtle curve to remind you just who's doing the driving." – Gabrielle Goldsby, author of *Wall of Silence* and *Such a Pretty Face*

"Black juggles the assorted elements of her first book with assured pacing and estimable panache…[including]…the relative depth— for genre fiction—of the central characters: Erin, the married-but-separated detective who comes to her lesbian senses; loner Patricia, the policewoman-mentor who finds herself falling for Erin; and sultry club owner Elizabeth, the sexually predatory suspect who discards women like Kleenex…until she meets Erin." – *Q Syndicate*

"*In Too Deep* is…an exciting, page-turning read, full of mystery, sex, and suspense." – *MegaScene*

"Ronica Black's debut novel *In Too Deep* has everything from non-stop action and intriguing well-developed characters to steamy erotic love scenes. From the opening scenes where Black plunges the reader head first into the story to the explosive unexpected ending. *In Too Deep* has what it takes to rise to the top." – *Independent Gay Writer*

"Ronica Black's debut novel, *In Too Deep*, is the outstanding first effort of a gifted writer who has a promising career ahead of her. Black shows extraordinary command in weaving a thoroughly engrossing tale around multi-faceted characters, intricate action and character-driven plots and subplots, sizzling sex that jumps off the page and stimulates libidos effortlessly, amidst brilliant storytelling. A clever mystery writer, Black has the reader guessing until the end." – *Midwest Book Review*

"*Wild Abandon* [is] a sexually-charged romance about two very different and guarded women….intriguing, original…" – *L-Word Literature*

"*Hearts Aflame* takes the reader on a rough and tumble ride…the twists and turns of the plot engage the reader all the way to the satisfying conclusion." – *JustAboutWrite*

By the Author

In Too Deep
Wild Abandon
Hearts Aflame
Deeper

DEEPER

by

Ronica Black

2008

DEEPER

ISBN 10: 1-60282-006-6
ISBN 13: 978-1-60282-006-7

THIS TRADE PAPERBACK ORIGINAL IS PUBLISHED BY
BOLD STROKES BO[...]
NEW YORK, USA

FIRST EDITION: FE[BRUARY 2008]

THIS IS A WORK [...]ON NAME[...], CHARACTERS, [PL]ACES, AND INCIDENTS ARE [...]NATION OR ARE USED FICTITIOUSLY. ANY RESEMBLANCE TO ACTUAL PERSONS, LIVING OR DEAD, BUSINESS ESTABLISHMENTS, EVENTS, OR LOCALES IS ENTIRELY COINCIDENTAL.

THIS BOOK, OR PARTS THEREOF, MAY NOT BE REPRODUCED IN ANY FORM WITHOUT PERMISSION.

CREDITS
EDITORS: JENNIFER KNIGHT AND STACIA SEAMAN
PRODUCTION DESIGN: STACIA SEAMAN
COVER DESIGN BY SHERI (GRAPHICARTIST2020@HOTMAIL.COM)

Acknowledgments

Thanks to my publisher, Bold Strokes Books, for your continued patience, support, and understanding.

Thanks to my editor Jennifer Knight for all your hard work, faith in me, and continued guidance.

Also thanks to editor Stacia Seaman.

Thanks to Cait Cody as always for your never-ending support and understanding.

To my friend D E, thanks for the feedback and your continued friendship.

Thanks to Sheri for another great cover.

My family, all of you, your continued support means the world.

Dedication

For Jay Adams and the many women who share in her pain.

PROLOGUE

Arcane, Alabama

The birdies. She concentrated, clenching her eyes shut and focusing on their sweet summer song.

A flood of hot tears ran down her face. Her cheek hurt. One eye was hard to open. Her shorts and panties clung around her ankles.

The stranger said something, sick pleasure high on his voice. His hand was knotted in her hair. He shoved her face up against the rough bark of the tree with every painful stab. She could feel her flesh tearing, felt a full burning between her legs. Why was he stabbing her there? She wished he'd just kill her. When he laughed she tried to rear back against him. But it only angered him more. He banged her head against the tree. Once, twice, then she lost count.

When she opened her eyes again everything was blurry. The birds sounded far away and distorted. She began to cry. Loudly. "Stop it, please." She tried to move but she was so dizzy she couldn't even raise her head. Her face was against the tree, drool and blood sliding over the earthy-smelling bark. Again she begged, "Stop, stop."

He smacked her upside her head, making her ear ring. She heard him talking to himself. Mumbling words that would get her a slap from her aunt Dayne. She held on to the tree. Clung to it until her nails ached. She thought of Lizzie. She couldn't let the man touch Lizzie. She fought off the looming dark tunnel, determined to keep the man from her sister.

Don't come back, Lizzie, don't come back, she prayed over and over. Her head swam and soon she could no longer feel. All she could do was listen to the birds sing.

"The birdies," she said. "The birdies."

"That's right." The man tugged on her hair and spun her around. "Listen to those birdies."

She swayed and swore there were three of him. She caught sight of the blood on his pecker and wondered why he had stabbed himself too. He gripped her hair again, forcing her down to her knees.

The birdies were watching. She was sure of it. Her aunt Dayne had always told her about angels. Angels watched over you. Angels protected you. The birdies were her angels.

The man smacked her again, this time hard and sharp across her cheek. He held her head upright because she could no longer do it herself. She could smell him, raw onions and something else. Blood and the scent of her own ravaged flesh.

"The birdies will save me," she whispered, feeling sick with dizziness and disgust.

"Those birdies cain't help you. They cain't do anything but watch." He yanked back on her head and looked down at her face. "What was your name? Jay?"

She stared up at him.

He leered. "Well, then…be just like them birdies up there. Be my little Jay bird."

❖

Valle Luna, Arizona
Twenty-two years later

A voice carried to him, deep and distorted, a demon whispering in his ear, a nightmare. His head was heavy and pounded with his pulse. He opened his eyes, but there was only darkness. He blinked. The dark was too dark. He tried to speak but only rough moans managed to escape. His tongue was fat and thick. Breathing was difficult, his throat feeling as if it would collapse upon itself. Panic seized him further, down deep into his burning chest. He concentrated as hard as he could.

"'Ello?" He tried to move but he hurt everywhere, pain shooting from his neck down his arms to his entire body. His panic grew, gripping every nerve.

A slit of light pierced his eyes. He stilled. Blinking, he realized he was blindfolded. He focused on the thin beam in an attempt to make out his surroundings.

He was on his back. A chair stood next to whatever he was lying on, a bed, he assumed. His feet were still clad in his socks, but when he tried to move them the pain shot out from his neck again. It made him gasp for breath, each intake of air jabbing his throat.

He wanted to cry but couldn't. The pain was too great.

A figure approached, darkening the slit of light for a brief instant. He moaned, hoping against hope for help. "He...help me."

Laughter resounded from the stranger, echoing through his head, shattering any and all hope. His sluggish mind searched desperately for where he was and who his captor could be. He remembered the bar, the promise of casual sex over two cocktails. Kisses, hot and heated. He tried to think further but nothing came.

"Money," he managed to say, thinking he must've have been knocked out in order to be robbed. "Take it." He didn't care. He just wanted to be left alone.

His mind churned wickedly over foggy thoughts.

All I wanted was a fuck.

Tuna salad. I had tuna salad for lunch.

The movie.

My role.

Fucking bitch.

Fucking bitch Adams.

The bed gave as the figure sat down next to him. Warm hands began massaging his chest, moving closer and closer to his neck. His shirt was gone. He was cold. He struggled for breath, again panicking. He didn't want the hands on him. Didn't want them anywhere near his painfully sore neck.

"Wha...what do you want?"

The bed squeaked as the stranger leaned in. He felt hot breath against his ear and then a wicked whisper.

"To watch you die."

Chapter One

M usic throbbed, alive and beating, surging its blood throughout the crowd, feeding them. Like vampires, the women were hungry for lust. Hundreds moved under the flashing lights, bodies scantily clothed, slick with sweat, a unison wave of purple, blue, and red. Hands in the air, hands touching neighboring bodies, hands feeling, gripping, owning. There were mouths set in dancing determination, mouths slightly open in enticement, mouths feeding on skin.

Wall to wall.

A carnival of women.

Elizabeth Adams watched the spectacle from the second-story VIP room with a strange detachment. On the raised platforms, her dancers entertained the crowd dressed in vintage carnival outfits. The lion tamer moved fluidly with whip and chair, keeping her animalistic partner at bay. Two sparkling red stars were all that covered her breasts beneath the open, long-tailed jacket. The lion was equally erotic, clad in nothing but brown and gold body paint, her hair standing out wild on her head. She growled at the tamer, showing off the whiskers above her lip. Two other women worked the vaudeville angle in tight black pants, striped long jackets, and painted-on curly mustaches, miming the introductions of various acts. The crowd oohed and cheered as one of them, a fire-eater, first swallowed and then blew pulsing flames. Jugglers positioned at the corners of the bar stood above the crowd throwing up glowing balls while a woman on stilts worked the edges of the room.

"Welcome to the show," Liz whispered, expressing the theme of the evening.

As if the DJ had heard her, the speakers pounded out "Ladies and

Gentlemen" by Saliva. She had to admit, this was her best event yet, another successful Saturday night at La Femme. Yet even though this particular night was special, she still had other things on her mind.

She ran a hand through her hair, noticing a slight tremble in her fingers. Grimacing, she lowered her hand and shoved it down into her black pin-striped pants pocket.

"Hi."

Liz turned and felt her face light up despite the darkness hidden inside. "Hey."

Erin McKenzie fell into her arms. Liz pressed her face into her lover's short dirty blond hair and inhaled, seeking the comfort it often brought.

"You're early," she grumbled, only half disappointed.

"The place looks great." Erin smiled brightly, looking around the club in awe. "Is this why Tyson looked like he swallowed a canary when I walked past him just now? Is this my surprise?"

"It was supposed to be." Liz forced a smile. She wanted to scream at Tyson and the other members of her security. The bouncers at the door should've stopped Erin and notified her immediately. This was supposed to be a surprise party.

Irritated, Liz reached up to check the earpiece she usually wore to communicate with her security. In disbelief, she realized she hadn't put it on. Damn. Where was her head? Nothing seemed to be going right lately.

The fake smile made her face feel like stone. Before it crumbled away, she asked, "Do you like it?"

"I love it." Erin moved in front of Liz to scan the crowd below. "The woman on stilts." She covered her mouth in surprise as her gaze continued on. "Is that cotton candy?"

"Uh-huh." Liz looked with her down at the woman spinning the pink fluff next to the bar. Across the room a woman popped fresh popcorn. They could already smell it.

Erin laughed. "How did you come up with this?"

Liz allowed the laughter to penetrate her anger. Instead of balling her fists, she leaned into Erin, placed her palms on her hips, and nuzzled her neck. Just the feel of her relaxed Liz's mind and set her more at ease. "Remember when we were on our little cruise?"

"Little cruise?" Erin leaned back into her.

"Okay, not so little. Do you remember the night we were on Lesbos and you had a bottle of wine?" Liz licked her ear as she spoke.

Erin stiffened, her arousal obvious. "It's a little fuzzy."

"I bet."

Erin reached back to pinch her legs.

Liz responded by biting her neck. "You were very talkative that evening, as you always are when you've had wine. And I asked what one of your favorite memories was." Liz paused, waiting to see if she'd remember.

"The carnival," Erin whispered. "I used to go every summer with my grandfather." She turned around in Liz's arms. Tears welled up in her eyes. "I…it was never like this…this is wonderful…this is…thank you."

"No need." Liz touched her face. Erin had such an effect on her, one she still couldn't believe. The soft warmth in Erin's eyes began to erode the walls Liz had erected around her heart. When she was able to speak, the words felt like fire, their truth powerful. "Your smile is all I need."

Erin swallowed and compressed her lips, obviously holding in her emotion. She hugged Liz tightly. Liz held her back just as tight, relieved that the night was still a success. Erin was happy. Nothing else mattered.

When they drew apart, Liz peered over Erin's shoulder once again to look down upon the crowd. It felt good to just be in the moment, just feel rather than think. She inhaled Erin's scent, smelled the shampoo and her sweet yet musky perfume. She studied her, always moved by her beauty.

Erin's gaze was on the platform dancers.

Liz whispered into her ear. "They don't look near as good as you do."

Erin blushed and ran her hands down her sleeveless black blouse and worn jeans. "I know how you like me in black."

"Do I ever." When she turned, Liz planted a soft kiss on her lips.

"I see you're dressed for the part," Erin said, looking Liz up and down, appreciating her pin-striped pants, white tank, and suspenders.

"For your birthday, anything."

"Mmm. Thank you." Erin licked Liz's lips as she ran nimble thumbs over her thinly veiled nipples.

Liz wished she could get lost in her completely, to dive so deep she'd never have to surface again. When she trembled, Erin's expression changed. Looking worried, she held Liz's face.

"What is it?"

"Nothing." Liz offered a tired smile. She could've forced a better one, but Erin had relaxed her.

Erin searched her eyes. "Are you still sick?"

"It's just a virus. I'll be fine." It was what she'd been saying every time Erin asked, trying to explain her odd behavior and weight loss. Erin felt her forehead and scowled. "How long do you expect me to believe that?"

Liz grabbed her hands. "For as long as I say it."

Erin looked unimpressed.

"I'm fine," Liz said. "Just a little under the weather."

"Then go to the doctor."

Liz shook her head. "I'm too busy."

"I heard about the fight with Joe."

Liz looked away and set her jaw. Suddenly her mood was far from relaxed. Joe was one of her new actors. She'd fought with him again about changing the script. But she hadn't wanted Erin to know. "I don't want to talk about it."

"You're *too* busy, Liz," Erin said. "You have so much stress. Maybe we should get away for a while? Take that trip we were talking about?"

Liz had been promising to take Erin anywhere she wanted to go for their wedding but time just hadn't permitted. She was busy with the new addition to her movie production company, not to mention the club. And she preferred it that way. If she was busy, she couldn't think.

"Soon, I promise." Liz decided to head off any more talk of worries. "Besides, if I didn't have my nose to the grindstone, I never would've been able to pull this off." She held out her hands at the carnival-like atmosphere. In truth, planning the party had been the one thing, other than Erin herself, that kept her going over the past few weeks, kept her focused.

Around them the DJ's seductive voice echoed throughout the club. "Ladies and ladies, welcome to the show."

The crowd cheered.

"Tonight's a very special night here at La Femme." More applause exploded. "One very special lady is having a birthday." The lights moved around sporadically and then focused on Erin.

"Wave," Liz said into her ear. "This is all for you."

Erin gave a small wave, overcome with the attention. The crowd cheered, many women waving back.

The DJ continued. "Ms. Erin McKenzie, each and every lady here at La Femme wants to wish you a very happy birthday. So without further ado…"

Liz signaled to the VIP bartender. Smiling, she then embraced Erin from behind and covered her eyes. The bartender, dressed as a vintage show girl, rolled an enormous cake toward them. Five tiers sat purposely off center, covered in black and white mosaic frosting and wild-colored ribbons. Thirty tall candles burned brightly, some sparkling like Fourth of July fireworks.

"Are you ready for the best birthday ever?" Liz asked in her ear.

Erin bit her lower lip in anticipation. "I think so."

"You think so?" Liz laughed.

"I'm nervous, Liz. God, there isn't a stripper, is there?"

"Do you want there to be a stripper?"

"What?"

"Because whatever you want, you know I'll…"

"No!"

"You sure?"

"Liz!"

"Okay. You're ready, then?"

Erin nodded.

Liz uncovered her eyes and cued the DJ.

As Erin turned deep red and stared at her giant cake in awe, hundreds of women belted out "Happy Birthday to You."

Erin kept looking around as if it all was a dream. Liz couldn't help but feel moved. Erin's happiness, it was like a drug.

"You better blow out those candles before the sprinklers go off," she said when the song was over.

Erin lifted her hands to her face, as if grounding herself in reality. "Very funny." She stood there, staring at the cake, the flickering light golden against her.

"Make a wish!" someone yelled.

Erin lowered her hands. "They've all come true already." She looked again at the cake and then back up at Liz. "Almost." She closed her eyes and took in a big breath. The candles went out in a whoosh and the crowd cheered. The music kicked up again, as did a few of the sparkling candles.

"What did you wish for?" Liz asked.

"If I tell you, it won't come true."

"But if you don't tell me, how can I make sure it will?" The words scraped her throat in their raw honesty. *Will I always be able to make her wishes come true? More importantly, will I always be able to keep her safe?*

They fell into one another and danced. Around them the club pulsed a life all its own and Liz's mind threatened to turn as dark purple as the strobe lights. She held Erin closer, tighter, and just breathed.

CHAPTER TWO

W e got another one over here!"
Homicide Detective Patricia Henderson turned toward the voice hidden beyond the desert brush. She was busy searching the ground about a hundred yards away, closer to the highway. Cars whizzed past, making it hard to hear who was speaking. She snapped on the latex gloves she'd pulled from her back pocket and wiped the warm sweat from her forehead with her wrist. The dry ground crunched under her boots as she followed a small legion of cops, all of them stepping carefully along the parched earth. The early spring wind blew warm, rustling the long, skeletal hanging trees and brush, the baked scent of the desert on its tail.

There was usually something peaceful about that smell, that it was the combination of just two things: the sun and the earth. That was it, nothing else. No rain, no shade. Just the sun and earth. And usually the smell comforted Patricia, but this wind was different. It had a hint of something ominous.

One of the officers pointed and she caught sight of an older man crouched down behind a palo verde, examining the dirt cautiously with a number two pencil. Patricia recognized him as a longtime employee for the county coroner.

"Bobby, what'd ya find?" She pulled off her shades and squatted close by for a better look. Her partner Gary Jacobs did the same.

"Not something that's gonna make you happy." Bobby, or Robert to those who hadn't known him long, scooted around some teeth with the end of the pencil. Working carefully, he unearthed what appeared to be part of a jawbone.

Gary whistled. Bobby dug farther, moving downward from the jawbone with his gloved fingers. After a short while he hit something and lifted what appeared to be the remains of a tibia and fibula tangled in a dirty patch of denim. There was little doubt that they'd just uncovered more human remains.

"That's enough for now." Bobby met Patricia's eyes. Forensics would need to recover the rest.

"The Corona County Sheriff's going to want this one," Gary said. "We're in their jurisdiction now, and God only knows how many more bodies there are."

Two sheriff's officers were already on scene. It would only be a matter of minutes before news of a second body would bring in half the department.

"Whoever takes it on is going to have to search the entire highway." Patricia added to his train of thought.

They should've done so all along. She'd said so months ago. Frustrated, she replaced her shades as she and Gary walked back toward the highway. She always hated being right under circumstances like these. Two months earlier they'd found a body about a mile south, just within the border of Valle Luna. A month before that the very first body had been found, a half a mile or so farther south. Today they'd been called out to examine a skull a hitchhiker had stumbled upon. Unsure of county boundaries, he'd called Valle Luna police and they'd come despite the jurisdiction issue. If the discovery was linked to their previous two bodies, they needed to find out all they could at the scene.

The skull was intact and nestled closely to the rest of the remains just off the highway. Now, within hours of investigating the skull, they'd located another body, farther out in the desert, perhaps the fourth victim of the same killer.

A chill ran through Patricia. "He's dumping here," she said. "This is his goddamned Green River."

She glanced up as a semi barreled past, blaring its horn. Gary moved closer as several other vehicles surged past.

"We don't know that for sure." He lifted his voice to be heard. "We don't even know if they're all related."

"They are, I'd bet on it." The first two had been strangled in the same fashion, both found soon after death. She didn't need forensics to confirm what she knew in her gut. She glanced back toward the latest discovery. "He started in this area. These remains are older."

The Green River killer followed a body dump pattern like this up in Washington state. The police there, too, had stumbled upon additional bodies when they investigated reports of remains.

"You're getting carried away," Gary warned.

Patricia sighed into the warm desert wind. Her partner knew all too well how her mind worked. That she wrapped up cases before all the evidence was in. A lot of the time, however, she was right.

She stared at the passing vehicles and imagined their killer. He dumped at night when no one could see. He would wait until there was no oncoming traffic or anyone behind him, then pull off the road, turn off his lights, and drag the bodies into the brush. It would take five minutes at most, then he'd climb back in his car and drive off.

She scoured the ground around them. Thousands of tiny shards of discarded glass shimmered in the sunlight as far as the eye could see. Then there were the black jagged strands of stripped rubber lying angry and coiled, like snakes ready to strike. Scattered among those shredded pieces of tire and glass lay small rusted metal pieces of at least a dozen vehicles, along with who knew how many different small pieces of trash and other discarded items.

Patricia frowned, knowing it was unlikely they would find any old undisturbed tire marks. But who knew? Maybe they'd luck out and find a cigarette butt covered in the victim's blood and loaded with the DNA of their killer. She laughed at her fantasy, knowing it wasn't likely, especially with everybody and their mother boning up on forensics courtesy of all the new cop shows on prime-time television.

"Have forensics look for any tire marks," she said and headed back to her Blazer.

She retrieved a hot bottle of water from the case she always kept with her. Going on call after call after dead bodies in the heat could get to a person. She looked to the pale blue sky, knowing soon enough it would be swarming with helicopters searching for more bodies. She closed her eyes, already imagining their loud sputtering sound along with the high-pitched barks of the search dogs.

The shrill of her cell phone disturbed her thoughts. She snapped it up quickly from her belt. "Henderson."

"Yeah, it's Stewart."

"What's up?"

Had he already heard of their new discoveries? Detective Martin Stewart had sided with her weeks ago when she suggested they search the entire strip of highway. But it wasn't his case and she'd been blown off, her request ignored in order to save the department time and money. Not to mention the jurisdiction issue and the permission they would've had to get from Corona County. Politics were a bitch, even when it came to justice.

However, if they could prove the new bodies were connected to the previous ones discovered in Valle Luna, the departments would be forced to work together.

"Get your ass over here," he bellowed.

"What? Why?"

"We got a dead fruitcake."

She flinched at his choice of words. Even though she'd worked with him on other cases, she never got used to his crass behavior. Usually she shot back with words of her own, but she was too focused on the mystery of the highway bodies to get into a shouting match with him.

"I'm not even going to ask what you mean by that." She eyed several more Corona County Sheriff's vehicles approaching along the highway.

"Get over here quick," he rasped.

"I can't, I'm up to my eyeballs with bones on the highway."

There was a pause and she could hear him struggling for breath, characteristic of his asthmatic, way too many smokes a day condition. When he spoke again, static began to break up the call. She pressed the phone tightly to her ear, trying to hear. Around her the uniformed deputies were walking and talking, catching up quickly to their situation. Wind blew her hair across her face.

Pushing the auburn strands aside, she said loudly, "Stewart, I can't leave." She started walking toward the cluster of men, needing to join Gary Jacobs in establishing control. But her snakeskin boots stopped dead as Stewart's final words suddenly came through crystal clear.

"I'm telling ya, Henderson, this one has Adams written all over it."

CHAPTER THREE

Erin McKenzie turned over in the king-sized bed, caught between sleep and wakefulness. She lay still for a moment as her mind stirred to life. Something had woken her. For a brief instant she panicked, unsure of where she was. Waking like this was a recurring nuisance, one she'd struggled with since her parents had sent her away at age thirteen to a facility for juveniles. But as she moved against the impossibly soft sheets and inhaled the cologne of her lover, she relaxed and breathed easy.

She was safe. With Liz.

She lifted her head to read the bedside clock. 7:16 a.m. There was still another half hour before the alarm. Sliding her arm over the warmth of her lover, she snuggled closer. They'd been together for over a year now and she still couldn't get over how wonderful Liz made her feel. She smiled and pressed her lips against the strong, smooth back. As Liz stirred slightly, mumbling in her sleep, Erin tugged her closer and settled deeper into the pillow. Her mind went back to their lovemaking a few hours before. No matter how tired they both were, once they were in bed, they couldn't keep their hands off one another. Liz was always busy with work, but she made sure they still had time for each other.

Her lesbian nightclub, La Femme, was the largest in the country. Women from all over flew into Valle Luna to experience the theme nights with hundreds of other dancing, sweating lesbians. Liz could easily live off the profits from her club, but she was savvy and had invested in the production and development of lesbian-centered films. With more women coming out than ever before, the market for quality lesbian entertainment had grown. Lesbians craved movies about their love and their lifestyle, and Hollywood just wasn't catching up fast enough. So Liz stepped up to the plate herself.

Erotique Studios was thriving, and Liz had recently added a gay line that was already paying off. Somehow she managed to balance it all, running her nightclub and film-production business with professional ease. Erin was proud to be a part of it and glad to help in any way she could. The movies were invaluable to many people, herself included. She could still remember the first one she'd seen when she was a still a cop, studying up on Liz for the undercover investigation that had brought them together. The storyline had moved her in ways she hadn't quite understood then, but the burn of desire was all too familiar to her now.

She stirred inside and nestled closer to Liz. *Happy. Protected. Loved.* She smiled as the words played in her mind.

Desired.

Yes, she had it all. Pure contentment weighed her down and she felt like melting into the sheets. This was happiness. She was just about to fall back to sleep when Liz turned to face her.

"Mmm, morning," Liz whispered, her voice not yet awake. She planted a kiss on Erin's forehead.

"Good morning." Erin heard a beep from somewhere in the distance. "Is that the gate?"

Liz groaned as she arched her back in a stretch. "It's probably Douglas wanting an early start on the yard. I told him not to come this early anymore."

"Should we let him in?"

"No." Liz snuggled down into the sheets. "I'm not ready for leaf blowers."

They lay in silence for a moment, Liz's hand lightly tracing the skin of Erin's abdomen.

"You all right?" Liz asked.

"Yeah." Erin stared at her lover's beautiful face. "I was just thinking."

Liz cracked a smile. "About your birthday?"

Erin flushed, remembering the wild lovemaking that had taken place in Liz's private room at the club. "Well, no," she stammered.

"You mean you already forgot?" Liz pinched her backside.

Erin squirmed. "Of course not. I mean, well, I've never, er... experienced cake like that before."

Liz had stripped her naked, placed her on the bottom tier, then smeared cake from the upper tiers all over her body and proceeded to eat it. The cake had been all over the both of them before long.

Erin felt a pang down deep as she recalled how hungry Liz had been. How hungry they'd both been. For pastry. She thought of Liz easing her back against the collapsed tiers, licking her way down until she rested between Erin's legs, where she couldn't seem to get enough.

Liz laughed as if she'd shared in the memory. She opened her eyes. Erin stared into their blue depths, mesmerized as always by how clear they were first thing in the morning. As if the night cleansed them of worries and clouds of pain.

"And you thought that big ol' cake was for everyone," Liz said softly.

"I did."

"How many times do I have to tell you that it's all about you?"

Erin warmed at the words. "I'm just not used to it. I don't know if I'll ever be." She had never been the center of someone's world before. As much as it thrilled her and touched her, she didn't know if she could ever take it for granted.

Liz's hands ran up and down her body, sending another type of thrill through her. "Turn around."

Erin shuddered. "Why?" But she obeyed, pressing her back up against Liz.

"I'm just trying to get you used to it." Liz breathed in her ear, biting her lobe.

One strong hand glided over Erin's hip to between her legs. She sighed as it slipped between her thighs and stroked her awakening clit.

"Liz," she whispered, covering the hand with her own, loving the way it moved, the way Liz made her feel.

"Yeah?"

"Mmm, think it might be working."

"Good."

The fingers spread knowingly, framing her now-engorged clit, stroking up and down, up and down, sliding easily in her arousal.

"Oh God." Erin clenched her eyes, moving against the hand. Her body was suddenly on fire, her entire being pulsing with Liz. She moaned as another sharp bolt of pleasure shot through her. "I take it you're feeling better, then?" she asked, amazed that Liz always seemed strong and healthy enough for sex, despite her apparent fatigue.

"You tell me," Liz responded.

Erin groaned as the fingers of pleasure stroked her internally, branching out within her body. "You're feeling...much...better."

There were beeps then, one right after the other. She thought it was in her mind, the firework effects of making love...but she was wrong.

❖

"Here we go again," Patricia said to herself as she exited the vehicle and approached the closed security gate. Beyond the rails loomed the large home of Elizabeth Adams, the dark desert mountains guarding it like an overbearing mother. She tugged on the gate and frowned.

Next to her Stewart cursed. "Fucking Fort Knox."

"Maybe you should use the call box," Gary Jacobs said from the passenger window.

Stewart adjusted his waistband. "I've been trying. Trying to give the bitch a nice little wake-up call."

Patricia checked her watch. It was after seven. The dawn light was gray, weak from the struggle of having to break through the darkness. She knew they should wait until at least eight to come knocking without a warrant, but she was in no mood for niceties. They had questions for Adams. Ones that couldn't wait. She crossed in front of the two unmarked police cruisers to the call box, pressed the large red button, and waited. Nothing. She tried again. No response.

"Hold it in and talk," Gary suggested.

"If you know how to work this, then you get out and do it."

She heard a vehicle's passenger door close as she bent over to examine the call box. Following her partner's advice, she held the button in and spoke.

"Elizabeth Adams. This is the Valle Luna Police Department." Static came screeching back.

Straightening, Patricia was surprised to see Detective Jeff

Hernandez next to her instead of Gary Jacobs. He pointed to the mounted security camera located on the wall above them. "It hasn't moved."

"Is it supposed to?"

"If she wanted to get a good look at us, it would." He indicated another camera farther down on the wall that surrounded the property. "That one hasn't moved either."

Stewart coughed and lit a cigarette. He was back to smoking again. It seemed every time he tried to quit he started back up, smoking even more than before. He shook the gate with his meaty hands and then tried to pull the two sections apart.

"Easy there, He-Man," Patricia said. The situation was bad enough. The last thing she wanted to do was give Stewart mouth-to-mouth when he had a heart attack from overexertion.

She approached her car and leaned on the open door. She couldn't believe she was here again. Elizabeth Adams just couldn't seem to stay away from trouble. The woman was dangerous, Patricia had been singing that same song for a long while now. She didn't need a trial and conviction to prove it.

"What makes you think she'll come with us without a warrant?" Gary asked.

Patricia slid inside the car and placed her hands on the steering wheel as he rustled open the morning paper and sipped his coffee. He was forever composed and calm, as patient as a patron saint. This morning his serenity was more annoying than assuring.

"She'll come."

He raised an eyebrow at her. "We're not exactly her favorite people."

Patricia focused in on the house in determination. "All we're going to have to do is say three little words."

"I hope you're right."

Patricia narrowed her eyes. "When it comes to Elizabeth Adams, I usually am."

CHAPTER FOUR

Erin jerked as Liz suddenly stilled. Her flesh was aching, starving. She started to move her hips, needing more, but Liz's breathing had changed. Instead of determined and hurried with desire it was clipped and sharp. Erin focused, her heart and body pounding, as they both sat up.

"What is it?" she asked.

"The alarm."

"What?"

The dogs started barking from beyond the closed bedroom door. Liz stumbled from the bed, turned on the bedside lamp, and slipped on flannel pants and a T-shirt. Bright light pierced Erin's eyes. Blinking, she got to her feet and quickly dressed. Liz examined the illuminated security keypad. Concern furrowed her brow. "Someone's trying to get in the gate."

"Who? Douglas?" Erin hugged herself, battling an anxiety she hadn't felt in over a year and hoped she'd never feel again.

"No, he wouldn't keep trying. He'd just come back later."

"Who else could it be?"

"I don't know, but you stay back, okay?" Liz squeezed Erin's hand, ever the protector. Her eyes were bright and alert.

Erin smiled at her. "I was once a cop, remember?" It seemed like years ago, now, but she'd once been a damn good one, especially on undercover vice.

"How could I forget?"

The beeping continued to echo from the speakers that were wired throughout the house and property. Erin hurried after Liz down the hall beyond the front door and sunken living room, past the kitchen to the opposite wing of the house. They entered the study where the security monitors were kept. Erin heard her curse loudly.

"What? What is it?"

Liz's face was stern and, Erin noticed, still unusually pale. "It's the cops."

"The cops? What could they possibly want?" Erin asked, feeling a bit sick to her stomach.

Liz punched in her code on the nearest keypad and silenced the alarm. Then she typed some more, opening the electric gate. She stalked to the large front door and shooed the two Dobermans.

"Liz?" Erin stepped up next to her, wanting to give and receive some sort of reassurance. But none was forthcoming.

Liz jerked the door open and stared with unmasked hatred as two police cruisers squeezed past the opening gate and screeched to a halt on the circular drive.

A rush of cool morning air pressed against Erin's clothes and blew Liz's dark hair away from her shoulders. The police cars sat in silence with their windshield lights flashing in the early dawn light. Erin trained her gaze on the small group of detectives heading up the walkway.

They all looked eerily the same, as if she'd just seen them the day before. Only these people were no longer her colleagues, and that fact was evident in the way they avoided her stare. The way they were acting, they might as well have been perfect strangers.

"Elizabeth Adams?" Detective Martin Stewart shoved his badge in their faces.

"We've met before, Detective," Liz said.

Erin's cheeks heated as she took in her former colleagues. Their stares were hard and unfriendly, aimed at Liz. The chill from the spring air suddenly seemed nothing in comparison to their intent.

"We would like to take you in for questioning," Detective Patricia Henderson said. Her tone was one of complete indifference.

"Is that why you were once again trying to break open my gate?"

"We didn't break it last time. The electricity was cut," Stewart interjected.

Liz glared at him. "Which I'm sure was your next option this morning. Seeing as how your lame attempts to pull it open failed."

"What's this about?" Erin asked, wondering what Liz had seen on her security monitors. What the hell were they doing here? Just when she'd thought they were finally going to be left alone. "You said yourself, Patricia, that Liz is free and clear of any charges."

Patricia had been there during those final moments when Kristen Reece confessed to all the killings. She'd shot Reece, saving both Liz and Erin.

"There's been another murder," Patricia said, her blue-green eyes fierce.

"What?" Erin said in disbelief.

Stewart thrust forward a photo taken at a crime scene. Erin grabbed it and scanned it quickly. She inhaled sharply at the familiar scene, this one a deceased male, discarded in the desert, his pants yanked down, his genitalia stabbed.

Liz leaned in and examined the photo with her. "This doesn't explain why you're here," she grumbled, scowling. "Get off my property."

"Look closer," Patricia demanded. "Look at his face."

"What?" Anger etched Liz's perfect features.

Erin focused on the dead man's face. Liz pressed against her and Erin felt her body stiffen as recognition settled in. Liz plucked the picture from her hand and stared at it long and hard. When her hand began to tremble, she forced the photo back toward Patricia. Erin squeezed Liz's hand, terror and shock rushing through her.

"Joseph Gillette," Patricia said. "He was working for you, was he not?"

Liz stood taller but Erin could feel her unease. "Yes."

Erin fought back tears. Joe Gillette was an actor Liz had hired for one of her new gay films. He was young and handsome but also cocky and stubborn. Seeing him dead and mutilated hit her down deep, even though she'd seen some dead bodies in her time. Seeing a dead person you knew was a whole different experience.

"We need you to come with us for questioning," Patricia said.

Liz stared at each detective with what Erin recognized as shock and disbelief. Eventually, when no one said a word, Liz looked away and her posture softened but her face remained hard. Erin had only learned to read her lover's subtle body language after months of being intimate with her. To everyone else Liz would seem calm and indifferent, but Erin knew she was hiding her fear.

"When did this occur?" Erin asked.

The detectives exchanged looks. Jeff Hernandez still refused to meet Erin's eyes.

"The body was discovered yesterday," Gary Jacobs said in his matter-of-fact tone.

"Time of death?" Erin shot back.

Stewart grumbled something inaudible.

"The coroner puts the time of death between seven p.m. and two a.m. the night of the fourth," Patricia replied after a brief pause.

Erin's mind raced. "That was Saturday. Liz was with me at the club. And then here at the house."

"You got a way to prove that?" Stewart asked.

"You know we do," Liz let out, smooth and deep.

Erin nearly cringed at the video surveillance her lover was referring to. It had proved Liz's innocence once before but had exposed them as lovers to the entire department.

"Oh, yeah." Stewart's eyebrows rose. "How could I forget?"

Liz took an angry step forward, but Erin gripped her wrist.

"Good, because we'll need to check," Patricia snapped. "Now in the meantime, get changed, we're taking you in for questioning."

"You have a warrant?" Erin asked.

"It's processing."

"Then she's not going anywhere."

"Witnesses say you fought with Gillette on Friday." Jacobs stared at Liz as if he expected an instant confession.

Liz didn't respond but Erin could see the skin darkening at the base of her neck.

"In fact," he pressed her, "we've heard you two fought a lot. Did those fights ever turn physical?"

"You son of a bitch," Liz seethed, ready to attack. When Erin pulled her back again, Patricia spoke.

"Jameson Marie Adams."

Both women tore their gaze from Jacobs to Patricia. Erin felt a shudder pass through Liz's body.

"What about her?" Liz asked.

"I thought she didn't exist?" Patricia taunted with venom. "Well, it seems she does indeed exist, even if Arcane, Alabama, has no legal record of her. I saw her with my own two eyes as well, of course." She paused a moment, seemingly for effect. "She was named after your grandfather, wasn't she?"

"Just tell me what you want, Detective."

"Come downtown, Ms. Adams," Patricia said. She turned away from them, unwilling to discuss it further, and headed back to the vehicles. After long, questioning stares aimed at both Erin and Liz, the other detectives walked after her.

Erin watched them in silence and closed the door. "You don't have to go."

"No, I don't. I can go out there and tell them to fuck off, to get off my property, even bang up their cars a little. But we both know they'll just come back in a few hours with a warrant. We've been through this before."

"But Jay didn't do this," Erin stammered.

Jay, Liz's sister, had been on the run for months. She couldn't have done it. Liz had sworn that Jay didn't kill, couldn't kill. Erin had to have faith in that. It was the only way she slept at night.

Liz stared down at Erin's fingers, still locked around her wrist. Her face was drawn. "Obviously they think she did, or she might know who did."

"But she's gone, right? I mean if she's gone and you don't know where she is…what would they want with you?" *Oh, God. No, please. Not again.*

"You saw the photo, Erin. I have to go."

Erin knew how much Liz loved Jay and how she'd protected her in the past.

"You don't know where she is, do you?"

"No." Liz detached herself from Erin's grasp. She turned and headed down the hallway.

As Erin watched her walk away, she hoped with all she had that Liz was telling the truth.

CHAPTER FIVE

Even though it was different than the one she'd been in before, the stifling interrogation room looked exactly the same, even smelled exactly the same. Like coffee that was way too strong and stale cigarettes. She hated both. The carpet was worn and charcoal gray, the walls a faded yellow-white, as if a thick layer of criminal filth covered it all.

The door opened and Liz released a long-held breath as her attorney, Cynthia Carmichael, eased into the room. Her arrival felt like a rush of fresh air. Impeccably groomed and levelheaded as always, she pulled out the ancient chair and sat down across from Liz. "Nice room," she said wickedly.

Liz sighed. The room was small, and there was no two-way mirror, ensuring their privacy.

Cynthia drummed her red nails on the table. She looked gorgeous in a dark gray skirt and jacket, red silk blouse underneath. "Sorry I'm late, but I had a facial at eleven."

Liz laughed softly, knowing she was only half kidding. "You're such a princess."

"That's right, but this princess takes shit from nobody." Cynthia smiled. "So what's new?"

"Not a damn thing. These cops are on my ass again."

Cynthia studied her through well-made-up eyes. "They gave me the rundown. They don't have anything in accordance to you. Erin gave me the tapes from the club and house and they confirmed your alibi." She paused and stopped drumming her nails. "You two have quite the sex life."

Liz stiffened.

"Don't worry, I only gave them what they needed and I only saw enough to make me want to head straight to the bakery."

"Thank you."

"I'm sorry, did you say something?"

"Don't push it, Carmichael."

Cynthia patted her hand. "Let's go. You've been here long enough."

"I don't think they're finished with me yet."

Cynthia raised an eyebrow. "Since when does that matter?"

"I can handle them." Liz knew these cops just as well as they knew her. Speaking with them didn't frighten her. She'd always been able to hold her own.

Cynthia sighed in obvious frustration. "Why the hell is it you pay me, Adams?"

Liz smiled. "To handle things when I can't."

"Jesus Christ."

"You didn't have to come down here." Liz had called her before she left for the police station as a formality and at Erin's insistence.

"I'm your lawyer. You call, I come."

"I can handle them. Just like I did last time."

Cynthia stared as if she were completely baffled by her. "They kept you for hours on end last time. Why in the hell you let them do that is still beyond me. You should've let me handle it."

"I was fine."

"You call getting yourself charged with murder fine?"

"I was innocent." She'd been at Patricia Henderson's that night a year ago, but she wasn't the killer the police were looking for.

"What about now, Adams? Do you know where Jay is?" Cynthia leaned back and folded her arms across her chest. "Because if you really don't, then you'd tell the cops to piss off and leave." She narrowed her eyes. "But if you do know where she is, you might play dumb just long enough to find out how much they know. Which I suspect was what you were doing the last time you were questioned."

Liz returned her stare. "You've got one hell of an imagination." Cynthia was the best there was and she was continuing to prove it.

"That I do." Cynthia pressed her dark red lips together. "You ever hear of attorney-client privilege?" She didn't wait for an answer. "You can talk to me, you know."

"I know."

"Then how 'bout it? Why not let me earn those big bucks you pay me?"

"I don't know where she is."

Cynthia again raised an eyebrow, waiting for Liz to continue.

Liz took a deep breath. "They know too much. Things I thought no one could ever find out."

"They've been investigating her for a while. You know that."

"I'm afraid for her. If she gets caught, she'll get hurt. She won't understand. She'll never make it in a prison. All she's ever tried to do is protect me. Why can't people see that?" Liz closed her eyes, more afraid of facing her emotions than she was of exposing them to Cynthia.

"Justice is blind," Cynthia whispered. "Literally and all the way around. All law enforcement sees is what she's been involved in. They don't care why." She patted Liz's hand again. "That's the way it works."

Liz opened her eyes and stared so hard into the wall she almost thought she could bore right through it. Then, her voice on edge, she said, "Let's go."

They stood and Cynthia smoothed down her skirt. Liz held the door for her. As they exited, Patricia and her superior, a short man in glasses, stood waiting.

Cynthia offered a practiced smile. "I think we're done here. My client has generously volunteered her time to answer your questions. Now she wishes to return home."

Patricia pinned Liz with a hard look while her sergeant stormed away. "Sooner or later, we'll find her," she said, her voice low but controlled.

"With this force, I'll bet on later," Liz responded, just as cold.

Cynthia cleared her throat. "Have a nice day, Detective." She linked her arm with Liz's and escorted her out of the building.

Liz squeezed her fists, still fuming over Patricia's remark, over the whole damn thing. Her heart sped up as she thought back to the graphic crime scene photos they'd shoved in her face. She forced them from her mind and squinted in the daylight.

Ahead of them, parked at the curb, Cynthia's silver Mercedes shimmered in the sun. Cynthia rested a hand on the roof and slipped on her shades.

"You know where she is, don't you?"

Liz looked beyond her to the busy street.

Cynthia took her silence as a yes. "When's the last time you heard from her?"

Liz didn't respond.

"Do you think she's involved?"

Liz brought her fierce gaze back to her longtime attorney. "Absolutely not."

"What makes you so sure?"

"Because I know her. I know her better than anyone."

"You thought you knew last time too."

Liz felt her skin heat. "She didn't kill anyone."

Cynthia opened the driver's side door. "If you're so sure, then you better get in contact with her." She slid inside and started the engine. "And, Adams?"

Liz raised an eyebrow.

"Watch your back. I don't like this. I don't like this one bit."

Liz pushed the door closed and stood staring as Cynthia drove away. As she headed back to her Range Rover, she thought of the two people that meant the most to her in this world. Erin and Jay.

How long could she protect them?

❖

Erin was pacing the length of the hallway when she heard the keys in the front door. Liz eased in, looking pale and exhausted.

"Oh, thank God." Erin threw herself into Liz's strong arms. "Why didn't you call? I've been worried sick."

Liz kissed her quickly on the lips, then slipped out of their embrace. "I'm sorry, I had a lot on my mind."

She walked into the living room and dropped her keys on an end table, then sank down into one of the feather-cushioned couches.

"So what happened? What's going on?" Erin had been on the phone first with Cynthia and then with Patricia. Neither had answered her questions. Patricia had even scoffed at her request for information on the murder. Erin had hung up the phone so frustrated she'd wanted to cry.

Liz shook her head as she stared off into space. "Nothing."

"What do you mean nothing?" Erin was unable to sit down. Her blood was pumping, her mind reeling, just like it did when she was on the force. She had to know everything. Now.

"They asked about Jay. They asked if I knew anything about the murder. I told them I knew nothing."

Erin stopped and stared. "This new murder...I'm scared, Liz."

Liz met her eyes. "I know."

"Who would do this?"

"I don't know."

"They think it's Jay." Erin shifted her gaze to the backyard. "The crime scene looked way too similar."

Liz stood. "There's one big difference. Joe was strangled, not shot."

Erin swallowed hard, knowing all too well what the difference meant. To shoot someone meant you could keep a relative distance. Strangling someone, on the other hand, meant personal contact. Intense anger and control, looking into someone's eyes as you squeezed the life out of them.

"Manual or ligature?" she asked.

"What?"

"Was it manual strangulation, as in they used their hands, or did they use something else, like a rope or cord?"

"They didn't say."

"Of course not. They aren't about to give away information. Something only the killer would know." Erin began pacing again. "What did the photos look like? Was there a purple line across the neck, a ligature mark, or did the bruises cover the neck more broadly?"

Liz frowned. "I don't know."

Erin made a frustrated noise. "You didn't see or you couldn't tell?"

"I didn't pay attention. I was too busy answering all their fucking questions, which sounded a lot like the ones you're asking now."

Erin halted. "I know, I'm sorry. I just...I hate not knowing." She used to be a part of it all. Being on the outside of an investigation was difficult. "Is Jay their only lead?" she asked a little more softly.

"Next to me, I would say so."

Erin approached, reaching out to touch Liz's face. "Are you okay?"

How much more could Liz take? How much more could their lives take? They had only just recovered from the previous investigation, and finally, with the suspicions gone, they'd started a new life together. They were happy, content, in love. Erin had moved beyond her past and she'd hoped Liz had as well. Their relationship couldn't take another blow to its still-fragile foundations.

"I'm fine."

"Are you sure there's nothing else? I keep thinking there's something you're not telling me."

Liz's blue eyes clouded. "What do you mean?"

Erin had tried to reassure her that it was safe for Jay to come back now that they knew Reece was the killer. Jay would be questioned, of course, but with Reece's confession and Jay's mental instability, Erin felt that Carmichael could protect her. At the very least Jay would get some help and she and Liz could rebuild their relationship without Jay having to run all the time. If only she could get Liz to see this.

"About Jay. I know you prefer to keep things to yourself, but you can trust me. Just talk to me."

"That's what you think? That I keep things from you because of trust?"

"I don't know."

"I don't need this right now, Erin."

"I'm not trying to upset you."

"Just…" Liz held up her hand. "Drop it. Please." But it wasn't a request. It was a demand.

Erin searched her eyes and saw the wounds and worry. Then she realized that next to sexual intimacy and their busy schedules with the club and studio, they didn't have a lot of personal time for discussions. Maybe it was time for that to change.

"Talk to me, Liz," she whispered.

Liz kissed her hand but her eyes remained guarded. "I'm going to go take a shower."

Erin nodded in silent defeat. Liz probably needed some time alone to deal with all that had happened. They were different that way. Liz kept things inside while Erin preferred to talk them out.

Liz started to walk away and then turned. "Then I'm going to work from here. I don't feel like going in to the studio or club today."

Erin nodded, keeping a brave face.

Once Liz had left the room, she sank onto the couch. "My God." She let her head fall into her hands. "It's starting again."

CHAPTER SIX

Patricia Henderson studied the latest crime scene photos, the ones of Joseph Gillette. Her heart raced even though her body felt fatigued. She hadn't been able to sleep much the past few nights, going over and over their questioning of Elizabeth Adams. No matter how smooth Liz thought her lies were, Patricia knew she was very much aware of her sister's whereabouts.

But what did that mean anyway? Was Jay really their killer? Patricia didn't think so but Jay Adams, next to Liz, was their only link to the previous murders. Gillette's killing resembled those murders, a fact no detective could ignore. So where the hell was Jay? Why didn't Liz give her up so they could clear her? Something wasn't right, and once again the Adams name was at the center of their inquiries.

"Here." Gary Jacobs breezed into the squad room. He plucked out two small white containers from the bag of Chinese food he was carrying. Patricia could smell the Kung Pao chicken she'd ordered as she opened first the container of white rice and then the greasy box that held the chicken.

Gary sat down across from her and licked his fingers before he tucked a napkin into his starched collar. After smoothing it over his shirt to perfection, he peeled open his chopsticks to dig into his Mongolian beef.

Patricia forked the hot food into her mouth and chewed, noting that it wasn't near spicy enough. She eyed the unfamiliar emblem on the bag. "This isn't Dragon Inn."

Gary kept chewing, responding with his mouth full. "They closed down."

Patricia stabbed her fork into the chicken. "They closed?"
He shrugged. "Yep."

"Since when?" They'd been eating there for years. It was the best Chinese in town. Did every good thing have to change? Patricia pushed the containers away, in no mood for mediocre Kung Pao.

"What's wrong?" Gary asked. "You wanted the sesame?"

"No." She sighed.

Again her eyes fastened to the crime scene photos of Joseph Gillette before shifting to the numerous other photos pinned to the wall. She'd just hung them an hour before, needing to visually group the victims in the different sets of murders. She blinked away fatigue, trying to focus. The first group of victims belonged to the Seductress Murders, as the press had dubbed them, due to the killer's MO. The victims were first seduced by a female with the promise of sex, then drugged and tied to a bed. The victims were all male, all married, prominent businessmen. Each was drugged, shot in the head, and mutilated in the genital region postmortem. Although Elizabeth Adams had been the main suspect a year earlier when these murders occurred, Kristen Reece and a young sidekick named Tracy Walsh had been found responsible.

End of story? According to the department, yes. So they'd let it go and the case was officially closed. But Jay Adams had not been ruled out over a possible role in the murders and she was still sought for questioning. So far, they'd had no luck in finding her. Elizabeth Adams made sure of that.

Patricia focused in on the next set of photos. The Highway Murders. She'd been working the case for a couple of months, but they now knew that the murders had been ongoing for at least two years, according to the initial report on the oldest remains. The police hadn't even been aware of the first few killings until they stumbled on additional decomposing remains when a recent victim's body was found. This meant that the Highway Murders had actually started before the Seductress Murders. Were the two cases related? How likely was it that two different serial killers were at work in one small area over the same period?

Kristin Reece had been dead for a year and had admitted her guilt, so none of the latest victims could be hers. Yet there were odd similarities in all the cases. They needed a break in the Highway case, someone who had seen suspicious activity or who knew a victim and could provide a clue to a possible suspect. A volunteer grid search was currently in the works, departments in both counties stubbornly coming together to find answers. In her gut, Patricia felt sure more bodies were out there. She wondered how many they would ultimately find.

She studied each victim photo and went over what she knew. They'd been able to identify three men thanks to wallets recovered with the remains. The victims were middle aged, middle class, and married. Their bodies had been dumped along the same highway leading out of Valle Luna. Two had been found before decay set in, strangled and with their wedding rings missing. Sex had played a role, though the investigators weren't yet sure just how much. One victim still wore a condom, and the other had traces of a lubricant on his genitals. Their wives had not known about any infidelities. In fact, all three of the victims who'd been identified were known to be cordial if not passive husbands. There was no apparent motive and no viable suspects. They'd been lucky to find those two bodies before decay set in.

Lucky?

Patricia considered the proximity of the bodies to the highway. They were closer to the road than the older bodies. Maybe the killer had wanted them to be found. She peeled the wrapper from her straw and sipped her large diet soda. She wished the forensic reports would come back on the one body they had yet to identify. She could only hope there would be a clue harbored in those remains.

Her gaze traveled back to the wall of death.

To Joseph Gillette. Her mind rattled off the facts. Twenty-four years old. Gay. A professional model/actor, looking for the limelight. No serious relationships, low on money, with a strong dislike for his new boss, Elizabeth Adams. According to the lab report he had ecstasy in his system. Not enough to harm him, but plenty enough to sweeten his surroundings. The Seductress Murder victims had been drugged first with GHB. Also like the Seductress victims, Joe was killed and dumped in the desert, his genitalia mutilated postmortem. His body had been posed the same way, lying on his back, his pants down around his ankles. Only rather than being shot, he'd been strangled.

Patricia's mind reeled as she absorbed it all.

"What are you thinking?" Gary asked, sucking on his drink.

"They were all men and all strangled. Gillette and the two Highway victims. Although Gillette's bruising seemed more severe. It's possible that the cases are related, although the victim profiles are different."

"Do you think Elizabeth Adams could be involved in all of them?"

"No, no." She shook her head. "I don't think she's involved at all."

"I don't either. But her sister…"

Patricia held his eyes. "Jay, possibly, yes. But not Liz."

There was no reason—Liz had a busy, happy life now. As much as Patricia still disliked her, she couldn't find a link with Liz in regard to the Highway Murders, and why would she kill Gillette? He was her newest actor, hired on for her newest investment.

"So how's Jay linked to the Highway Murders?" Gary asked. "I can understand the link with Gillette and the Seductress Murders, but not all three."

"I don't know. It's just a thought. They all seem weirdly similar." She lifted the Gillette photo she had on her desk, seeking something she wasn't seeing. "I don't know. Maybe they're just all running together in my head. Maybe Jay's not involved at all. Maybe it's someone else, someone who's fucking with all of us." She paused, then gave voice to the obvious. "There are just too many dead men in this town."

Gary tossed her a fortune cookie. He sat back to open his. "The MOs are somewhat different. Dump sites different. And I see what you mean about the profiles. Gillette is younger than the Highway victims. Unmarried, openly gay, struggling financially."

Patricia opened her cookie and extracted the tiny strip of paper, which read, "Love will find you soon." She scowled and threw it in the food bag. "But Gillette is similar to the Seductress victims."

"In some ways, yes. In some ways, no." Her partner crunched on his fortune cookie. "It's probably a hastened copycat. Someone kills Gillette, panics, then remembers what he read in the newspaper. He pulls down the guy's pants and stabs him. Or maybe the killer just had a lot of rage toward Gillette. Sexual rage."

"You don't see any correlation with the other murders?" She trusted Gary and valued his opinion. They kept each other focused and she needed him to reel her back in if she was venturing off path.

"All of them?" He wiped his mouth with his napkin. "Not likely. We simply need to find Jay Adams if we can and question her. Only because she's our best lead right now. If she's cleared, then we move on and drop the link to the Seductress Murders or cough it up as a poor attempt at a copycat."

"You're probably right. What do I know, anyhow?"

He laughed softly. "Way more than most."

She scoffed. "I'm beginning to doubt that, my friend. I'm beginning to doubt that."

She stared at the wall of death and thought over the cases, her life, and her loneliness. She thought of Mac and how happy she seemed living with a woman once suspected of murder.

Perhaps her own judgment was clouded by her feelings. Patricia still cared about Mac, and for that reason, if she were completely honest, she didn't want Liz to be guilty of anything. Yet at the same time it was impossible to trust the woman. Liz was hiding something, she was sure of it. Jay? Probably. But she wasn't positive.

Maybe that was her problem. Maybe she really didn't know as much as she once thought. Maybe she knew nothing at all.

❖

"There's something you don't know," the well-muscled woman whispered. She wore a white tank, baggy jeans, and a newsboy cap. "Something I got to tell you."

She leaned into the dark-skinned woman in the blue church dress and hat. They stood against a worn barn door with an old tractor behind them, a hot Southern sun glistening their skin.

"I can't know…" The dark-skinned woman turned her face away, as if shying from dangerous knowledge.

The strong woman reached out and gently guided the other woman's chin so that their eyes met. "Coral, you must know. I—"

"No, please, Miss Hazel." A tear slipped down her cheek. "You can't."

"But I do." Hazel tore off her newsboy cap and a long braid tumbled down past her shoulders. She dropped the cap and held Coral's face with both hands. "I love you."

"No," Coral whispered. "The town, what they would do to you if—"

"Shh." Hazel pressed her lips to Coral's, stifling her words. Coral gave a soft whimper of protest and halfheartedly tried to push her away. The kisses were short and full of ragged breath. Coral's hands fell in defeat and her posture softened as if she would melt right then and there. Hazel leaned into her, holding her, pressing her against the barn. Their mouths nearly touched, their bodies trembled.

Hazel stared into her eyes. "You feel it too, don't you?"

Coral touched her own lips as more tears slipped down her face. "Yes."

"Don't you see that I don't care what this town thinks?"

"It's not safe, Miss—"

"I won't let anyone hurt you. I swear it on my daddy's grave." She took Coral's hands. "You can move in here with me, I'll tell everyone I've hired you as my house maid. No one will argue with that. Lord knows I need one." She smiled.

"I can't."

"Tell me you don't love me."

Coral said nothing.

"Tell me you don't feel the same, and I'll leave you be."

More silence. Then Coral said, "I can't do that, Miss Hazel. I can't tell you I don't love you. Because that would be a lie. A bald-faced lie. And I don't lie."

Hazel pressed into her again with a kiss that quickly deepened and then exploded into a frenzy of desire. She tore her mouth away and kissed Coral's neck. "I love you, Coral," she whispered. "Oh, God help me, how I love you." She bunched up Coral's dress as the kisses continued.

"Miss Hazel, what you are doing to me." Coral sighed.

Hazel thrust forward, her arm swallowed up inside the dress. Coral cried out in pleasure and bit her lip to stifle her moans. She buried her face in Hazel's shoulder as the strong woman rocked into her. Tears continued to run down her face as her fears turned to pleasure.

She closed her eyes and held tight to Hazel.

"Oh, what you are doing to me," she said one last time before she shuddered in orgasm.

"And…cut!"

Erin jerked at the director's sharp interjection. The two actors stilled and drew apart, both smiling but clearly exhausted. Erin wiped away a tear.

"That was beautiful," she told Liz.

"It was good," Liz replied, her focus serious. She moved quickly to the director with the script in hand, which they both pored over and spoke about softly.

Erin sighed, still trying to adjust to the fact that the story wasn't real. Around her people moved about, changing the lighting, changing the set. "Coral" stood in the corner with a cell phone pressed to her ear while "Hazel" downed a bottle of water.

Rather than continue staring at the actors, wishing their characters were real, Erin took in her surroundings. Erotique Studios was housed in a brand-new building not far from La Femme. Every time they pulled up in the parking lot in front of the large building, Erin was amazed. Liz had taken a small dream of making movies and turned it into a reality. Erin envied and respected her for that.

Liz returned from her conversation with the director and scribbled on the script. When she looked up Erin noted the dark patches under her eyes.

"You sure you're okay?" Erin asked.

Liz had been especially quiet the previous few days. She'd holed herself up in the study at the house, working well into the night and crawling into bed long after Erin had tossed and turned herself to sleep. In the mornings, she rose before Erin, showered, and headed back into the home office. Her face was perpetually drawn and pale, her reassuring smiles tired and strained. Erin only bothered her to pop in with meals, since her attempts at casual conversation failed every time.

"I'm okay." Liz gave a weak smile. "You okay?"

"As long as you are."

They kissed softly. It was the most contact they'd had in days. Erin closed her eyes briefly, allowing the feel and smell of Liz to linger. She was starved for her lover, missing her touch, her laugh, her presence. She gave Liz a smile. She didn't want her to know just how worried she was and how lost she felt trying to help her. At least today they'd left the house. Erin hoped the change in scenery and getting back into the swing of things would help them both.

As they headed back toward the offices, a loud voice brought reality smack-dab back in front of them. "Oh, my God. Is it true? Please tell me it's not true!" Antwon De Maro shrieked, running up to them.

He fixed Liz with stricken eyes but she brushed past him to

continue into her office, the topic obviously off-limits with her. When his gaze swung to Erin she nodded solemnly.

He covered his mouth with his hand and squealed in horror, "Oh, my God!"

Erin wiped away tears of her own as she enveloped the makeup artist for a brief hug.

He continued to share his scattered thoughts, just as he always did. "Who would do such a thing?" He touched Erin's face. "Are you and Ms. Adams okay?"

Erin held his hand. "We're fine. Just a little shook up."

They moved farther into the building and Erin offered the other employees a soft smile. Some walked away, content to go back to work, while others remained staring, discreetly whispering.

"The cops were here, asking all kinds of questions. Even about Ms. Adams." Antwon sniffed. "Arrogant pricks. Of course, they wouldn't answer any of *my* questions. They wouldn't even say what happened. They said I wasn't next of kin, so they weren't obligated to say anything. Bastards."

"They're just doing their job, don't take it personally."

She sat down at the desk she'd been using for weeks and pulled her laptop from her soft briefcase, anxious to do more prodding into the Gillette murder. She'd been compiling the newspaper articles and trying to put the pieces together in her mind. She typed in her password and gave Antwon a pointed look, hoping he'd catch the hint that she needed to work.

He hugged himself as if he were cold and didn't budge. His small muscles rippled under the tight-fitting red T-shirt that contrasted nicely with his dark mocha skin. Raising perfectly trimmed eyebrows that matched his goatee, he leaned forward and whispered loudly, "They were asking about Ms. Adams like she might be the one who offed him."

Erin held up a hand. "Antwon, I assure you, it was just a routine formality."

"I mean, I know Joe and Ms. Adams had their differences, but that doesn't mean she killed him. Even I thought Joe was a pompous ass, but would that lead me to murder? No, of course not."

"Antwon." Erin tried to calm him down, but it was always difficult to curtail one of his verbal tirades.

"Bastards. Why in the world would they do that? Come in here like that, asking all sort of crazy questions."

"They think she did it," another voice added, even and confident.

Both Erin and Antwon focused on the two men who'd just emerged from the sound stage. Reggie Lengel and Don Altman. Don was one of their biggest financial backers and Reggie was one of their bookkeepers.

"At least that's the impression I got," Don added.

Reggie nodded and gave Erin a regretful look. "Me too."

"But why would they think she did it?" Antwon asked, the drama obviously building in his mind.

"Probably because of her past. This isn't the first time she's been accused of murder," Don answered matter-of-factly.

"Falsely accused." Erin stood, the conversation quickly getting on her nerves.

"That's true," Reggie said, but he sounded uncomfortable. It was obvious the whole thing bothered him. He seemed to live a simple, straight and narrow, predictable life and he tried to apply those principles to his work, much to the dismay of some of the other more outgoing employees. "She was cleared of all charges."

Erin wanted to scream but she held back. "That's right. And I don't think this conversation needs to go any further. Liz had nothing to do with Joe's or anyone's death. The cops are just doing their job. Now I suggest we get back to ours."

Reggie and Don walked away toward Don's desk and Erin eased back into her chair. Antwon was still watching her, his eyes full of fear.

"I'm scared," he said. "If it could happen to Joe, it could happen to anyone." He looked around and pointed at some of the lingering actors. "Blake, Tommy, James, any of us." He glanced back to Don and Reggie. "Even them, the straight guys." He looked back to Erin. "Or you. Or one of the other lesbians."

Erin stopped him, unable to take any more. "Antwon. I'm scared too. So is Liz. But you're safe here, okay?" She held his gaze. "Just go back to work and try not to think about it. We've got two more scenes to shoot this afternoon."

"But what about Joe?"

"What about him?"

"How are we gonna shoot without him?"

"Shit." Erin looked to Liz's office. The blinds were closed. "We'll have to find someone else and do his scenes over. Go ahead and get the others ready. We'll shoot something without Joe's character for today."

She looked down at her laptop. The cursor blinked in the Google box. She folded down the lid. The murder would have to wait. At least for now. She left her desk and headed for Liz's office.

CHAPTER SEVEN

W hat's up?" Liz stopped pretending to scribble, knowing she wouldn't be able to fool Erin.

"I just realized that the scenes we were supposed to shoot today involve Joe."

Liz looked away. The image of the young actor dead and dumped raced into her head. She cleared her throat and regained her composure. "I've already spoken with the alternate. He can start tomorrow. I've got it under control."

"I know," Erin said softly. "But I was thinking that maybe we should just cancel today's shoot altogether, at least until tomorrow. Give everyone a little break."

Normally Liz would scoff at such a suggestion. Time was money. But everyone had continued to come in to work since the news of Joe's death, with the exception of her and Erin. Maybe Erin was right.

"Antwon's a mess, and the others are talking. I think everyone is freaked out. I know I am."

"Leave it to you to worry about everyone's feelings." Liz smiled.

Erin smiled in return. "Someone has to. You're a ball buster."

Liz took in her lover's shapely legs under the pressed chinos and the weight of her breasts under her tight, thin sweater. Sometimes she couldn't decide if she liked Erin better with or without clothes. She was beautiful regardless.

"Come here," Liz murmured.

Erin walked around the desk and came to stand before her, straddling her thigh. Liz gripped her backside and pulled her in closer.

"Do you know how much I love you?" Liz felt her throat tighten with emotion. She hadn't been able to do anything but throw herself into work for the past few days. Her mind wouldn't stop and Erin was so full of questions she couldn't answer that she had just tried to avoid her, and that hurt. What was she going to do?

Erin touched her face, bringing her back from that cold desolate place of fear and confusion. "Tell me," she whispered.

Liz held her hand and kissed it softly. "I wouldn't know what to do without you."

Erin shuddered as Liz's breath tickled her palm.

"Someday soon I'm going to marry you. I promise. Things have just been so hectic and..." Liz held her gaze for a long moment. "I'm sorry about all this."

"About what?"

"All this. This new mess, the old mess. Trouble seems to follow me. Maybe you'd be better off without me." The thought had stabbed at her insides for a long while. Saying it aloud nearly killed her.

"Hey." Erin held her face. "Don't ever say that again. Don't even think it."

Liz started to protest but Erin placed a finger over her lips. "I mean it. You aren't responsible for any of this."

"I'm responsible for you. And for Jay. I need to protect you..."

Erin dropped down to her knees. "All I need from you is love."

Liz swallowed back the stinging anxiety. She managed to smile, her heart swelling in her chest just as it always did when Erin looked at her like that, so full of unconditional love and compassion. But her ribs were tight and confined with guilt. She flinched inwardly, hating those dark feelings. Erin was before her declaring her unconditional love. She should enjoy it. Take it.

She cupped Erin's face and drew her in close for a soft, lingering kiss. Erin moaned and Liz felt her own flesh ignite when Erin's tongue pleaded for permission to enter. She plunged her tongue into Erin's mouth, this time groaning as Erin kissed her back. Their tongues made love. They swirled and caressed, hungrily, hurriedly. She was always amazed at just how easily and quickly Erin could turn her on. Head and heart pounding, Liz gasped when Erin forced some distance between them, pushing against Liz's chest.

"I didn't come in here to do this," she rasped before Liz could speak. "We should talk about Joe, about the studio, about what happened. We haven't talked in days."

Liz tightened her grip. No, hell no. Not now. She'd finally torn the situation from her mind and needed the time out. "Let's not."

"But, Liz, it's not going to go away."

"I know. But for right now, let's just focus on us." She inched up Erin's sweater. "Help me get this off." She hadn't touched her in a week and the sudden feel of her hot mouth and warm skin made Liz want to throw her against the wall and consume her. She had to have her. Now.

"The door," Erin said, concerned.

"It's locked. You know that. It locks when you close it." They'd gone through this countless times before.

"I know, but I can't relax until the dead bolt's locked." Quickly, Erin stood and rushed to the door.

Liz watched as she set the top lock and turned back to face her. A knowing smile spread across her face as she walked slowly toward the desk. With each deliberate step she exposed more skin. Liz watched carefully, so wet she could already feel it saturating her underwear.

"You are so beautiful," she said. Her cell phone rang, breaking the intensity for only a moment. She silenced it and tossed it aside.

Erin pinned Liz with a lustful look and then pulled off her sweater and tossed it to her. Liz caught it with one hand and stood, unable to take much more. She rounded the desk but Erin held out a hand to stop her. She unhooked her bra and draped it around Liz's neck.

"Fuck," Liz whispered.

Erin laughed and pulled her closer by tugging on the bra. "Is that the best word that comes to mind?"

Liz took in her light brown nipples, already puckering, and imagined them in her mouth. "At the moment, yes."

She reached for Erin then, growling as she bit and sucked on her neck. Erin made a noise, one of aching desire as she arched into her. Liz fed furiously, unable to get enough. The scent of her lover, the taste of her skin, the sound of her soft moans, all of it drove Liz's libido into a tailspin. Hurriedly she unbuttoned Erin's pants and shoved them down as best she could. She knelt to help Erin out of them and stared in disbelief at Erin's light brown hairs.

"Where are your panties?"

Erin laughed not so innocently. "I must've forgot."

Liz kissed her thighs lightly and felt her quiver. "Well, here's to your poor memory."

Erin laughed again and then yelped a little as Liz lifted her onto the desk. "What happened to the couch?"

"Not today." Liz pushed her back so she was lying down, neat stacks of papers pushed to the side. She ran her hands all over her body, relishing her warmth, her softness, her pleas for more.

"Take me," Erin said, her green eyes full of fire.

It didn't take much. A few light touches, a few heated kisses, and Erin was always starved and eager for more. Liz spread her legs wide and groaned when Erin took her hand and placed it where she wanted it most. Liz nearly closed her eyes at how hot and impossibly wet she was.

Erin moaned at her touch and gripped her shoulders. "Now, baby. Now."

Head spinning, Liz thrust into her with three firm fingers. Erin cried out and lifted her head and shoulders off the desk, her mouth open, eyes wide with pleasure. Liz pushed onto her and their mouths locked in a dangerous kiss. Liz fucked her mouth and her body, thrusting and pushing, giving and demanding. Erin clung to her, crying out into her mouth.

Faster and harder Liz fucked her until she felt Erin dig into her shoulders with her short nails. Then Liz slowed, pulling in and out, long and hard and deliberate. She sucked on Erin's tongue, keeping time with her fingers until Erin groaned loudly.

"More, Liz. Please, baby. Harder."

Liz felt her tighten, felt her throb with need. She kissed her again, feeding her need, pushing her fingers up deep inside. Erin's body sucked her fingers. Hot, tight, wet walls of spongy muscle clung to her, encased her. Erin cried out again. Liz laughed devilishly as they rocked together, her own swollen flesh grinding against Erin's thigh. Oh, she felt so good. So perfect, so demanding, so giving.

"Liz," Erin panted over and over, her voice giving way to short, rapid breaths as Liz fucked her, faster and faster, deeper and deeper. "I'm gonna come. Oh, God. I'm gonna come."

Liz sucked on her ear lobe and whispered, "Come for me, then. Come hard."

Erin clamped her mouth to Liz's neck as her body shook hard with the climax. Her cries were stifled and Liz knew she was trying her best to keep quiet.

"Just let it out, Erin. Just let it out." Liz pulled away to watch her.

Erin arched her back and opened her mouth, but no sound escaped. Liz leaned in and licked slowly up her straining neck, loving every second. Erin coming was the most incredible sight she'd ever seen. And each time was more and more captivating. Liz pumped into her, her own fingers collapsed against one another as Erin's body held tight and fed.

"I. Love. You," Erin finally managed to say, the last of the orgasm sparking through her.

Liz smiled through the impending darkness, her fingers still up inside where she wished she could disappear forever. "I love you too."

❖

Erin smoothed down her sweater and tucked the short strands of her hair behind her ears. She moved quickly but caught the knowing glances from more than one of Liz's employees. It seemed that no matter how careful or quiet she was, everyone seemed to know what went on in Liz's office. Of course, exiting with swollen lips and marks on her neck didn't help any.

"Shit." She felt her face heat. She wasn't used to people knowing about her personal life, especially her intimate life. But try as she might, she just couldn't tell Liz no, no matter where they were.

Erin wound her way through to the large wardrobe and dressing area where Antwon sat talking with a couple of the actors. His voice trailed off when he saw her and he stood, a perfect eyebrow lifted curiously.

Erin willed the heat in her cheeks to cool. "The shoot's off for today. You guys can go home and get some rest."

Tommy grinned. "You did some convincing?"

"Don't you all thank me at once."

"Damn, girl. You must be good," Antwon teased.

Erin rolled her eyes. "I did it for you. I thought you were frightened."

"We are. Can't you tell?" He stood looking like a little teapot, one hand on his hip the other up in the air.

"Go on, get out of here."

"Doing the boss in her office. That's hot. Damn hot," Tommy said. "You should write that down."

"It would make a great movie," Blake, another actor, added with an amused grin.

"I can see it now." Antwon ran his hand through the air. "*Dykes on Desks*."

Erin's flush deepened. "Get out of here before I have her fire your asses."

Laughter erupted as she walked away. With a sigh, she sat down at her own desk and concentrated on her search.

Joseph Gillette.

"Damn." Nothing new. Part of her was grateful, knowing that anything else might spark talk of Liz and her possible involvement. For now the cops had kept her out of it.

She scrolled down the recent serial killer articles to a few links that read THE HIGHWAY MURDERS. She'd been following it closely, unable not to. She'd done all the research she could and more than once she'd thought about picking up the phone to call Patricia about it.

She eyed the phone once again. *I could just call her and ask again for information on the Gillette murder. I'm only trying to help.*

As if on cue the phone rang, startling her. "Erotique Studios."

"Ms. Erin?"

"Yes, Tyson?" Erin recognized the deep smooth voice of the head of security at La Femme. She'd told him a thousand times to call her Erin, but he refused, sticking with his impeccable manners instead.

"I've been trying to reach Ms. Adams but I haven't been able to."

Erin closed her eyes, remembering the ringing of Liz's cell phone during their tryst in the office. Liz had tossed it across the room before lowering herself to feast between Erin's legs. Erin flushed again and squeezed her legs together when they throbbed in response to the memory.

"What is it?" she asked Tyson.

"The cops are here."

"At La Femme?"

"Yes, ma'am. They seem to be staying a little longer today."

Erin glanced at her watch. It was nearing three. Too early for the patrons to arrive at the club. "What do they want?"

"They're asking the girls questions."

"Do they have a warrant?"

"No. But they aren't searching. Just hanging out and talking to the employees."

"Thanks, Tyson. I'll let her know."

"What should I do?"

"Nothing. There's nothing you can do."

"Ms. Erin?"

"Yes?"

"Does Ms. Adams really have a sister?"

Erin sighed. "You'll have to ask her that question yourself."

Liz had done her best to keep everything away from La Femme. The murders, Kristen Reece, and Tracy Walsh's involvement. She didn't want anything spoiling the spirit of the club. Even though La Femme was full of new employees, Erin knew that they'd all probably read the papers, along with Tyson. But Liz was adamant about not discussing what had happened with her head of security or anyone else. What was done was done, she said.

Erin ended the call but kept the receiver to her ear. She buzzed Liz's line.

"Hey," Liz answered, her voice extra deep as it often was after lovemaking. "You calling for more?"

Erin grinned as her skin erupted in flames once again. "No."

"You sure?"

"I need to talk to you," Erin said.

"You sound serious."

"Tyson called. He said he's been trying to reach you."

She heard Liz sigh in frustration. "When I want to talk to him, I will."

"Oh, so you know he's been calling?" Erin was a little surprised by Liz's tone. She waited for an explanation, but Liz offered no clues as to why Tyson was suddenly annoying to her.

"He probably left you a message or two."

"He never leaves messages," Liz said. "He knows better."

For a brief instant Erin wondered why. "Well, you should've called him back, because the cops are at La Femme asking questions."

Silence.

Erin continued. "They don't have a warrant but they seem to be sticking around this time."

More silence.

"Liz?"

"I'm here."

"What do you want to do?"

"What can I do?"

"We can go down there."

Liz's voice hardened. "No, that's what they want. Let them ask questions. It's still early. The evening crowd won't arrive for another few hours so they aren't hurting business. Let them sit there."

"You sure? I thought you'd be furious."

"I am."

"I'm sorry."

"Don't be. It isn't your fault."

Erin thought long and hard, hating what Liz must be feeling. "I'm doing some research on Joe. We'll find this bastard…"

"No."

"No, what?"

"I don't want you anywhere near this, Erin."

"But—"

"No, it's dangerous."

"I'm a cop."

"Not anymore."

"Liz—"

"No, Erin, no. I won't have you involved." Liz didn't wait for another protest. "I've got to go. We'll leave here around five and head over to the club."

"Liz, wait—"

But the line was dead.

Erin sat dumbfounded and then softly replaced the receiver.

Arcane, Alabama
Twenty-two years ago

"Shh, don't cry, little birdie." She held the soft bundle up to her face and rocked with it in the darkness. The feathers were like silk and she rubbed them on her cheek. The scabs on her skin had finally fallen off and her face no longer showed the pain she still felt.

The doctor had said she was lucky no bones had been broken.

Why did she *feel* broken?

She rocked with the bird she'd found by the big hickory tree in the front yard. It had been flapping helplessly in a circle. She'd tried to save it. Plucked it up and brought it inside to feed, but it was no longer breathing. Still, she had to keep it. She had to keep it safe. It had been with her in the woods. She was sure of it. It had helped to save her from the bad man.

She stroked the feathers, now moist from her tears. "Don't cry," she soothed. "It's okay. It's okay."

She began to hum. A light clicked on in the far corner, Lizzie's corner.

"What are ya doin'?" Lizzie sat up in her bed, rubbing her eyes.

Jay quickly wrapped the bird and placed it under her covers. "Nuthin'."

"Why was you hummin'?"

"I wasn't." She continued to rock, clutching her pillow instead.

"Are you okay?"

Jay wiped her eyes. "Go back to sleep."

Lizzie turned off the light and lay back down.

Jay stared into the grays and blacks of night. Outside the window the big hickory swayed in the wind. In the distance she heard the muffled sounds of approaching thunder. Lightning flashed soon after, quick camera-like flashes that illuminated her hands, her chest, the long strands of her hair. She focused on herself in the reflection of the window. Her hair hung long and dark. She fingered it, stroking it much like she had the bird. Only the soft silk of her hair didn't comfort her, it tortured her.

Instantly she was back in the woods. The man was grunting and tugging on her hair. He held her by her hair. Clenching, knotting, pulling, pushing.

She couldn't get away.

He was pulling her hair so hard she could feel some give way as it was torn from the roots. He had her. Had her by the hair.

"No!" she screamed. She ran from the bed and pounded against the glass pane, slamming, banging, trying to destroy.

"Jay, Jay!" Lizzie was at her side, dragging her away.

Jay fought her, still screaming. More lights came on. There were voices, the sound of running feet on old wood floors. Her aunt Dayne grabbed her by the shoulders. She shook her, yelling over her. "Jay!"

Uncle Jerry held her arms down.

"No!" she screamed.

"Let her go!" Lizzie cried. "She's scared." She pulled their aunt from her, then started in on Jerry. He let go when Lizzie began to scratch him.

Jay collapsed in Lizzie's arms, trembling. She felt Lizzie stroke her hair.

"Leave us alone," Lizzie commanded. "She's just scared."

Jay heard her aunt and uncle eventually leave the room, Dayne still voicing her concern. When all was quiet they walked to Lizzie's bed and climbed under the covers. Snuggled close, Lizzie again stroked her hair.

Too exhausted to care, Jay let her eyes drift closed.

Her hair, he had her by the hair.

CHAPTER EIGHT

L ove and Rockets sang "So Alive" as the go-go girls moved seductively on their platforms, wearing miniskirts and crop tops, their hair big and makeup wild. Eighties night was in full bloom, and had it been a different time or she in a different profession, Patricia would've actually enjoyed it. Instead she sat at the bar, chewing on her swizzle stick, swallowing her libido and a down-deep yearning for irresponsible fun. Around her, women poured into the club, tired from a long day at work but excited about meeting friends and ready to dance the night away.

"Get you another?" The bartender's bored tone let on that she had way more interesting things on her mind than Patricia's club soda.

"No, thanks."

The bartender, whose name was Madelyn but who preferred to go by Mad, held her eyes a moment longer than necessary and then moved on. She was young, too tan for early spring, and had dyed dark red tousled hair. Her tank top was white, her breasts ample and showing through nicely. She was a hot-to-trot femme, very confident and very promiscuous, which hadn't been hard to find out. She'd even looked Patricia up and down a few times with interest just before Gary whipped out his badge. As always, Patricia and her colleagues weren't exactly welcomed with open arms. The mood in the near-empty nightclub had changed dramatically then. The laughter of the bartenders and maintenance crew vanished, replaced by whispers and stares.

Like the rest of the employees, Mad answered their questions with attitude and indifference. No one knew Jay, no one had ever even heard of her. Ms. Adams didn't have a sister. What were they? Fucking stupid?

Patricia watched Mad a moment longer and thought of Tracy Walsh. She too had been a loyal bartender for Elizabeth Adams, but her loyalty had spilled into obsession and she became easy prey for Kristen Reece. Under Reece's influence, she became a killer. Patricia still couldn't stamp out the image of a crazed Walsh breaking into her house, trying to kill her. The thought made her mouth dry. She licked her lips and eyed her drink.

"Wow, what else can that mouth do?" Mad was back, and resting on her elbows, still looking bored with her job but trying to intrigue the cop who'd been sitting there for hours.

"You aren't supposed to talk to me, remember?" Patricia finished her club soda.

"Says who?"

"Your boss."

"Adams?" Mad twirled the mangled straw around inside Patricia's empty glass. "Adams never said I couldn't talk to you."

"Then what's with the attitude you gave us?"

"I don't like cops."

Patricia laughed. "Who does?"

"You're cute, though."

Patricia looked into her dark brown eyes. "Thanks."

"No, I mean it. If you weren't a cop..."

"Yeah, and if you didn't work for Adams..."

"Touché."

They both smiled.

"Let me know if you need another drink." Mad slipped Patricia a business card. "Or anything else."

The card read "Mad for Women" and had two phone numbers listed. Patricia gave a small, amused grin and surveyed the crowd once more. Her body still tingled from the bartender's flirtatious hints. She forced herself to think rather than feel, and wondered if she was suddenly distracted because of her frustration over the case. As she looked around she recalled the dozens of women who threw themselves at Adams, wanting her at any cost. Erin had given up everything to be with that woman. Everything, including Patricia.

Jealousy ran hot through her blood. It still stung and she wondered if it always would. What was it about Adams? Patricia had been intimate with her once a long time ago, had even attempted a relationship. While the sex was beyond intense, she wouldn't ever sacrifice anything of herself for the woman.

The crowd parted slightly near the bottom of the VIP staircase. Patricia slid off the bar stool and stood on her tiptoes expecting to see Adams, but the woman of interest was shorter and blonder. Erin McKenzie moved through the crowd with ease, smiling slightly and looking downward at the attention. Patricia smiled herself, remembering her former colleague's modesty.

"Hi." Erin was suddenly standing before her.

"Uh, hi," Patricia stammered, Erin's wanting to talk to her unexpected.

"Come on." Erin clasped her hand.

Patricia nearly melted as she was led to the back wall of the club. A few women stood fully engulfed in one another, making out. *How long has it been since I've been touched?* The truth thorned as she remembered the way Erin kissed. Hungry. Needful. Hot. She forced back thoughts of that night over a year ago, when they'd lost themselves in one another for an amazing but brief few minutes.

"What are you doing here?" Erin asked and reality slammed back in.

Patricia stared. "What do you mean?" They had to speak loudly over the music. She knew the song from her high school days, Oingo Boingo singing "Dead Man's Party."

"Are you here to harass her, is that it?"

Patricia shook her head. Erin was not only accusing but protective. Patricia hated Adams all the more. "I'm here enjoying the evening." She looked toward the bar where Mad gave a wave. Patricia returned it.

"Yes, I saw that you made a new friend."

"Oh, I see. You and your significant other don't like me talking to the hired help."

"Please. If we minded we would've interfered." Erin glanced down, as if she'd said too much. "Look, we both know you're not here for entertainment, so don't lie to me, Patricia."

"Don't lie to *you*? You've got some nerve saying that to me, after your bullshit about Jay."

Erin had disclaimed all knowledge of Jay Adams during the

Seductress Murders investigation, putting Liz before her job and the case. Patricia still couldn't believe she'd done it, or understand why.

"Look, if you're here to ask questions, you've done that, so move on."

Patricia stared into the beautiful green of Erin's eyes. She'd gotten lost in them once. "What's happened to you?" she asked, thinking aloud.

"Me?" Erin replied with disbelief. "I'm not the one accusing innocent people of murder. I'm not the one harassing an innocent woman."

"I'm doing my job. You know, the one you left. For her."

"I was fired."

"That didn't happen without cause. You made your choices long before that."

"Yeah, and I see how well the department's doing without me."

"What's that supposed to mean?"

Erin's tone softened. "The Highway Murders. Joe Gillette."

"What about the Highway Murders?"

"You don't have a single lead, do you?"

Patricia didn't answer. She couldn't.

"I've been doing some investigating of my own." Erin hesitated. "If you'll just give me a chance, maybe I can help."

"Are you kidding me?"

"What do you have to lose?"

"I don't believe this. First you yell at me over your way-less-than-noble lover and now you're trying to worm your way into an investigation after you've lied and kept things from the department."

"Worm my way?" Erin's face clouded with hurt. "I thought we were friends."

Patricia breathed deep, forcing herself to calm down. "Mac, I will always care for you. I will always be your friend." It was true. She knew Erin was a good person. More sensitive than most. Even if she couldn't have her, she would always be there for her.

"Then why are you here? Honestly?" Erin demanded, her voice high in pitch.

Patricia met her eyes. "We're trying to find Jay."

"We don't know where she is."

Patricia didn't respond. She took in the large diamond engagement ring on Erin's finger. Just how well did Erin really know Adams? Did she really truly trust her enough to marry her? The Elizabeth Adams Patricia knew was far from trustworthy, on all levels. Hardly marriage material.

"What makes you so sure Liz doesn't know?"

Erin looked away. Before she could answer, a familiar voice cut into their discussion. "Detective Henderson."

It didn't matter how many times Patricia heard the low, even tone, it always sent shudders of hate and excitement right through her. Both emotions bothered her. She wished she felt nothing at all.

"Liz." She offered a brief, disinterested glance. "Long time no see."

Liz looked past her to Erin. "Am I interrupting?"

"Would it matter?" Patricia snapped.

"We're fine." Erin's expression was one of incredible guilt. "We were just discussing some things."

Patricia caught the tight look Liz gave her.

"Enjoying your evening?" Liz asked, patronizing as always.

Patricia forced a smile. "I am, yes." She glanced around at the scantily clad bodies dancing on the elevated platforms. "What is it, hooker night?"

Liz laughed. "No, it's desperate, lonely author night."

Patricia caught her breath. The comment stung. Deep.

Erin whispered something to Liz, obviously unhappy and embarrassed. But Liz kept smiling.

"Since you've been here for hours, it seems safe to assume you're thoroughly enjoying yourself."

"You know, there's one thing I can't figure out," Patricia said.

Liz's stare was something colder than ice, something harder than stone.

"Why the stab wounds to the groin?"

Liz's posture stiffened even further. "Leave," she breathed out.

"I think maybe Jay was the victim of a sexual assault. Because that would definitely explain it."

"My sister is no business of yours."

"She's every bit my business. She's involved."

"You're wrong. Dead wrong."

"Well if it isn't Jay, then who? You? We all know how you feel about men."

"That's enough," Erin interjected, looking more frightened than worried.

"Fine." Patricia shrugged. "I guess someone just happened to hate this particular man? Someone who has sexual issues? I don't know, I just don't buy it. No, I think I'll dig deeper into Jay. Something tells me there's more to her story."

Liz tried to lunge but Erin held her back. "Get the fuck out of my club."

Patricia knew she should smile at her victory—Adams most definitely would have. But she didn't feel victorious. Her intentions were no longer about vengeance with Adams, they were about something deeper. She wanted to get to the bottom of the murders, to see the absolute truth for herself.

She watched as the couple parted the crowd and headed up the stairs. She could see Erin talking to Liz, no doubt soothing her. Patricia was still fuming over the confrontation, trembling as she fought to contain her anger. Dealing with Adams always left her rattled and emotionally distraught. She let out a shaky sigh.

Just what the hell was it about Elizabeth Adams?

❖

Erin stood by helplessly as Liz tore through the house in a panicked search for wiretapping. The calm indifference she'd been showing was suddenly gone, replaced by a quick-tempered paranoia.

"They wouldn't bug the house," Erin said as Liz shoved everything aside on the shelves in the sunken living room.

Liz turned on her, eyes wild. "How you can even say that? When you came in my house undercover, wired yourself?"

Erin felt the blood leave her face. She had no response.

"Besides," Liz continued, refocusing on her task, "the cops may not be the only ones after me."

"The house is secure, Liz. The alarm's working, the security monitors show no signs of movement," Erin said softly. "Why are you so worried all of a sudden?"

Liz stepped back to eye the room, searching for any last little corner she hadn't touched. "You think I'm just now worrying?" She didn't wait for a response. "The cops have questioned me, yet they're still coming around my places of business. That means they have little to no other leads. The heat hasn't let up. They can't find Jay, so I'm their focus."

"You're afraid they're going to try and nail this solely on you, just like before?"

Breathing hard, Liz ignored the question and stalked toward the master bedroom. A few moments later Erin crept a little ways down the long hall and heard Liz rummaging through the room. She moved closer, trying to decide what to say. There was no way someone could've snuck in and bugged the house. Not with all the cameras and security Liz had installed. That was one of the reasons Erin had gone undercover in the first place. Liz was so well guarded the cops couldn't get to her.

Erin entered the room as Liz slammed something angrily in a drawer. "Honey, the house is safe."

"Nothing is safe!" Liz's face was contorted in anger.

"Calm down. Everything will be okay."

Liz brushed past her. "Don't tell me to calm down."

"Why are you talking to me like this?" Erin was frustrated and hurt. Liz had done nothing but snap at her since they left the club.

"I don't want to talk about it." Liz stormed down the hall and Erin chased after her.

When she reached the kitchen, Liz jerked open the fridge and twisted open a bottle of water. She sipped slowly, blue eyes as cold as artic ice, staring straight ahead.

"Liz!" Erin couldn't believe what she was witnessing. "You snap at me, tell me what I can and can't do, and then you say you don't want to talk about it? What's wrong with you? Why are you treating me this way?"

Liz turned on her, face set in stone. "What way?"

"Like some goddamned piece of property."

"Is that how you feel?"

"It's how you're treating me. Telling me I can't research Joe's murder, and I can't talk to Patricia."

"I told you, I don't want you involved."

"I'm a cop, I can handle my own."

"You *were* a cop. You're not anymore." Liz opened the fridge and shoved the bottle of water back inside, slamming the door shut.

"I don't need anyone else reminding me of that." Erin tried to keep the quiver from her voice.

"Really? Did Patricia tell you the same thing?"

Erin didn't answer. Her throat was tight and burning.

"Why were you even talking to her? Whose side are you on?"

Erin could see the hurt and fear in Liz's eyes. Tears ran down her own cheeks. "Yours."

"It doesn't sound like it."

"Why won't you talk to me? Every time I bring up Jay or the case you run or you try to distract me by making love."

"There's nothing to say," Liz replied.

"There's nothing to say, or there's something you won't say?"

"I see you've made your own assumptions, just like Patricia. I hope you know she'll use you to get to me."

"No, it's not like that," Erin said quickly. She didn't want Liz to think Patricia would do something like that.

Liz glared at her. "Why do you keep defending her? Just what is it with you two?"

"Nothing."

"You're lying."

Erin suddenly felt panicked, not expecting to have to defend her friendship with Patricia. "She's my colleague…was my colleague. And she's a friend."

Liz's eyes bored into her. "I don't believe it," she whispered fiercely. "All this time and I never would let the thought in. All this time it's been right in my face."

Erin shook her head, not liking the look in Liz's eyes. She stepped backward as Liz moved toward her. "When was it?" Liz backed her to the wall but didn't touch her.

Erin heard her hurried breathing, felt her racing pulse as she held on to her shoulders. "Liz, calm down."

"Answer me." The demand was low and firm.

Erin tried to embrace her but Liz stood erect, ice eyes ablaze.

"Answer me, Erin."

"No." Erin began to cry, unable to stop herself. Why was Liz doing this? Why was she attacking her? "She's my friend. That's all."

Erin felt so lost at that moment. Torn. Her insides ripped. Liz pushed her hands away and stepped back, her eyes full of pain.

"You don't have sex with someone who's just a friend." She turned and walked away.

Erin rushed after her. "Liz, wait, please! Don't do this. We have to talk."

Liz strode down the hallway and slammed the bedroom door. Erin slumped against it, her throat so tight she could hardly breathe. Suddenly, an intense anger surged through her. She was hurting and pained and now, the accused.

"You fucked her. You fucked complete strangers, how dare you preach to me."

Liz's opened the door and her upper lip trembled. Erin tried to reach out and touch it but Liz swatted her hand away.

"So it's true." She seemed barely able to speak. "You slept with Patricia."

"It was a one-time thing," Erin said. "I was confused. I don't understand what the big deal is. You've been with her, with countless others—"

"Was it before or after me?"

Erin realized what she was asking, what she thought. "Oh no, honey. It happened before we—" She stopped herself. "It happened during the case."

Liz swayed a little as if she were going to fall. "After the night at the club?"

Erin's first intimate encounter with Liz. "I can't remember," Erin lied.

"Bullshit!"

"Liz, I—"

"You know exactly when it happened," Liz seethed. "It was after me, wasn't it? You fucked her while you two were hiding away at her house, didn't you? Or did she fuck you? Or maybe you did each other. After she read to you from one of her mushy romances? The ones you told me you wrote?"

Erin could hardly speak. It was all coming out now. The issues she thought Liz would never want to talk about. The fact that Erin had lied to her, had been undercover in order to gain information to pin the murders on her. Liz was hurt by those acts, something she could no longer hide. Erin didn't know how to even begin to make it right. "I was confused and—"

"Confused?"

"Yes." Erin sucked in shaky breaths. "About you, and the way I felt and the way you made me feel."

"So you fuck her to feel better? Did it help with your confusion, Erin?"

"Stop it!"

"Did it?"

"Yes!"

Liz looked taken a back for a split second as if she hadn't expected Erin to answer at all.

"It made me realize my true feelings. That it was you that I wanted."

"I don't believe you."

"Why did I risk everything for you, then, Liz? My job, my life as I knew it. All of it. I did it for you."

"Well, maybe you shouldn't have."

"Why would you say that?" Erin cried.

"Because I'm bad, Erin. Just like Patricia says. Just like I'm sure she's always told you."

"No, you're not."

"I am. I don't give a shit about anybody but myself."

"That's not true. You love me. You love Jay."

"I'm not what you want me to be, Erin. I'm not Patricia. I'm not one of her perfect characters out of one of her books."

"I never said I wanted you to be that."

"You don't have to."

Erin looked away.

Liz continued. "I'm real. I'm flawed. I'm fucked up. And that's not what you really want."

"Yes, I—"

"No, you don't," Liz cut her off again.

"How can you say that? After all I sacrificed, after all the secrets and lies I had to swim through to find the real you?"

Liz dug through the drawer she'd slammed earlier and held up Patricia's latest lesbian romance. She tossed it at Erin, looking as if she'd crumple to her knees at any moment.

"You had it hidden under the bed," she whispered. "Who's keeping secrets now, Erin?"

She walked away, leaving Erin all alone staring at their empty room, Patricia's book clutched to her chest.

CHAPTER NINE

L iz awoke with a start, her heart racing in her chest. She sat up
and blinked, convinced a killer stood in the darkness, staring
her down. But no one was there. She turned and saw the emptiness
beside her. She was alone. Erin hadn't come to bed.

The dream had seemed real. A figure entering the room, laughing
as bloody hands were held up before a featureless face. "I'm going to
kill off everything that's dear to you," a voice had said.

It shook her to the core, but what unsettled her most was the sudden
pang inside telling her that she knew the killer. Just like before.

Liz flung her legs over the side of the bed and stood. She hugged
herself as the sweat that coated her body met the chill of the morning
air. She glanced at the alarm panel and her heart sped up again as she
realized it wasn't set.

Hurriedly, she ran down the hall, a nervous ball in her throat. She'd
been hurt and stubborn the night before, too caught up in her own pain
to make sure Erin was safe inside with the alarm set. She slammed to
a stop as she caught sight of Erin asleep on the largest couch, snuggled
tight under a light throw blanket. It was the first night they'd slept apart.
The reasons still tore at her insides.

She approached quietly and tugged the blanket up higher. Her
worry for Erin's safety ceased as a book fell to the floor. All she'd been
doing was lying on the couch reading. Relieved, Liz picked up the
paperback and glanced at the cover. Patricia's book. It opened to a dog-
eared page. Her chest tightened as she read. It was a love scene. One
of the characters strongly resembled Erin. Feeling sick, Liz turned the
book over to read the back blurb. Her stomach fell to her feet.

Erin. Patricia had written about Erin. It was plainly obvious. The character not only looked like Erin but she was a detective, a woman trapped in an unhappy marriage, who eventually fell for her lesbian colleague.

Liz dropped the book and stared at her lover, her fiancée. The woman who'd breezed into her life and turned it all upside down. The only woman she'd ever let into her heart. Erin.

She looked so peaceful when she slept. So beautiful.

Liz fought back the burning tears. Erin deserved better. Erin wanted different. Liz couldn't offer her the pure life that Patricia could. She couldn't even offer her safety. Or the truth.

Feeling like dying, Liz left her asleep on the couch and went to get ready for her day.

❖

The breeze was warm, promising more than mild sunshine and big-rig fumes. Patricia turned into it, hoping whatever was promised would be a major clue. It was a quarter past nine and by the look of the crowd, everyone was present and ready. She was dressed similarly to the others, in worn jeans and sturdy boots, ready for a long day of searching through the dry desert. Her navy VLPD T-shirt was already threatening to stick to her if the breeze let up even for a few minutes. Summer was beginning to take over from spring.

Around her a dozen or so Corona County cruisers were parked together, facing off the Valle Luna PD cruisers. She could almost hear their engines revving, ready to attack each other like thick-necked lineman on a football field. Beyond them sat more vehicles, unmarked cruisers and numerous volunteer's cars and trucks. The morning sun reflected off the mass of metal, bathing them all in equal light regardless of jurisdiction.

She headed toward the large crowd of people, wondering if like the cars, the positions had already been drawn in the sand. When she heard Sergeant Eric Ruiz barking out orders, she knew the answer right away. He was pointing at the enormous map spread out on the hood of a Valle Luna PD Ford Explorer. His short frame was stretched to reach the outer areas of the map and his voice was cracking from having to shout over the passing traffic. But he wasn't about to let up. Ruiz had the heart of a lion and the tenacity of a pit bull. He was relentless when it came to getting the job done and vicious about guarding his territory. The man next to him wearing a Corona County vest didn't stand a chance as he tried to offer his input. Ruiz simply didn't have the patience to listen.

The search had been put together hurriedly, both departments anxious to get their hands on more remains, desperate for new evidence.

Patricia watched the uncomfortable exchange for a moment and then glanced over to the dog handlers. Some had SAR on their backs, others wore orange vests. The labs, shepherds, and bloodhounds were anxious to get started, barking in high pitch, tugging on their leashes. Overhead she heard the repetitive thump of an approaching helicopter.

"Henderson?"

Patricia shaded her brow as Gary Jacobs strolled toward her. She caught her breath at the sight of the woman next to him. The stranger walked with confidence, not arrogance, the difference being attitude. Her shoulders were back, her physique muscular and strong. She moved with ease but kept her gaze level and her posture open. She looked like she could handle any situation while remaining levelheaded in the process. Patricia's heart rate kicked up as she studied the khakis that clung to her legs and the dark brown CCSD polo shirt that hugged her ample breasts.

She willed her face not to burn, and blamed Erin McKenzie for awakening her libido from its long hibernation. "Been looking for you," Gary said.

Patricia tore her eyes away from the woman's short, light brown hair, which was worn in tousled layers. She noticed that Gary sounded different. Guarded.

"I had to park way in the back," she said.

Her partner nodded, his tie lifting in the breeze. Even though he would spend the better part of the day in the desert, he still wore a tie, this time with jeans and L.L.Bean boots. He captured the tie with an irritated sweep of his hand and looked nervously to the woman beside him. "This is—"

"Detective Audrey Sinclair." She smiled slightly and extended her hand.

Patricia caught herself gazing into the reflection of her aviator sunglasses. She also noted the large-faced aviator watch. A pilot, perhaps? "Detective Patricia Henderson," she responded, releasing Sinclair's warm, strong hand just as quickly as she had taken it.

Trying to fend off an instant reaction to the brush of the detective's skin, she focused on Sinclair's thick brown belt and strong-looking forearms. Her senses told her that it was very likely Sinclair was gay. She cleared her throat with unusual nervousness.

"Sinclair has been assigned to the Highway Murders for the CCSD."

"Oh?"

Sinclair gave another small smile that showed a deep dimple on the right side of her face. Patricia wanted to look away but couldn't.

"I was hoping to meet with you to go over the case," Sinclair said. "I'm doing my best to play catch-up."

Gary looked to Patricia. She knew he didn't like the idea of sharing information, but it had to be done. Of course the real issue was claim. Sergeant Ruiz would have a fit if CCSD marched right in and solved the case when Valle Luna had put in all the hours. They also needed to work quickly before funding for the case began to dwindle, which often happened when cases went cold.

She knew this game and had played it a long time. She didn't want to just give away all that they'd found thus far, and that included theories as well. Just how much should they share? Wondering if Sergeant Ruiz had been introduced to the attractive detective yet, Patricia chose her words carefully. "As long as we get credit where credit is due, I don't see a problem."

Sinclair's face gave nothing away. "Glad to hear you aren't territorial, Detective Henderson. After all, we are on the same team."

Are we? Did that have a double meaning? Patricia fought off a blush and focused. "We may be on the same side of the fence, but we aren't on the same team," Patricia corrected.

Sinclair stood taller. "My mistake. I thought we were all out for the safety and well-being of our citizens." She ran a hand through her short hair in a manner that suggested she did it often, when she was frustrated. "I'll call you so we can set up a meeting." She turned and walked off, headed back toward the army of people who were now walking through the desert brush at an arm's length apart.

"That went well." Gary exhaled.

"Yeah, thanks for backing me."

"Hey, I'm not messing with that woman."

"Why not?"

"Because she can bench-press me, that's why. Besides, she's top notch. Former federal agent."

"What?"

"Yeah. She's new. Been with CCSD less than a year."

"What was she, ATF or something?" Patricia could imagine Sinclair in black SWAT clothes storming into a run-down shack after dozens of illegal weapons.

Gary sank his hands into his pockets. "FBI."

"No kidding?"

He nodded and they both watched as Sinclair stopped to speak with the man next to Ruiz.

"What is she doing here in Valle Luna?"

Gary shrugged. "That's where the story ends. I only got as much as I did because Hernandez's cousin works for CCSD. They're both here today, so I got the rundown on her."

"She left the FBI for Corona County." Patricia faced into the blowing wind, wondering what Sinclair's story was.

"They're paying feds shit these days." Gary clued her in on his theory. "A rookie on Valle Luna PD makes more than a G1."

Patricia was snapped out of her trance when Ruiz came walking up like a bull in a ring full of bloodthirsty matadors. He adjusted his wire-frame glasses, sweat sprinkled across his brow. His eyes were wide and paranoid, and he seemed jumpy. His intensity was palpable.

"I want you both out ahead of the others walking with the dog handlers. Anything's found, I want you all over it."

"Yes, sir," Gary replied.

"Sir, even if we find something, if it's in their jurisdiction it's theirs," Patricia said.

His eyes flew up to hers. "I know that, Henderson. But this is our case. I can't afford for them to fuck it up. So I want you here, investigating like it's yours, understand? If there's a discovery on their turf, I want you to take pictures right away, get as much info as you can."

She sighed and nodded, and he stormed off, already yelling to the next guy.

"This is not going to be fun," Gary said as they started walking. "I feel like I'm ten years old again and playing capture the flag."

Patricia laughed softly. "I hear ya. But I just keep hoping that we'll find the one clue that breaks the case."

Gary glanced over at her. "You better hope it's found on our turf."

❖

Erin laid the phone down on the end table. It was the tenth time she'd called Liz that day and still no answer. She'd left message after message, but Liz hadn't returned a single call.

She'd woken to an empty house, alone on the couch with the Dobermans lying at her feet. In the bedroom, she found their bed already made and the fresh scent of Liz's cologne in the air. Erin had been crying ever since, feeling completely lost and alone.

Wiping away warm tears, she rose from the couch to fetch her keys. The dogs followed her to the door and gazed tenderly at her as she set the alarm and headed outside for her car. The small Toyota SUV still smelled new. She'd resisted Liz's attempts to buy her something more expensive. Erin started it up and followed the circular drive out through the gate. She drove in silence, her nerves on edge. She'd been patient long enough, had given Liz her space time after time. She could wait no longer. After forcing herself to drive the speed limit the entire way, she pulled into a rare parking space in front of La Femme. She took a deep, anxious breath and exited the vehicle.

Music thumped in her ears as she crossed the parking lot. She wondered if Liz was watching her, and what she might be thinking. The two large female bouncers at the door nodded entry toward her as she stepped in front of the long line.

The club was hot and crowded, wall to wall with sweaty lesbians dancing the workweek away. Erin swallowed against a tight throat and realized she felt just as nervous as she had the first time she'd entered the club all those months ago.

Only now she had different questions that needed answering.

Angling through the mass of people, she squinted against the dimness and flashing strobe lights and headed directly for the staircase.

Tyson stood watching the crowd and she could tell by the surprise on his face that Liz had yet to spot her.

He greeted her with his usual courtesy but his dark eyes kept shifting.

"Is she here?"

He looked worried, then ashamed.

"She won't return my calls," Erin shouted over the music. She'd even tried to contact Tyson, but he too had avoided her calls.

"I'll let her know you're here," he said, pushing in on his earpiece.

"Since when do I need an invitation?"

Erin unhooked the red velvet rope and ascended the stairs quickly. The darkness thickened as she climbed. She slowed as she reached the top, taking in the poorly lit room outlined by numerous couches that were all occupied by women talking, laughing, making out.

Erin approached the bar, the only illumination in the room. The bartender gave her a wave and motioned toward the far railing. Erin followed her line of sight and stopped in her tracks. Liz leaned on the rail next to a blonde Erin recognized as one of La Femme's regulars. She was a yoga instructor, and Erin knew without asking that she'd been a lover of Liz's. She accepted that as history, along with the countless others that Liz had been with before her.

Erin watched as the two began to laugh.

Liz was laughing. She hadn't seen Liz smile in days, much less laugh.

Liz turned slightly toward the other woman and Erin caught sight of a satellite phone clipped to her waistband. Erin hadn't seen one since the night Kristen Reece had had tried to kill them all, Jay included. Liz told her she'd given the phone to Jay but hadn't heard from her since.

So why did Liz now have a replacement? One she hadn't told Erin about? Erin felt her stomach collapse as the blonde leaned in and whispered in Liz's ear. Her hand lingered on Liz's upper arm, the fingers lightly stroking up and down.

Liz smiled her crooked smile in response, the one that drove Erin wild. The one that whispered, "Oh, yeah."

The Studio Kings came over the speakers singing "Let's Have Sex" and the two women began to dance, dangerously close. They kept their hands to themselves but the intent was evident, evident in their eyes and in the way they moved. They were speaking without talking, fucking without touching. The music kept on, pounding and pounding, insisting that Erin see. Liz moved as she'd only moved with her. Hips, rhythm, eyes, lips. The blonde responded, inching closer, raising her hands into the air, offering and taking as if Liz were kissing her neck, holding her hip and thrusting into her with her fingers. They were fucking. And oh so enjoying it.

A sharp cry escaped Erin's throat as Liz stepped into the blonde and held her. Erin clasped her hand over her mouth and tried with all her might not to erupt in tears. Liz looked over and her grin vanished. She mouthed the word "Erin," and took a brief step toward her.

Erin turned, unable to stand the look on her face. Liz's motives were written all over her, and the pain of seeing it and knowing it burned painfully in Erin's gut. She ran for the stairs and nearly toppled down them to the bottom. She stormed past a questioning Tyson and ran in a mad sprint to her car. Sobs rocked her body as she leaned against the SUV. The pain she felt was unlike any she could ever have imagined. Jealousy, betrayal, confusion…as if she didn't really know who Liz was. The pain kept hitting her over and over again, hard smacking punches that just wouldn't let up. Just like the fucking pounding music she could still hear. It just wouldn't stop.

Desperate to get away, she began pushing buttons to unlock the car, but accidentally set off the alarm. She cursed and cried, managing to shut it off and unlock the doors. She climbed inside and started the engine. As the SUV came to life she glanced back at the entrance to the club.

Liz wasn't there. Liz wasn't coming after her.

She pulled out of the parking lot, her insides being eaten alive.

Liz, she cried to herself. *Why?*

❖

"Do you want me to have her followed?" Tyson asked, looking to his visibly distraught boss.

"No." Liz stared through the crowd to the main entrance where Erin had fled.

"If you don't mind my asking," he began cautiously.

"I do mind."

He clamped his mouth shut for a couple of seconds, but his concern overcame his well-disciplined respect. "I was going to ask if everything's okay."

His boss stood still, her eyes fixed on the door. He couldn't quite read her but he could tell she was worried, and hurt. It was evident in her eyes, even if her body seemed stoic. He thought briefly about reaching out to touch her arm, as if somehow to ground her in reality, but when she turned to look at him, he lowered his hand quickly. Eyes as hard as stone yet full of insurmountable pain bored into him.

"No, Tyson, everything is not okay." She flung the velvet rope to the side and headed back up the stairs.

❖

Once in her lair, Liz focused intently on the security monitors. She felt her body go numb as Erin's SUV drove out of the parking lot. She had to let her go. Nothing was okay anymore. It was time to stop pretending.

She clenched her fists as her painful emotions hardened into anger.

Someone had to pay. Someone had to pay for all of this.

And she was going to make sure they did.

❖

Tyson unclipped the velvet rope as his boss hurried down the stairs.

"Lock up tonight," she instructed. "I won't be back."

"Shall I forward any calls to your house?" It was standard procedure. Any calls or questions he couldn't handle, he forwarded to her.

"No. I'm not going home."

"To your cell phone, then?"

"No." She stopped for a moment, obviously frustrated. "No calls. Not tonight."

He watched as she brushed by him to weave through the crowd to the back exit, where she punched in her code to unlock the door.

"Yes, ma'am," he whispered as the door closed behind her.

❖

Erin silenced the alarm and shooed the dogs, too upset to greet them. Her brain was awash in liquid pain. Edges blurred, reality fogged. She filled bag after bag with her things. Shirts, blouses, jeans, socks. Drawers opened so hard their guards jammed. Her hands dug madly, tossing out her belongings, flinging them over her shoulders. When her fingernails scraped a drawer bottom, she stopped and yanked open the next one. Her body shook, her throat burned, but none of it seemed real.

When she was finished with the dresser she slid open the mirrored closet doors. She worked furiously, careful to leave anything Liz had given her. Robbed hangers swayed, shoes clumped in landing outside the doors. In a rage she attacked Liz's hanging clothes, tearing them from side to side, the very scent of them too much to bear.

After collapsing in a crying fit she stood in the middle of the large closet, turning in a slow circle, taking in what was once her whole world. She and Liz together. She gazed past what appeared to be a small gray box on Liz's side twice before she reached up to where it sat on the top shelf. She pushed the hanging clothes aside, exposing the safe.

She was somewhat surprised, having assumed Liz kept everything she valued locked up in her study. Her mind alerted her to the fact that she still didn't have access to some of those locked drawers, a fact she normally pushed out of her mind or made excuses for.

But tonight things were different. Erin breathed deeply, trying to calm herself enough to focus. She stretched to her tiptoes but still couldn't quite reach the electronic keypad. She searched the closet in vain and then went into the master bath to retrieve the vanity stool. Placing it at the foot of the hanging clothes, she braced herself in Liz's wardrobe and pulled herself up. She wiped her wet cheeks and concentrated. Her heart beat madly, numb with pain but surging with a fear of what she might find.

She punched the keypad, entering first Liz's birthday. Then

her own. Then the date she knew was Jay's. Nothing. She tried the alarm code to the house, the alarm code to the studio, to the club. Still nothing. Addresses, zip codes, phone numbers, any and all number combinations.

"Damn it."

She thought as hard she could. About anything and everything that was important to Liz. She thought about Jay again. Liz rarely spoke of her sister, but when she did, Erin had found her recall from their childhood extremely vivid.

Erin jolted. She stretched upward and tried one more set of numbers.

7, 1, 85.

The lock beeped. Her temples pounded in anticipation as she pulled open the door. Tentatively, she reached inside.

She felt something. Paper. Stacks of it. She pulled it out. It was money. Three large stacks of hundred dollar bills. She fumbled through the cash, fanning it out, confused. There had to be fifty thousand dollars. She reached back inside the safe and ran her hand along the base. A folded piece of paper flew out, caressing the air like a falling feather. She returned the money and stepped down to pick up the paper. As she opened it, a small photograph slid out. She caught it before it fell.

She turned it over and focused on the faded photograph of two young girls with hair as black as night. Tears came to her eyes as she realized the smaller one was Liz. She appeared to be humoring the photographer with a forced smile. Both girls sat on a weathered porch swing.

Erin ran her finger across Liz's smile. A little girl lost.

She focused on the child next to her, who could only be Jay. The faces were so similar, the eyes a familiar blue. Jay's hair was cut short in uneven strands, as if another child had tried to cut it. She wasn't looking at the camera, but at Liz, a sad, distant look on her face. A little girl pained.

Erin knew without a doubt that the photo had been taken shortly after the man in the woods. After July 1, 1985. Liz had told her of Jay's withdrawal, of the incessant hair-cutting. Erin fought back her tears as she concentrated on the paper. A series of numbers was written in the center in Liz's hand.

Erin repeated the numbers several times until she had them

memorized, and then returned everything to the safe. She returned the vanity stool and busied herself stuffing her bags and zipping them closed.

The dogs followed her down the hallway, their confused stares examining her bags as she set them down. She knelt and patted their heads, kissing them both on the snout, then stood and looked around. The pain had eaten away at her, leaving her hollow inside. She swallowed a fiery sob.

"Why didn't you just tell me?" she whispered into the air.

She heaved up her numerous bags and set the alarm. Then, without looking back, she walked out the door.

Chapter Ten

L iz gripped the steering wheel as she drove. Her mind was vicious, replaying the images that kept her foot pressing on the gas.

She could smell wet grass. The screen door slammed over the loud buzz of the cicadas. The throb in her forearm sang just as loud as she ran into her aunt's house.

"Oh, my Lord." Aunt Dayne jumped up from their old brown plaid couch and hurried to her.

Clutching her badly broken arm, Lizzie cried, "Jay." She could hardly speak. "Hurry."

"What is it now?" Uncle Jerry walked lazily in from the kitchen, a can of beer in his hand.

"It's Jay! A man has Jay!"

"What?" Jerry lowered his beer. "What did you say?"

She tried to control her crying. "A man. He took Jay. He has her."

"Oh, my Lord!" Dayne covered her mouth.

"What man?" Jerry demanded.

"I don't know. We found this dead body and—"

"A dead body!" Dayne shrieked.

"The man was by the body," Lizzie continued. "And he took Jay."

Jerry crossed to the television set, set down his beer can, and lifted his CB radio mic. He stared at her hard. "This better not be one of y'all's little games."

She shook her head. "It's not. No, sir. I swear it."

Jerry clicked the mic. "Earl, come back."

"Jerry!" Dayne began to sob, hysterically. "What if he's taken her, what if he's gone?"

"Shut up!" Jerry shouted.

Dayne tugged Lizzie to the couch and examined her arm. "It's not that bad," she said over and over again, as if to convince herself.

Jerry cursed and called again. Earl and his brother Roger lived just down the road.

Static came over the radio, then a voice. "Go ahead."

"Git Roger and your guns and git over here quick," Jerry said. "Somebody's took Jay."

"Come again?"

"Somebody's took Jay."

"10-4."

"We should call Sheriff Bowman," Dayne said, still clinging to Lizzie. "We should call everybody."

"Dayne, shut up! I'm taking care of it. Me and the boys is going to take care of it."

"But the sheriff..."

"There ain't no way he can get here fast enough and I ain't waiting." Jerry crossed the room to Lizzie and placed his hands on her shoulders. "Where are they?"

Lizzie shook her head, panicked." I don't know where he took her."

Jerry shook her. "Lizzie. Lizzie, where was you and Jay at?"

"In the woods. At the ravine."

"Down by your Papaw's?"

She nodded.

He released her to approach his gun cabinet. After placing a worn Red Man ball cap on his head, he loaded his shotgun. Lizzie kept hearing the man's evil laughter, hearing Jay telling her to run as the man dragged her behind the tree.

Dayne went into the kitchen and returned with a wet washcloth. She placed it on Lizzie's arm. Lizzie stared through her, hating all of a sudden how weak her aunt always was. Bowing down to Jerry, unable to handle anything, numbing herself with booze. Lizzie threw the rag to the ground and hurried after her uncle, who stood near the screen door stuffing ammo into his pockets. Beyond the screen door, she heard Earl's truck skid to a stop on the slick grass.

Jerry slung his shotgun and rifle over his shoulders and shoved two revolvers into the waistband of his jeans. He banged out the door and ran down the porch steps. Roger climbed out of the truck to let Jerry in. Her uncle paused, catching sight of her hurrying down the steps.

"Go back inside, Lizzie."

"But I wanna go with you."

Roger bowed his head, as if too overcome with emotion even to look at her.

"This ain't for you to handle." Jerry nodded toward the porch where Dayne stood looking ashen. "You go on inside and let Dayne tend to your arm."

"But Jay—"

"We're gonna go git your sister. I promise you that." He and Roger climbed in the truck with Earl, and the three men sped off into the Alabama woods.

Liz pulled off the paved road and followed a bumpy trail carved into the barren desert. After driving for about ten minutes she reached a clearing and put the Range Rover in park. She sat staring into the thick beams of her headlights. Dust hung heavy in the air. She glanced at the clock and grew all the more anxious.

Then, as the dirty air settled, she saw movement, a lone figure emerging from the darkness.

❖

"Interesting place."

He walked slowly through the house, noting the lack of photos or artwork on the walls, the mismatched old furniture, and numerous dark stains on the carpet. He could smell the staleness of the air. Lack of taste resonated from every room, and a coat of dust covered every surface. The place probably hadn't been cleaned in months. It almost looked as though it wasn't lived in. As if it were just kept on the side for doings he could only begin to imagine.

He entered what, in an average house, would be the dining room.

He stopped and ran his hands over a foosball table. It appeared to be on the newer side. On the adjacent wall hung an electronic dartboard. At least two dozen framed and signed photos of professional athletes, most of them baseball players, lined the walls. Had he given a shit it would have been quite impressive.

He shook his head, confused by the choice of décor.

He tried not to think of that, though.

A home makeover wasn't why he was here. He cocked his head as a small ripple of unease stirred in the back of his mind. Why exactly was he there?

He turned as he heard footsteps approaching from behind. A cold drink was offered to him, along with a disarming smile.

"Why, thank you." He took the drink with a smile of his own and downed several sips. One thing was for sure, it was going to be an interesting evening.

❖

What the hell am I doing? Patricia asked for the tenth time as the bartender's hands went up under her shirt, thrilling her skin.

You're getting laid. Now shut up and enjoy it.

Madelyn was now under her bra and pinching her nipples. Patricia caught her breath in pleasurable surprise. Mad laughed in her ear.

She's a La Femme bartender.

Tracy Walsh was a La Femme bartender. So was Kristen Reece. Killers.

Mad worked her nipples harder and bit her neck, pushing her firmly against the wall, forcing the thoughts out.

"I'm so glad you called," she purred, rubbing her thigh against Patricia's crotch.

Her apartment was tiny and cluttered, the taste eclectic. It smelled of incense and dryer sheets. Clean but overwhelming.

"I don't usually do this," Patricia confessed.

"What's that?"

"This. Casual sex."

Mad grinned devilishly. "Well, maybe that's your problem." She rolled Patricia's nipples and tugged on them.

"Mmm." Patricia couldn't speak. She was too caught up in the battle between her paranoid mind and starving body.

You've checked her out. She's clean. Not even into drugs. Now relax, she wants you.

Her eyes rolled back in her head as the wonderful sensation of a hot wet mouth on her skin spread throughout her insides. It felt so good. It had been so long. Seeing Erin the other night had only worsened her state of mind, leaving her feeling vulnerable, confused, and hungry once again. Then there was Audrey Sinclair. The stunning cop had also stirred her blood. Suddenly her body *demanded* service.

"You are really fucking beautiful," Mad said. The bartender had been ready for her, pouncing on her the second she'd walked in the apartment door. "I can't wait to taste you. I bet you're already soaking wet."

She lowered her hand to hastily unbutton Patricia's jeans. As her nimble fingers inched their way down into her panties, Patricia began to doubt her decision. "Wait, maybe we should…"

Oh, God. It's…fuck…it's so fucking wonderful. Patricia closed her eyes, overcome.

Mad laughed again, having found her aching flesh. "Yeah, baby, feel me." She moved her hand up and down, her fingers sliding along the sides of her clit.

Patricia's head banged back against the wall as Mad's fingers skimmed over the tip of the engorged head. Her legs trembled, threatening to give.

Do what she says. Just feel it.

Yes. Anything.

Anything to get free from my mind.

A ringtone sounded and Patricia jumped, making Mad pull her hand away. Patricia plucked her cell phone off the sagging waistline of her jeans. The digital clock told her it was after midnight and the caller was Gary Jacobs. She had to talk to him.

"Henderson," she said, gasping for breath.

"Where are you?"

Caught off guard, she fingered her hair with a shaky hand. "I'm out, just you know, out." She felt guilty and defensive. "Am I not allowed to go out?"

All she did was work. Work and write. She never did anything socially for herself.

"What?" Gary sounded confused but quickly moved on. "We got another one."

Patricia felt the blood rush from her face. Her mind was still way behind her body. Dazed, she said, "What?"

"We got another one that looks like Gillette."

Patricia swayed a little as her blood rushed back to her head. "Where?"

"East Valle Luna, practically in Adams's backyard. The station got an anonymous call an hour ago. I'm just now on my way."

"I'll be right there."

She ended the call and stuck her phone into her pocket as she hitched up her jeans. *What am I doing here?* Suddenly her harmless little get-together seemed more than obviously wrong. Mad worked for Adams. They were investigating Adams. Not to mention the fact that Patricia didn't have casual sex. Especially with someone who was known to have it often. Had she learned nothing from her relationship with Adams? She felt sick with shame and guilt.

"I have to go." She buttoned her pants and adjusted her shirt and hair.

"That's too bad," Mad raised her hand to lick at her fingers. "I was just getting started."

Patricia ignored her, upset at her body for still responding to her. She moved to the door with Mad close behind.

"Come back anytime, so we can finish." Mad leaned in and planted a firm, wet kiss on her lips. Maybe we can whip out those handcuffs."

Patricia forced a small smile. As she turned to walk out she knew without a doubt that she would never be back. The handcuffs would remain cold forever.

❖

Jay Adams watched it all from her position nestled into the side of the mountain. Down below, red and blue flashing lights went around and around, lighting up the walls of the surrounding hills. She hugged herself against the chill of the night air.

Lizzie.

Her sister's large home was down and to the left. The body, now covered in a sheet, was only a couple hundred yards away.

Things had to be done. Like it or not.

She squinted as more portable floodlights were turned on. Anxious detectives and forensic people milled around the crime scene, working like misguided ants to examine and preserve the area. Car doors slammed as more arrived.

It was right that she came back.

For her, her sister whom she loved more than anything in the world. The one she'd sworn to protect always.

CHAPTER ELEVEN

Patricia climbed out of her Chevy Blazer, exhausted.

"Is it true?"

"Oh, my God." She clasped her chest, at first in fright and then in relief. She caught her breath. "You scared the shit out of me, Mac."

She'd just arrived home after examining their latest victim and crime scene. It had been a long night.

"Sorry." Erin approached from the edge of the driveway.

"Is what true?" Patricia removed her sunglasses and squinted at her in the harsh sunlight.

"That there's been another murder? One connected to Gillette's?"

"Yes." Patricia studied her closely. She looked weak with fatigue and confusion.

"Is it true the victim is linked to Liz?"

"Yes."

Erin's body appeared to go limp, but she fought to hold herself upright. "Who…who was it?"

"We've been trying to find you," Patricia said. "No one's seen you. Adams isn't speaking to us." Patricia took a step toward her, noticing the instability in her stance. "Mac, are you okay?"

"Just please, tell me who."

"De Maro. Antwon."

"Oh, God." Erin nearly collapsed, but Patricia caught her in the nick of time.

"Come on," she said, "let's get you something to drink."

She helped her into the house where the security system beeped. Her Jack Russell terrier, Jack, caught their scent and stood and stretched on his little bed in the corner. Patricia hurriedly typed in her code to silence the new security system she'd installed. A strong sense of déjà vu overcame her as she watched Erin kneel on the Spanish tile to pet Jack. It hadn't been that long ago. Her heart rate kicked up as she recalled the stormy night when Tracy Walsh and Jay Adams had broken into her home.

Erin straightened and looked at her as if she knew what she was thinking. "You got an alarm."

Patricia forced a calm smile. She had to put the past behind her. But it was difficult when it was staring her right in the face.

"Are you okay with my being here? I mean, after everything." Erin shook her head as if she were frustrated with herself for even asking. She headed for the door. "It was wrong of me to come."

Patricia reached for her arm. She had such mixed emotions over Erin, feelings she might never figure out. But she couldn't let her leave. Not when she looked as if she might crumple at any moment.

"It's all right," she said, relieved when Erin allowed herself to be escorted to the living room.

Patricia eased her down onto the leather couch and left her with an affectionate Jack. As a cop who had experienced malice on her own turf, she was now adamant about keeping the doors and windows locked at all times even with the addition of the alarm.

After securing the house, she poured a glass of iced tea for each of them and sat down on the couch a few feet from Erin.

"Mac, are you hurt?"

She had no idea where Erin had been or with whom. There were no physical marks of harm, but pain, as she knew, could be held deep within. Erin looked completely washed out and appeared barely able to hold herself upright. As if she were a drawing on a page and the artist had simply run the side of his hand over her, smearing her existence.

"I'm okay." Erin took the tea and sipped it, while patting Jack on the head. He licked her hand for a while and then darted into the kitchen where they heard him rocket through his doggie door.

Erin laughed a little. "I forgot how much I love him." She grew quiet.

Patricia toyed with the idea of asking the question pressing on her mind: *Where's Liz?* But she could sense Erin's stress. Any extra pressure could drive her away.

Erin smiled, her chin tilted up. "Seeing him makes me miss the Dobermans. Did you know Liz named them after the dogs on *Magnum P.I.?*" When Patricia didn't answer, she continued. "Higgins had two Dobermans. Zeus and Apollo. Liz used to love that show, and when she got her dogs she thought of it. Only she named hers Zeus and Ares after seeing just how much like Ares the little puppy was." Erin again stared off in silence.

Patricia fought off her urge to bad-mouth Liz. "I didn't think Liz watched television."

Erin met her eyes. "As a child sometimes it was her only escape. After what happened in the woods, she and Jay didn't leave the house much. Jay was almost completely agoraphobic and Liz didn't want to leave her."

"What happened in the woods?"

Erin looked a little surprised. "You mean you still don't know?"

Patricia felt herself flush with anger. She had never understood the tight bond between Jay and Liz. "How do you expect us to know anything when we get no cooperation?"

"You're including me in that statement too, aren't you?"

"Yes."

Erin had lied and kept things from the department. Patricia had tried to forgive her but she still held some resentment and anger.

"I'm sorry," Erin said.

"Are you?"

Erin shifted on the couch. "Of course I am."

"Then tell me about the woods."

Erin cleared her throat. "It's not my story to tell."

"For God's sake, Mac." Patricia stood, upset. When Erin and Liz had told them "everything" the year before, they hadn't mentioned why in Arcane, Alabama, the Adams name was either unknown or very hush-hush. All along, Patricia had suspected a history. Every family had secrets. Maybe theirs would explain why Jay was willing to do anything for Liz. And vice versa. "Look, what happened to Jay and Lizzie is their childhood, their memory, their nightmare. Not mine. I can't go behind their backs and talk about it."

"But it has everything to do with what's going on now."

Erin looked away. "I don't think so."

"Bullshit."

"This isn't easy for me."

"It's not about you, Mac. It's about murder. Where the hell is Jay?"

Jack returned, jumping quickly onto Erin's lap. She stroked him softly. "I don't know where she is." She met Patricia eyes. "I swear I don't." She continued to pet Jack. Her face took on a far away look, as if Jack's fur were hypnotizing.

Patricia sighed. "Mac?"

"I'm sorry, I'm just so…lost." She began to cry. "I've been driving around. And thinking."

Patricia asked the obvious. "What's going on with Liz?"

She knew Erin hadn't been with her. Adams had been less than cooperative the night before, telling them to fuck off and then threatening violence. When they'd inquired about Erin, she nearly tore their heads off. The tantrum had landed her a night in jail, where she refused to answer any questions. Carmichael had breezed in, just like always, but this time she had no alibi tape. Adams only was released because they had nothing substantial on which to hold her.

"I left her," Erin said.

The admission shocked Patricia. It hadn't been that long since Erin had stood before her and the department and defended Adams. The idea that their relationship was in trouble, or over entirely, was almost unbelievable.

"I'm sorry." Patricia didn't know what else to say. While she hated Adams, and had once wished for Erin to be her own, she truly felt bad.

Erin lifted her head, her eyes wet and pained. "Aren't you going to say 'I told you so'?"

"I…" Why wasn't she saying that? Erin was watching her, expecting it. "I don't want to see you hurt."

"Yeah, well, I am. And you were right."

"I don't want to be right. That's not what this is all about."

Watching her cry, Patricia realized just how much she still cared about her. Erin was in pain and it was Adams's fault. Her protectiveness kicked in. "Why did you leave her?"

Erin didn't answer for a long while. When she did, her face was troubled and ashen. "I don't think I really know her."

Patricia felt her stomach rise up to her chest as if she were descending on a steep roller coaster. "Did you find something tying her to these murders?"

"No."

Patricia breathed out a long sigh. "You're sure?"

Erin nodded. "She's been behaving strangely. But she's not killing people."

"Strangely how? It's important that I know. What you think is insignificant may not be to the case."

"Don't you think I know that?"

"Do you, Mac? Because you're still keeping things from me."

"What do you want me to tell you?"

"The truth!"

"You want to know the truth? Well here it is." Erin stood, her knuckles white as she fisted her hands. "She's been acting strange. She doesn't eat, she doesn't sleep. She won't tell me why. We argue over everything." She swayed a little and Patricia stood to steady her but Erin swatted away her hand. "Then last night I caught her dancing with another woman. They were flirting. They were nearly fucking right there in front of me. So I went home and packed my bags."

"I had no idea," Patricia murmured, half to herself. They had intentionally pressured Adams, hoping for her to crack and tell them where Jay was. It hadn't occurred to Patricia that doing so might cause problems for Erin.

"Why would you know? We're not friends anymore."

Stung, Patricia said, "You're wrong about that, Mac. I never stopped being your friend."

Erin wiped her eyes and her face softened. "I found this number." She dug in her pocket and pulled out a folded piece of paper. "It was in a safe in the closet. I memorized it and wrote it down." She opened it up and handed it to Patricia. "I found an old photo of Liz and Jay and a large amount of cash with it."

"It's a satellite phone number." Patricia's heart jumped.

"I think she knows where Jay is," Erin said in a thin, sorrowful voice. "All this time she knew and she didn't tell me. I thought she told me everything. Things she never told anyone else. So why didn't she tell me about this?"

"Come on," Patricia said. "Let's get you in a bed before you collapse."

Carefully and full of concern, Patricia led her down the hallway to the spare bedroom. She eased her down onto the bed and removed her shoes. Erin lay back against the pillows as Patricia covered her with a light blanket.

"Get some rest." Patricia said softly. "When you wake we'll talk some more."

Jack jumped on the bed and snuggled down next to Erin. Patricia watched them for a moment before leaving the room. Deep in thought, she headed down the hallway to her office, staring at the phone number in her hand.

Finally. A lead on Jay Adams.

❖

Liz sat on the king-sized bed and flipped slowly through the magazine full of pictures from the Caribbean. Erin had dog-eared numerous pages, hoping that they would soon be able to escape and marry in the tropical paradise. Liz had eagerly made the promise, letting Erin choose where she wanted to go. Liz could still recall how Erin's green eyes would sparkle with excitement when they talked about their plans. For a long while, it seemed to be all she could think about.

Those dreams were gone now, discarded like the magazine Erin had left on the floor. Liz could read the message, that their love had been thrown away. She cursed herself. She should've married her back then, but she'd been self-centered, putting her businesses before their relationship. Erin hadn't complained. Instead she'd stepped up to help.

Because she loved me.

Liz wiped away a stray tear as she glanced around the room. Drawers hung open and empty. Erin had taken her pillow, leaving the bed unbalanced. She was gone. Nothing had ever hurt so bad. Liz felt as empty as the room, a mere shell with nothing of value left on the inside.

She rose and absently fingered her wrists. They were still sore from last night. The handcuffs had been too tight and left on too long before she'd been shoved into an overcrowded cell. But she hadn't cared. She'd wanted to kill the large, rude cop who'd made a comment about Erin. He'd asked where she was, whether they had been fucking in the pool again. Then, upon seeing her face, he changed his verbal assault tactic.

"Or maybe you've been fucking somebody else and she threatened to leave," he gloated. "Maybe you killed her. Maybe you killed her like you did those men. Yeah, that's it. She found out the truth and you had to kill her."

Liz had lunged at him then, wanting nothing more than to tear his fucking throat out. She knew how to. She'd been trained well over the years in mixed martial arts and she knew how to kill just as she knew how to protect herself. If another cop hadn't held her back, she honestly didn't know if she could have stopped herself.

And now Erin was gone. Erin had left her. She thought about Patricia's book. It hadn't taken long for Tyson to confirm that Erin's SUV was at the detective's house. Maybe Erin was where she truly belonged.

Liz looked into her closet and caught sight of the abandoned hangers. Her insides felt the same—ripped, torn, and left completely skeletal. That's all she was now. Bones.

She moved her clothes to open the safe. Antwon's body had been found right next to her house. She shivered as she turned the dial. Her hand shook as she opened the paper to look at the photograph. Walking back into the room, she grabbed her satellite phone and dialed.

❖

Flash.

Patricia blinked against the white light as Gary Jacobs moved around the metal gurney, snapping photos of the body.

Flash, flash.

"Antwon De Maro. Twenty-eight-year-old male. Five foot ten. Hundred and fifty-seven pounds, African American descent." She paused, examining his nude body. "In excellent physical shape. Well nourished, though on the thinner side. Pubic hair well trimmed. Head of the penis pierced once with small half-ring in place. Four stab wounds to the genital region, two flanking the penis and two on the testes. No other visible wounds. All bruises and abrasions appear to be on the neck."

Gary took close-ups of the throat.

"Significant marks on the front and sides of neck. Cause of death has been determined as strangulation." She stared at the purple reddish marks. One was higher up than the others, a demonic red grin on the upper neck. A ligature mark, made by something other than hands. The killer had strangled De Maro more than once.

Gary moved the head from side to side with a gloved hand. "Just like Gillette," he said. His face was serious and he was chewing on the inside of his bottom lip, his mind obviously working a mile a minute.

Patricia clicked Pause on her recorder and breathed deeply, thankful for Gary's cologne. "Maybe the repeat strangulation was out of choice rather than need. Maybe he purposely tortured them." She imagined the scenario in her head. "He strangled them again and again. First with a cord or rope here," she said, pointing to the thinner, higher mark. "Then he used his hands. Or maybe vice versa. But my gut tells me he probably preferred to finish them manually."

Gary lifted the young man's hands. "He didn't try to fight back." The fingers were free of bruising or abrasions, the nails clean and intact, just as Gillette's had been.

"He was probably drugged." She studied the body closely, looking over every last inch of skin. He'd already been combed for trace evidence and everything had gone to the lab along with his clothes. They were waiting for the results.

"He must have been nearly unconscious not to fight back while being strangled."

"What did Gillette have in his system? Ecstasy?" She knew but she needed him to answer. They often thought aloud.

"Yes. Not enough to cause unconsciousness."

"So if De Maro's drugged, and let's assume he was, our killer gets him a little relaxed with the ecstasy and then strangles him. For whatever reason our victims don't try and fight back. There's no indication that their hands were bound. Then, out of rage or in some sort of sick copycat fashion, our killer stabs his genital region after he's dead."

She brought the recorder to her mouth. "But why? Why didn't the victims fight back? Was this erotic asphyxiation? If so, why the stabbing of the genitals?"

"That's the million-dollar question," the coroner, Dr. Nat

Burroughs, said, strolling into the room. Patricia hadn't known Nat for very long, but she knew his sense of humor was as wicked as his mind was sharp. He was a tall, thin man with dark brown skin and an infectious smile, bald on top with thick and curly hair on the sides and numerous gray sprouts. His shoes were covered like a surgeon's and made a shuffling noise as he moved to stand next to the body. He'd obviously stripped out of his scrubs to come talk to them.

Patricia could smell the hand soap he favored, a powerful ginseng that she'd often asked about because she liked the scent. She relaxed with his arrival, glad that they would soon be finished. She hated this place, and never got used to the finality it represented. They were in the icebox, the large back room full of metal drawers where the bodies were kept cool. Filing cabinets for the dead. There was no cutting here, no sawing, no poking or draining. The bodies that were here had already been through all of that. De Maro was no exception—the large "Y" stitched on his chest and abdomen made him look like a human baseball, roughly sewn together.

Nat stood hunched over the gurney, one arm across his chest while his other hand stroked his five o'clock shadow. He shook his head. "Poor boy."

"Got anything good, Nat?" Gary asked.

Their routine was simple. She and Gary would look over and photograph the body, then depending on whether he had the time, Nat would either walk in and verbally give them his report or they would have to settle for the typed version. The coroner before Nat had never offered his time, preferring to work almost solely with his silent patients, leaving dealing with the living to other staff. Patricia was thankful that somebody more social and willing to help had come along. And today, they were lucky. Nat had the time.

She turned on her recorder as Nat recited his observations, no chart needed. He sank his hands into the deep pockets of his worn lab coat. The lab coat, along with soft corduroy pants, was what he always wore when he met them in the icebox.

"Well, let's see, you know the basics, right?"

Patricia nodded. "He was strangled, possibly drugged beforehand because of the lack of defensive wounds. Dumped in the desert very soon after death."

"Right, right," Nat said as he began to move.

Gary backed up, allowing the doctor to circle the body, just as he always did when he gave a report, as if he were winding himself up.

"The body was very clean, despite having sustained stab wounds. He most likely bled little because the wounds were made postmortem, but still, there was very little blood on him. A few small stains on his underwear, that sort of thing." He met Patricia's eyes but continued to move. "He was sexually active, within twenty-four hours of the time of death."

"Any semen?" DNA heaven. She held her breath.

"No, none. There were, as with Gillette, some abrasions in and around the rectum."

She nodded. The information was helpful, but she had already confirmed that both men had led very active sex lives.

"There is one thing I think you'll find interesting and it's why I called." He moved to the long stainless steel countertop against the side wall, where he snapped on some gloves. Crossing back to the body, he said, "Do you remember the small crucifix on Gillette?"

"The tattoo?" Gillette had several.

Nat grunted softly as he lifted De Maro up a ways to show his back. "We found a small crucifix on Gillette's back, which we assumed was a tattoo. But when we washed the body after the autopsy, the ink faded. It was drawn on. My secretary called your precinct to let you know. I wasn't sure if it was something significant or not."

Gary nodded. "Yeah, I remember. Now it seems as if it is."

"Come have a look," Nat said, still holding up the body.

Patricia quickly rolled an examination lamp over and switched it on. A crucifix was inked on the skin of his lower back. The ink was faded as if it had been washed.

"Sweet holy mother of God." Gary bent down to take a photo.

Nat let out a boisterous laugh. "That's a good way of putting it." He touched the cross with his finger. "It's definitely drawn on."

"There's absolutely no question now," Patricia said. "We got another serial."

CHAPTER TWELVE

The diner was small and overcrowded, the strong scent of coffee and the sound of clanking silverware filling the room. Erin tapped her fingers on the table after pushing away the plastic menu offering just four choices: Breakfast. Lunch. Dinner. Pie. Nervous, she gazed out the window and watched a light breeze blow the trees against a gray, smoggy backdrop of a sky. The scene fit her mood. She was nothing but a lone tree, blowing whichever way the wind demanded.

The past few days had been a surreal hell spent tossing and turning in a bedroom she'd never expected to be in again. Asking herself questions she knew she'd most likely never find answers to. Dying inside. Dealing with the rejection. Dealing with the fact that she might never have really known Liz. Jealousy clawed at her soul, tearing her open each and every second of the night. All of it was too much.

It was pain she never could've imagined.

"Holy shit," a voice said, the body quickly following, sliding into the booth across from her. "It's my old friend Mac."

Erin grinned at her longtime friend J.R. Stanford and squeezed his hands as he greeted her.

"How you been, sister girl?"

She laughed, loving how no matter what, J.R. could put a smile on her face. He motioned for the waitress and ordered a slice of apple pie. "And make it big," he instructed, "I'm a growing boy. And," he said, gently grabbing the waitress as she was leaving, "coffee. Black." He looked to Erin. "You order yet?"

"I'm fine."

He grimaced, hand still on the waitress. "And the same for my friend here."

The waitress nodded and walked away. J.R. patted Erin's hand affectionately while slinging his other arm over the back of the booth. His shirt was trademark loud, wild-looking tropical trees growing in all directions. His eyes were lively and kind, and his mouth was already clearing a path for his mind.

"So, *qué pasa?*" he asked in his Spanish lisp. "How long has it been? Like a year or something?"

"Yeah, I think so."

"How you been?"

She forced a smile. "I've been okay." She paused, hoping she sounded believable. "You?"

"Ah, you know, a bit of this, a bit of that. I think what they did to you was shit, by the way. So you fucked a suspect?" He shrugged. "She was hot. You're hot." He lifted his eyebrows. "That tape was hot. And she ended up being innocent."

Erin closed her eyes, torn between wanting to laugh and wanting to cry.

J.R. continued, unperturbed. "You were a good cop, the best undercover I've ever worked with." He scoffed. "Stupid motherfuckers."

Erin cleared her throat, trying to rid herself of the emotion his words brought on. "I did wrong. They were right to fire me."

"Whatever. They shoulda done their job better."

They sat in silence for a moment. Erin felt her body threaten to tremble. She hoped he didn't notice.

"So I heard you and Adams are engaged or some shit like that." He looked to her hands on the table, knuckles white from their grip on one another. He frowned and she assumed he was looking for a ring.

"Actually..." She took in a breath. She had to tell him. She was about to spill over with pain and sorrow. "We're separated."

He raised an eyebrow. "Separated?"

"I left her."

"Fuck." He leaned back in surprise. He seemed to think heavily for a moment. "Why?"

She let out a long breath. Her chest shook. "It's a long story."

"I got all day. Fuck the job."

"Thank you. But that's not why I'm here." She held his eyes. "I need your help."

A large pot of coffee came between them, their mugs were turned upright and filled. When they were alone again she continued.

"I was hoping you would help me. It's about the new murders. Gillette and De Maro."

"The ones Henderson has?"

"Yes."

"I don't know, Mac. I'm not anywhere near those cases. They're big deals. With those and the Highway Murders, people are talking FBI involvement. Ruiz and the whole department are walking around like hot pokers are up their asses."

"I know. And I don't want you to do anything that could cause you trouble. But I was wondering if you could put your ear to the ground, so to speak."

He slurped his coffee. "How so?"

"De Maro and Gillette were gay, big on the club scene."

"I see."

"I was hoping you could ask around, find out who they were dating or hanging out with."

He slurped some more and winked at the waitress when she delivered their pie. He cut into it with his fork and shoveled a big mouthful. "Tell me why."

"Because everyone thinks Liz has something to do with it. The victims both worked for her. I knew these guys, J.R."

"What about you? You think she has something to do with it?"

"No. But I'm afraid she knows more than she should."

"You left her, though, so why do you give a shit?"

She looked off again at the blowing trees. "Because I love her." Despite it all, that was the painful truth. That was why it hurt so damned bad.

He chewed absently. "You really do love her, don't you? Sacrificing your job, leaving behind the life you had, all that for this woman."

"I do, J.R."

"But you left her."

Erin wrapped her hands around the hot coffee mug, needing to feel the sting. "She's troubled and she's not herself. She pushed me away and kept something from me and…no matter what, I just want her to be happy. Even if it's without me."

"Wow. That's some classic dyke melodrama shit right there." He pointed his fork at her. "But she did something else too, for you to leave her. She cheated on you, didn't she?"

Erin lowered her eyes. "I'm not sure."

"Uh-huh. I knew it. I knew when we went under after her. She's a player." He spelled it aloud for her. "P-L-A-Y-A." He shook his head. *"Mentirosa."*

Erin sighed. "She's just not being herself. The secrecy, her behavior…"

"Mac, you ever think that's who she really is? That you're finally seeing the real Elizabeth Adams?"

"I don't know anymore. But I know I saw a part of her no one else has. A good part. A loving part."

"But again, you left her."

"Yes, I did. I don't think she wants me anymore. But still I…I want to help her." She knew Liz didn't want her. That much was obvious. But the reasons tore at her. What had she done? What hadn't she done?

"So you want me to sniff around a bit about these dead twinks."

"If you wouldn't mind. Did you know them?"

"Nah, saw the one, De Maro, around a few times. But we never spoke."

They sat in silence for a moment as more orders were called out and waitresses scurried about delivering them. J.R. lowered his mug. "So, are you okay? You have a place to stay?"

Erin finally took a slow sip of the coffee. It flooded her mouth with warm comfort. "I'm staying with Patricia."

J.R. grinned from ear to ear. "No kidding?"

Erin rolled her eyes. "It's not like that."

"The hell it isn't. She's always had it bad for you. Written all over her uptight little face."

She fought off a blush. "We aren't like that, J.R."

"Not yet." He grinned again. "She know you're poking around the case?"

"No. She wouldn't be happy." But she was going to keep trying. Liz didn't deserve to be hounded for something she didn't do. It wasn't right, and Erin would do anything to help. Anything less would seem like a betrayal of all they'd shared.

"Well then, poke her first." He winked. "Then you might get somewhere with the case."

After they paid the check, they walked outside and parted with a long hug. J.R. kissed her roughly on the cheek and made her promise to call him if she needed anything. She nodded and waved, watching him drive off, car thumping to the beat of a local Latino station. The blowing breeze caressed her cheeks gently. She wished it could lift her up and carry her away. Her heart ached, dull and irritating, a small, black rock beating in her chest, keeping her alive and moving, but nothing else.

She was surprised when she found herself behind the wheel of her Toyota, the sun shimmering off the hood, soothing her. She drove eastward, staring straight ahead, entranced. When she reached Erotique Studios, she again felt the small sting of surprise. What was she doing here? She didn't know.

She climbed from the car and headed for the door. Her index finger punched in the code but the door didn't open. She stood staring at the small monitor screen, numb. A whoosh caught her attention. Don had pushed open the door and was smiling at her.

"Erin, come on in."

She tried to return the smile but couldn't. She followed him inside. The building smelled the same, like new office equipment and industrial carpet. She trembled when she caught the lingering scent of Liz's cologne.

"Is she here?" The voice was hers but she almost didn't recognize it.

Don stepped backward toward her, cupping her elbow. "Yes." His eyes were bright and concerned. "Are you okay?"

"I need to see her."

Just then the door to Liz's office opened and Liz stood in a dark business suit, eyes cast downward on the papers Reggie was holding. They had apparently been in a meeting. Reggie nodded and walked away, but stopped midstride when he saw Erin. He looked back to his boss.

Liz stood very still, her gaze fiercely fixed on Erin. Her face gave away nothing. Erin felt Don stiffen next to her. She gave him a small smile of thanks and walked toward Liz. When Liz didn't move, Erin stepped beyond her and into her office, where she waited by the desk. Her small, desolate heart began to beat wildly in her chest, spreading the blood through her body. Seeing Liz, smelling Liz, it was killing her. She wanted to die, to collapse in Liz's arms, but she fought to stay strong. She waited, refusing to turn around.

Liz came to the desk slowly, rounding it to stand by her chair. Her face was strong and striking, yet pale and wounded. Erin wanted to touch it. She wanted to caress it. She wanted to place kisses along the jawline.

"Something I can do for you?" Liz's voice was as cold as her blue eyes. But Erin saw the hint of red at the base of her throat, the jump in her pulse.

"You can tell me what the hell it is you're doing," Erin rasped.

Liz's fingers gripped the top of her chair. "Excuse me?"

"Why are you pushing me away?" Erin had to know. Couldn't rest until she knew.

"I'm not the one who left."

Erin wanted to scream but she was too weak. "Don't play games, Liz. You wanted me to go." She braced her hands on the large, antique desk, resisting the memory of having made love on it just a couple of weeks ago. "Did you cheat, Liz?"

Liz pushed the intercom button on the phone. "Reggie, I need those latest numbers."

"Sure thing," he responded.

Erin forced her voice up her raw throat. "Answer me."

Liz began rearranging papers. "There's nothing more to say." But Erin heard the hesitance in her voice.

"Did you fuck that blonde just to get rid of me? Or had you been doing her all along?"

"You can see yourself out," Liz said, avoiding her gaze.

Erin rounded the desk, causing Liz to straighten with surprise. Erin grabbed her shoulders. "Tell me. I need to know."

Liz's jaw flexed. "There's nothing to say."

"Tell me you don't love me."

Liz stared.

"Say it," Erin demanded. "Say you don't want me."

A knock came from the door. Liz reached down to push the button to grant entry but Erin caught her by the wrist.

"You say it first. You say it and I'll leave you alone, Elizabeth Adams. I'll walk out that door and out of your life."

Liz tensed and Erin caught sight of a bruise ringing her wrist.

"What's this?" she asked. "What happened?"

Liz pulled her hand away. She didn't even blink. "I don't want you." The words came out as a ragged whisper.

Erin felt the jolt of their meaning stab deep into her bones. She heard movement behind her and turned. Reggie hovered in the doorway, looking about as ashen as Erin felt. The tension in the air was stifling. He offered her a polite smile but she couldn't return it.

She walked from the office to the outer door, ignoring hellos from other employees. When she stepped out into the sunshine, her eyes and body recoiled at its brightness, as if she were an angry vampire.

She wiped away tears. She imagined them to be black. Black like her blood.

Chapter Thirteen

It did a strange thing to Patricia's heart to know that Erin was at her home and that she had someone to make dinner for. Her chest filled with warmth as she glanced over at her, as if her heart were full of love and contentment and then someone had squeezed it so its insides flooded her chest. She felt really good despite the stress of her current caseload. She'd worked nearly three days straight after De Maro's body was found and she was exhausted, more than ready for a relaxing evening of cooking and chatting with Erin.

"You're making dinner, I see." Erin slid onto a bar stool, her eyes trained on the salad.

"Therapy," Patricia said with a soft smile. "It helps me unwind. I hope you're hungry."

A sad look overcame Erin's face. That's when Patricia noticed that her eyes looked dull, as if drained of color.

"I haven't been," Erin said.

Patricia grabbed a large tomato and began dicing. The chicken and potatoes were in the oven, warming the kitchen with their scent. She hoped the home-cooked meal would cheer them both up, revitalize them.

"Where have you been going every day?" she asked, tying to sound lighthearted. She knew Erin had been going out. She'd called the house and get no answer. She got the same thing when dialing Erin's cell.

"Today I went to the library."

"Oh? Get anything good?"

Erin was staring beyond her, as if in her own world.

"Mac?"

"Huh?" she snapped back.

"I asked if you got anything good? As in books?"

"Oh. Yeah. Sure."

Patricia studied her for a few moments. She'd lost some weight and Patricia knew she wasn't sleeping well, having heard her up and moving around in the middle of the night on more than one occasion. She was worried about her, and hated that she hadn't been at home to help her more during this emotionally trying time.

"How have you been feeling about things?" she asked. "Any better?"

"About the same."

"Have you heard from Liz?" She asked the question gently, her curiosity getting the better of her. It wasn't like Adams to just let something go. Especially if Erin was the one who did the leaving. The Adams Patricia knew would be doing all she could to win Erin back.

"No."

Patricia dropped the chunks of tomato in the salad. "Do you want to talk to her? Maybe you should make the first move."

She didn't know why she was suggesting anything at all in regard to Adams. Actually, Erin was better off without her. But still, Patricia couldn't stand to see her so sad and so defeated. Erin wasn't like other people she knew. When Erin felt, she really felt. Down deep.

"I've tried," Erin said. "I went to see her at the studio. It's no good. It's over."

Silence.

"I'm sorry," Patricia offered yet again. She didn't know what else to say. Erin looked as if she would shatter into a million pieces and blow away in the wind. "Really, Mac, I am."

Erin gave a small laugh, surprising her. "If Liz could only hear you now."

"What do you mean?" She stirred in some of her homemade dressing and tossed the salad with large wooden salad tongs.

Erin seemed a little hesitant all of a sudden and didn't answer.

"What? What is it?"

"She thought you hated her. Thought that you would do anything to ruin her or to come between her and me."

Patricia set the tongs down. "Is that what you think?"

It was true, she did have feelings for Erin. Feelings that went beyond friendship. And a small twinge of hope lurked deep in her chest now that things were over with Liz. But try to come between them? No. She wanted Erin's happiness. First and foremost.

"No." Erin met her eyes. "I've always defended you. In fact, that's what the last fight was about."

Patricia didn't speak.

"She found out about us," Erin confessed.

"Us?"

"The night we were...together."

Patricia looked away, the memory nearly overwhelming. The twinge grew arms, thick, veiny branches, and then turned inside her gut. "You told her?"

"I didn't have to. She figured it out." Erin glanced down at her hands. "And she found your book. The latest romance."

Patricia picked up the salad bowl and carried it to the table. She needed to move. Her blood was moving hot and thick under her skin. She crossed back to the kitchen drawers to retrieve knives and forks. Erin remained at the bar, looking at her hands, obviously deep in thought.

"Was it about me?" Erin asked.

Patricia stiffened as she placed the knives next to the forks on the table. She looked over at Erin, who sat very still, looking so lost and confused. Yet she was still so beautiful with her all-knowing, all-loving green eyes and heart-melting smile. She was still as modest and as kind as she ever was.

Erin's appeal, her beauty, her ability to love and care so deeply was what had driven Patricia to write the book. She hadn't been able to get Erin from her mind after the Seductress Murders case was closed. She'd written a book about the murders and then returned to the precinct with cabin fever, eager to throw herself into work once more. But her head kept returning to Erin. Writing about her was the only way she could manage her emotions. Liz might have taken Erin off on a yacht, but Patricia had had Erin all to herself in her mind.

Erin was watching her. And Patricia knew she could see the answer on her face.

"I think the chicken's done." She moved to the oven and slid out their dinner. After placing the chicken and diced potatoes and peppers on two plates, she returned to the table.

Erin rose to pour them both some iced tea.

"I think I'd like some wine," Patricia said, sliding a bottle of merlot from the wine cooler on the adjacent counter.

Her nerves were rapidly firing and she could feel Erin's eyes on her, feel her questions. *She knows about the book. She knows it was about her. She's read the love scenes. She's crawled inside my mind.*

This wasn't good, not with the way her libido had been screaming at her lately. She was extremely raw and Erin had just peeled back her last layer. Her hands shook as she pulled down the wineglasses. Hurriedly, she set them down and opened the bottle. The red liquid made a glugging noise as she filled the glasses. She took several large sips before joining Erin at the table. She liked her merlot chilled. And at the moment, she liked it a lot.

"How's the chicken?" she asked before either of them had time to try it.

Erin stared at her. "Are you okay?"

"Hmm? Yes, I'm fine." She cut into the chicken and forced herself to eat. Then she had some more wine.

Erin also drank the wine and allowed Patricia to refill it. Eventually she asked, "How are things going? I heard you found two more bodies during the search."

"You heard correctly."

"Anything new? Anything useful?"

Patricia chewed slowly. The change in topic was welcome, yet not especially warming. "We're not sure yet."

"How was the condition? Too decomposed to tell much of anything?" Erin cut her chicken into small pieces as she asked her questions.

"You know I can't divulge that kind of information."

Erin's knife and fork slid to a stop, nestled in the chicken breast. "Forgive me, I forgot." Her tone was clipped and her eyes remained down.

Patricia lowered her fork. "It's not that I don't want to tell you."

"It's not?" Erin lifted her eyes and pinned her with a thorny look. "Because that's what it sounds like. Like you don't trust me, like I'm some sort of crazy civilian obsessed with a case."

"You are a civilian," Patricia said softly.

Erin released her silverware and shoved her plate away. "And..." She rose. "You don't trust me."

Patricia stood as well, placing her hands palm down on the table. "I can't forget the fact that you compromised a previous case, no. Or the fact that you were released of duty from the department for that very reason. Those are serious issues and I still don't understand why you did it."

Erin stood across from her, arms folded over her chest. She seemed wound so tight she could lose her balance if slightly nudged.

"What if it was me? What if I was accused of murder, Patricia? And you knew I was innocent but no one believed you. What would you do?"

Patricia stared at her, trying to make sense of her words. "I don't understand."

"Would you let me go down? With the way you feel about me?"

Patricia felt herself go heavy with the weight of the question. "What?"

"Would you try and help me, no matter what the costs, because you love me?"

"I..."

"Would you sacrifice your job for love, Patricia? For me?"

"I would do what was right," she finally said.

"Which would be what?"

"I would follow the law." There was no question. No doubt in her mind. It was who she was.

"The law." Erin looked away. When she looked back to her, her eyes were full of tears. "Well, that's the difference between you and me. What's right to me, it isn't governed by any law. The law has nothing on love."

She turned then and headed out of the kitchen toward the living room. Patricia followed, unsure of her motives but very much aware that Erin was hurting. "Wait," she whispered, coming up behind her, placing a hand on her shoulder.

"Don't, please." Erin turned. Her eyes were crystal green again; the tears had brought back the color.

Patricia reached out and thumbed away a tear. Her heart bled for Erin. "I'm sorry."

"For what? For hiding your feelings for me? For falling in love with me and writing a fucking book about it without telling me? For letting me in your house, letting me sleep in the next room while completely untrusting me?" She sucked in a quick breath. "What exactly are you sorry for, Patricia?"

Patricia couldn't speak. Her hands seemed to melt into Erin's face. Hot tears glued the two of them together. Erin was there. In her home. In her arms. Something she'd wanted for so long. Something she'd dreamt of and never thought would happen again. She pulled her closer. Erin's full rose lips beckoned, parted in raw emotion.

"I'm sorry for all of it. I'm…" She stepped into her then and kissed her lips, the final words needing to be pushed into her rather than spoken. One word after another. *I'm sorry. I love you. I need you.*

Erin made a small noise of surprise. Their lips pressed together in moist warmth, once, twice, three times. Hot breath spilled from them both.

"The book," Erin whispered. "It was about me." She wasn't asking. She wanted Patricia to tell her. To say it.

"Yes." The word eased up and out of her chest. A hot mist of truth.

"Why?"

The reasons why were right in front of Patricia, mixing in the very air she breathed. Yet there were no words. The words had already been said. Stamped in ink on hundreds of pages. "You, Erin. That's why."

"Why didn't you tell me?"

Patricia was still holding her face. She couldn't let go. Wouldn't. "You were happy. With Liz."

Another tear slipped down her face. It slid under Patricia's palm. "I love Liz," Erin whispered.

Patricia smiled at the confession. Erin's honesty warmed her. "I know." She stared again into those beckoning lips. "I know."

She kissed her again. Hot, wet. Tears, love. Erin kissed her back, first with a soft moan, offering her surrender. Patricia reacted quickly, pressing her harder, leading her up against the wall.

"I wish I was in the book," Erin said, drawing away. "That the story was real, something I could open up and dive into, leaving this world behind. I don't want to be me anymore, Patricia. I want the fantasy. Even if just for a little while."

"Okay." Patricia understood what she needed. She understood it better than anyone else could. Getting lost in the fantasy was the very reason she wrote.

Erin's hands rose to tangle in her hair. Then her tongue slid over Patricia's lower lip. Patricia heard herself groan and then she met Erin's tongue with her own.

Sweet, slick velvet bliss.

They stood fused, Patricia pressing Erin against the wall, Erin clinging to her, kissing her hard. They moaned, short and loud. Patricia kissed her just as hard, struggling to breathe. She shoved her hands beneath Erin's shirt, pushing her bra up, eager to graze the firm nipples. When Erin cried out, Patricia pulled her mouth away to lower herself. She met the right breast with her hungry flattened tongue, marking it heavily with her saliva. Then she closed her mouth over it and fed.

Erin clawed at her scalp. She slammed her head back against the wall, hissing in pleasure. Patricia sucked her so hard she almost came from the feel of the full breast in her mouth. She tore the shirt up over Erin's head, discarding it with the bra.

Erin stood breathing heavily, breasts heaving, one wet and red from Patricia's mouth.

Patricia stepped into her, kissing her again. She couldn't get over the taste of her mouth. So luscious and hot and needful. Suddenly, she had to feel the other part of her too. And taste it. She shoved her hand down the front of Erin's loose-fitting jeans. The cotton of her panties was warm and moist. Patricia eased her fingers farther. She found Erin's short curls were equally moist and twice as warm. With a groan, she went further, feeling the lips just below the curls.

"Mmm." Erin bit on Patricia's lower lip, taking possession, just as Patricia was.

She could wait no more. She pulled away and tugged on Erin's hand. "Come. Now."

They hurried down the hallway to Patricia's bedroom.

"I can't." Erin's voice was ragged. "Not in here."

Patricia understood immediately. Too much had happened in there that night; their very lives had been threatened. She tugged Erin into the spare bedroom. "In here okay?"

Erin nodded.

"Good."

Patricia pushed her onto the bed and straddled her leg. Erin's fingertips grazed slowly up Patricia's sides to her bra, unlatching it in the front, letting her breasts spill.

"You're…" Erin started but then stopped.

"What?" Patricia asked as the bra was tossed aside. Her breath hitched as Erin's fingers rubbed over her breasts.

"So…" Erin didn't finish the sentence but instead tugged her down into another deep kiss.

Patricia found herself grinding into Erin, rubbing her thigh hard between her legs, needing the pressure. They rocked like that for a few moments, their mouths promising what was to come. They kissed and rocked. Again and again. When the sweet, dark bliss of orgasm began to tunnel her vision, Patricia moved away, her crotch throbbing for release, angry at the loss of contact. Ignoring its fierce pangs, she hurriedly undid Erin's jeans and yanked them off along with the cotton panties. Breathless, she looked down upon Erin with the hungry desire she'd endured for over a year.

"I have to have you in my mouth," she whispered.

Erin stared up at her, eyes full of raw emotion. "You want me," she said, not quite a question, not quite a statement.

"More than anything."

"Say it again."

"I want you."

Erin closed her eyes. "Liz doesn't want me." She breathed heavily for a moment. "I need you. I need you to want me."

"And I do."

"Take off your pants," Erin said, her voice low with hastening desire.

Patricia climbed off the bed and stripped.

Erin was watching. "Your panties too."

Patricia removed them. Erin sat up on her elbows, bathed in the moonlight that slanted in through the vertical blinds. Her gaze moved hungrily yet slowly over Patricia's body. Patricia had never felt her skin so ablaze before. When their eyes met again, no words were needed.

Patricia crawled onto the bed. Her mouth felt full and plump with saliva and blood, a starving being cradled over the feast of a lifetime. She opened Erin's legs, pressing gently on her thighs. Erin obliged and the moonlight glistened against her wet flesh.

Patricia snaked out her tongue and licked up one thigh and then the other. She caught Erin's scent and her eyes threatened to roll back in her head. Then she kissed where her tongue had been. Full, thick, sucking kisses that fell upon sensitive bare thighs. Erin began to claw at her head again, moving upward beneath her.

Anticipation shot to Patricia's lower abdomen in hot, exquisite waves. When she finally came to Erin's flesh, she closed her eyes and allowed her nose and cheek to feel her first.

Wet. Hot. Heady with scent.

She closed her mouth over her and lapped at the folds of flesh. Erin called out and lifted her hips, eager for more, offering herself. Patricia responded, fueled by the slick taste of her, excited by the firm knot of her desire. She swirled her tongue over it, loving how it twitched but did not move as she massaged it. *It's anchored there. Anchored and awaiting the pleasure I am bestowing upon it and around it. It will never move. It is forever mine.*

Her brain began to rapid fire as she feasted, the neurotransmitters saturated. Erin kept crying out, her body pulsing for more. The sound of her raspy voice, coated in thick pleasure, made Patricia swoon. Caught up in her, nestled between her legs, she was helpless. Tasting her, pleasing her, having her.

She kissed harder, licking longer and heavier. She slurped her juices, loving the silky hot feel against her tongue.

When Erin began to buck she ran her tongue all over her, all over her clit, all over every fold of flesh. And then she sucked up the wet tracks.

Erin thrust up into her, head thrashing from side to side. Her words were clipped and muffled, her stomach muscles tightening and twitching. "I need this," she kept saying. "I need this."

Loud clouds thumped in Patricia's ears, like buzzing heavy cotton, allowing her to block out everything else and keep going. It wasn't until she felt Erin tug especially hard on her hair that she paid attention.

Her mouth left Erin's flesh in a smack. "What?" She could barely speak, her mouth full of sweet silk and swollen with exertion.

"Come here." Erin pulled on her upper arm.

Patricia crawled to her side, confused.

Erin kissed her palm, her eyes full of tears. "I need to taste you too. At the same time."

Patricia nearly fell over. Her own flesh was beating between her legs, its demands as intense as the thumping in her ears. But the emotion she saw in Erin's eyes caused her to pause.

"Hurry." Erin reached for her.

"Are you sure?"

"Please."

Patricia swallowed and did as instructed, lifting her leg over Erin, her back to her. She felt Erin's hot hands on the back of her hips, guiding her. When she felt her hot breath on her inner thighs, she nearly came.

"Now," she heard Erin say. And then she felt Erin's wet mouth tugging on her flesh.

"Oh!" She pressed back, unable not to. She heard and felt the smacking of her mouth, hot, wet bolts of it shooting up through her body. Erin was starved for her just as much as Patricia was starved for Erin. The overpowering pleasure took over. Her hips began to gyrate. Her eyes drifted closed. It had been so damned long. She bit on her lower lip. Oh, God. Oh, God. She was close. It wouldn't take long now.

Hurriedly she lowered her mouth back down to Erin, and they fed off one another, hungrily, desperately. Patricia wrapped her hands around Erin's thighs for support, moving her mouth heavily against her, sucking her, swirling her tongue all over her. They moaned into one another's flesh. They thrust together in a groove.

It couldn't get any sweeter. It just couldn't.

Erin moaned louder. Patricia sucked harder. Oh, God. It was heaven. Yes, this must be heaven. She was sure of it. She felt Erin yank her mouth away. She felt her struggling breath as a cry of raw-sounding emotion escaped her throat. It was deep and throaty. She held her hips up off the bed, her fingers digging into Patricia's legs. She came long. She came hard. Patricia never stopped trying to drink it all in.

Erin was coming. Coming beneath her. It kept replaying in her head. She sucked it in. Swallowed it, and sucked some more. She knew deep inside that it would never happen again. So she took in as much as she could, relishing the moment. She could feel Erin warming down her throat and into her chest.

It was so good, so bittersweet.

Patricia groaned. Erin was sensitive and bucking. Patricia licked at her while her own flesh was being pulled and sucked, again and again.

"Come here," she heard Erin say.

Patricia sat up, her hands on Erin's slick stomach, her body moving in a rhythm against Erin's mouth. Erin groaned, enjoying giving. Her tongue was a hot missile, shooting up inside her and then licking back to her clit. Patricia moaned as each bolt of pleasure lit up inside her. She began to pant Erin's name. Nothing had ever felt this good before.

Erin gripped her harder, holding her hips firmly as she took Patricia's flesh in her mouth and sucked hard.

"Oh my Go..." Patricia cried out.

Erin kept sucking, harder and faster. It was time. They both knew it. And Erin was insisting.

"Erin...Erin..." Eyes squeezed shut, Patricia came, pushing up with her arms, her spine a straight, hard, hot bolt of lightning. "Ahh... ahhhh...ahhhh!" she cried, rocking, rocking, rocking.

Her voice vanished but her body continued to move involuntarily, desperate for every last ounce of pleasure. After what felt like an eternity, Erin let up and Patricia slowly stopped moving. They were still and silent then, their skin lit up and slick with sweat.

Patricia stared hazily at the streetlight coming through the blinds. Lazy, tiny particles of dust floated down upon them. Her heart beat warm, heavy blood throughout her body. Her bones had melted. She eased off Erin, moving carefully, fearing she might collapse. Erin watched her with heavy-lidded eyes. Patricia crawled up next to her and nuzzled into her neck. She could feel Erin's heart beat, smell both their scents mixed with sweat. She thought she could die at that very moment and be happy.

When she looked up she found Erin's eyes glazed over and full of tears.

"It's going to be okay," Patricia said.

Erin didn't respond. She merely curled into her, sobbing uncontrollably. Patricia stared up at the ceiling fan. She kissed the top of Erin's head.

"Shh, it's all right. It's going to be all right."

As she said the words, she didn't quite believe them. Erin's future was unknown. But their future together was minimal.

Her few moments of bliss had passed.

Never to return.

❖

Erin buried herself in Patricia's neck, feeling safe nestled in the soft skin. She didn't want to move away from her, afraid of what lurked beyond Patricia's scent and softness. She didn't want to face what she'd just done. She wished it would disappear into the darkness of the night.

She thought she needed the sex, needed the connection. But she was wrong. What she needed was love. What she needed was Liz.

CHAPTER FOURTEEN

Y ou'll plead no contest to the charges," Cynthia said with a self-assurance Liz usually took solace in. But at the present, she felt nothing but fear. And fear, Liz despised.

She pressed her thumb against the long lip of her plastic pen cap. Bent it until the blue plastic whitened and then snapped. She glanced at the door and imagined Erin there, walking seductively toward her, inching her shirt up as she moved. The thought made her throat tighten, and her mind flashed to a few days before, when Erin had stood at her desk looking lost and alone and betrayed. Then she recalled how she'd confirmed those feelings.

"I'll do my best to ensure the judge hears of the situation and the claims of officer harassment," Cynthia continued. "But honestly, I don't think it'll do any good. You might be looking at some jail time here."

"They set me up. Taunted me." Liz hated them. They had ruined her life with their accusations and pursuit of Jay.

"They taunt suspects all the time," Cynthia said. "It's called interrogation."

Liz squeezed the phone until her hand hurt. "I'm not a fucking suspect. I've done nothing." She pounded the desk with her fist.

"I know. I know. Listen to me." Cynthia paused and Liz could almost picture her lipsticked lips pressed to the receiver. "You have got to remain under control. No more temper tantrums. Lay low and do as you're told. Cooperate and be polite. I want you to be the best damned citizen in Valle Luna. Understood?"

Weak with fatigue, Liz conceded. "Yes."

"Good. I'll call you next week. And you call me if they so much as glance your way, okay?"

"Yes."

"And be careful. No stunts. They're most likely watching you."

Liz heard the click and lowered the phone, lifting another handset immediately. The bulk of the satellite phone was somewhat comforting. She spun in her chair and peeled back the blinds to search the parking lot for anyone sitting in a vehicle. Cynthia was probably right. The cops were most likely watching her. Liz had done her best at countersurveillance for the past few days, switching lanes, driving fast, exiting the freeway at the last second. She'd also checked her vehicle for GPS tracking devices, but she couldn't be sure.

She left the office, her pace determined. The back door declared Emergency Exit Only, but she pushed through it just as she'd done countless times before. The sunshine warmed her head and shoulders. The blacktop behind the building was vast and empty save for a cement cylinder filled with sand and dozens of short standing cigarette butts.

She glanced around to make sure she was alone, then extended the antenna on the phone and dialed the three-digit code. At the prompt she dialed the remaining twelve digits. She knew them by heart. They were her lifeline.

She paced. Then she heard background noise when someone answered.

"Elvira," she said into the phone.

She heard more noise, then a voice. "Hey, Lizzie."

The Oak Ridge Boys sang loud, only their voices were low and distorted. Like they were a chorus of demons underwater.

"El...vi...raaaaaa" played in warped slow motion.

Lizzie hated it. She used to think it funny, but now it was evil.

The screen door banged over the drone and Lizzie jumped, shoving her fingers in her ears, unable to take the noise anymore. Jerry came storming in, equally annoyed, his eyes ablaze. He grabbed her arm, popping her finger from her ear. He lowered it quickly, mindful suddenly of the cast.

"Turn that shit off!" he screamed at her.

Lizzie could smell the beer on his breath. She knew he meant business.

He shot a look to the large chair by the window. The room was dim but they could just make out Jay, who sat curled up there, rocking back and forth, lost in the world of "Elvira." Jerry shook his head in frustration. When he spoke, though, his voice softened a bit. "Turn it off."

He left the room, leaving Jay to her. They'd all been doing that. Leaving Jay to her. They were too afraid to say much to her, so they let her be. When something needed to be said, they said it to Lizzie.

She rose from the couch and approached the record player. It was sitting on an old end table, the volume all the way up, the speed on the wrong setting. Jay played it like that for hours every day. Talking to no one. Just sitting and rocking.

Ever since that day in the woods.

Lizzie switched it off. Jay stopped rocking but she didn't look away from the window.

"Hey," Lizzie said, walking up to her.

Jay stole a glance at her but said nothing. Lizzie opened the thin curtains. If Jay was going to stare out the window, she might as well have a good view. The afternoon light spilled in and Lizzie gasped. From somewhere in the house she heard Dayne scream.

"What the hell?" Jerry called out.

Lizzie hurried into the hallway. The light was on in the small bathroom and her aunt was on the floor crying hysterically, her knees in a dark pool. She reached down and grabbed fistfuls of the darkness, raising it up.

Lizzie stared. It was Jay's hair.

"Why?" Dayne cried. "Why would she cut her hair all off? What's happenin' to her, Jerry? What's happenin' to her?"

Lizzie returned to Jay and sat on the armrest of her chair. Jay was still staring out the window. One hand was up and tugging on a short strand of hair. She'd cut almost all of it off, leaving only a few patches here and there, no more than a couple of inches.

Lizzie reached out and took her hand. Jay's blue eyes seemed endless. A void. And Jay was somewhere, lost in their depths. Lizzie leaned into her.

Jay began to hum "Elvira."

Lizzie hummed with her.

Both of them staring out the window.

❖

Erin came in through the back door, little Jack hot on her heels. She'd been sitting outside for hours, staring into the pool. She'd been doing that for the past few days, thinking about her life, about Liz, and about Patricia. They hadn't spoken much since the night they'd been intimate. Erin really didn't know what to say; so many different emotions swam through her when she thought about it, guilt being the most prominent.

Her heart belonged to Liz, whether Liz wanted it or not.

Patricia seemed to know this and even accept it, and that only made things all the more confusing. Erin knew she'd have to talk to her at some point. The gentle hand squeezing her shoulder while she sat in the morning sun would soon need to elicit a response.

She walked into the living room, turned on the TV, and sat on the couch, wanting to see if there were any news updates on the murders. As if on cue, she heard, "A sixth body has now been added to the Highway Murder list. Police released the information today at a press conference where many more questions were raised than answered."

Erin thumbed up the volume on the remote control as Sergeant Ruiz came on screen. He stood gripping a podium, his face and eyes stern. His glasses glinted as he angled his head to speak, reflecting light at the numerous reporters gathered in front of him.

"At this time we are only able to say that the latest bodies found have been positively linked to the other bodies, bringing the total death count to six."

"Do you have any leads?" someone shouted.

A man scooted in close to Ruiz, and Erin recognized the chief of Valle Luna PD though it had been a while since she'd seen him. Chief Lawrence Gentry regarded the crowd sternly, as if he disapproved of the press conference. He towered over Ruiz but when he spoke, his tone wasn't near as fierce.

"We cannot discuss that at this time."

"Chief, is it true that truck drivers are being questioned?"

"Are people safe to travel the highway?"

"Is there a motive?"

The press was hungry for information, and Erin leaned forward, hungry herself.

"We encourage everyone to continue on with their daily lives, including travel on the highways," the chief said.

"Chief! Chief! Are the victims all male?"

Ruiz leaned in toward the microphone. "Yes."

This fed the fury. Like chum to circling sharks. A barrage of questions followed. Ruiz began to darken and Erin knew his blood was boiling.

"Sergeant, are the two recent murders of the young gay men in any way connected?"

"No."

When the crowd continued to shout over one another, Chief Gentry said, "We are here to discuss the Highway Murders."

His remark seemed to fall on deaf ears. The mass of reporters went on with the thread.

"Are men safe to walk at night?"

"Does that then bring the death toll to eight?"

"Is the killer killing at random? How are these deaths related?"

"Chief, is it true that lesbian night club owner Elizabeth Adams is once again a suspect?"

The questioning stopped. All that could be heard were the clicking of cameras.

Chief Gentry answered, "No more questions at this time."

Erin felt her body heat with anger and fear. Angry for Liz and fear for what she herself didn't know, what she might never know. She raised the remote to extinguish the picture but stopped when an attractive deputy sheriff maneuvered in front of the microphone. Ruiz moved aside, but his look of contempt was not well hidden.

"Good afternoon," she said with calm confidence. "I'm Detective Audrey Sinclair. I'll be speaking on behalf of the Corona County Sheriff's office."

Immediately the questions started once more. Ruiz and Chief Gentry whispered madly at one another, obviously upset at being upstaged. Sinclair took a moment to let the room quiet down. She looked professional in a bone-colored button-down blouse and medium-sized platinum hoop earrings. Her badge shone from her front breast pocket.

Her short light brown hair was tousled just right. She appeared at ease with the press and Erin was at once impressed with her command.

"Autopsy and lab results confirm that all six of these bodies are linked to the same killer," she said. "We cannot disclose evidence, but we believe this is the work of a serial killer."

"Is there any apparent motive?"

Erin expected her to say no, but Sinclair had other plans. "We believe the killer may be sexually motivated."

Erin felt the blood in her body rush to her face. What was she doing? The press went insane, arguing among themselves about what "sexually motivated" could mean.

"Are you suggesting Adams is killing out of her hate for men?" someone asked.

Ruiz and Gentry stood ramrod straight, completely taken aback.

"We also have a description." Sinclair took a piece of paper from a colleague and held up the composite drawing for all to see. "Our suspect is five foot ten to six feet tall. Short dark hair, Caucasian, may be driving an SUV. If you think you know who this is or have any information whatsoever, please call the number provided. Thank you."

Erin was dumbfounded. The sketch could've been anyone, really. Right away she realized it wasn't Liz. But it was the eyes that gripped her, sending a small jolt along spine. They were familiar. But she couldn't place them. The sketch could've been male or female. Sinclair had intentionally left the suspect's sex out of the equation.

Erin thought of Jay, knowing her former colleagues would be doing the same. She'd seen Liz's sister only once before but she remembered that her hair was similar to the hair in the sketch. The chill continued to crawl up her spine.

She switched off the television and grabbed her car keys.

❖

"What the hell does she think she's doing!" Ruiz slammed his fists down onto the table.

Patricia jerked even though she'd known the reaction was coming. Stewart closed his mouth midchew and swallowed the juice from his gum. Heavy silence stifled the room. Chief Gentry began mumbling into his cell phone. They all sat and waited. She, Gary Jacobs, Stewart, and Hernandez.

The press conference had been a disaster. A complete disaster. And at the helm of the shipwreck was former fed and now Deputy Detective Audrey Sinclair. Patricia couldn't believe what she'd done. But maybe now that she'd blown it on Corona County's behalf, they'd get their case back.

Gentry snapped his phone shut. "Sheriff Paxton stands by his detective."

"What?" Ruiz snapped, way louder than the snap of the phone.

"He also refuses to meet us today. His secretary suggested sometime next week."

Ruiz nearly foamed at the mouth. "What do they think they're doing?" Again the fists came down, rattling the table. "She compromised the entire investigation."

They all sat in silence, too afraid of Ruiz to speak. Gentry's phone rang and he mumbled something about the mayor and stepped from the room to talk.

Ruiz began to pace. "Did any of you meet with her? If you did, you'd better speak up now."

They all shook their heads.

"Henderson?"

"No, sir. She requested a meeting but it never happened."

"Where the hell did she get her info? How, people, does she have a composite when we have nothing?"

"I don't know, sir," Patricia said.

"You don't know?" Ruiz pushed back on the bridge of his eyeglasses as he stared her down. "Well, that's pretty fucking obvious, isn't it. And what about the motive? Where the hell did she get that when we haven't yet been able to come up with one?"

No one said a word. Patricia felt the vein along her neck throbbing with her anger. When Ruiz turned and stormed out of the office, she rose to her feet, a new mission in mind.

CHAPTER FIFTEEN

L a Femme throbbed. Its heart was alive and beating, the dancing women its blood flow. Erin shouldered her way in, pulling the ball cap down to avoid being recognized. She moved as she felt, like a creature of the night, in and out of the shadows. That was who she'd become, a mere shadow of her former self. Dim and empty. She spoke to no one, looked to no one. Just moved. Quickly and silently.

Skin slick with sweet-smelling sweat rubbed against her as she wove her way through the mass of women. Bodies waved in unison, pulsing and thrusting. Eyes were focused on eyes, limbs tangled with limbs. Sex was heavy in the air. Lesbians lusting after lesbians.

Erin could easily have gotten caught up in it, or simply just stared as she often did, amazed by the erotic energy. But she wasn't there for lust or wonder. She was there for love, for what little she had left inside. She looked up toward the platform dancers as Alice in Chains surged "Grind" from the speakers. The dancers moved like animated sex in ripped jeans, Dr. Martens, and plaid flannel shirts. Beyond them hung huge murals, one of Kurt Cobain in a black and white striped shirt, one of the Smashing Pumpkins, and one of Pearl Jam.

She'd had all those albums once, some on cassette, most on CD. It seemed like only yesterday, yet so far away. Her gut felt empty at the thought. So much had changed and continued to change. Her mother had called earlier, demanding to know what was going on. Her shrill voice seemed to play right along with the riffs of "Grind."

"What's going on, Erin? Where are you?"

"I'm fine, Mother. I'm at a friend's."

"I called that woman's house about a million times."

"Her name is Liz."

"Why aren't you there?"

"We split up."

"What? I thought you said you were in love? You said you were a…lesbian!"

Erin had gripped the phone tightly. "I am. On both counts."

"You left Mark for that woman and now you're not even… together?"

"It's a long story."

"And now, this morning, your father gets the newspaper and she's wanted for murder. Again! What is going on, Erin Lynn?"

She could hear her father in the background. "Tell her she should just come home."

"We're very upset," her mother continued. "We're worried."

"Everything's fine. Really. I'm staying with a friend."

"Who? We want to know where you are."

"I'm at Patricia Henderson's."

She heard her mother gasp. "Isn't that where you were attacked?"

Her mother and father begin to argue.

"Mother. Mom?"

"Come home, Erin. Just come home."

"Listen, I've got to go, okay? I'm fine. I'll be fine."

"You know, Mark may have moved on but there are lots of other eligible men. And the whole lesbian thing, so many people are doing it, I'm beginning to think it's a fad. I'm sure there are plenty of men who would overlook that as just a little experimentation."

"It's not a fad, Mother. I'm gay."

"Nonsense. You shouldn't label yourself. I'll make up your bed in your old room."

"I've got to go, Mom. I'll call soon." She paused, and heard her mother start in on another breath. Before she could speak, Erin said, "Give Dad my love," and hung up.

The memory of her mother's voice faded out with Alice in Chains. The mass of plaid cheered, throwing up fists of approval for Stone Temple Pilots and "Wicked Garden." Erin focused in on a few dancers, saw the winks of their white tanks beneath the plaid. It was almost primal. The skin on each woman's neck slick with sweat.

The deejay chimed in, drawing Erin's attention, her voice as raspy as the music. "Grunge night is on full fledge. Get your requests in now."

Erin made her way to the VIP staircase, thoughts of Liz flashing in her mind. She remembered how her body glistened in the moonlight, the hard, etched muscles pebbled in sweat. The way she came so hard she sometimes pulled the muscles in her neck. Erin missed her. Missed them.

The large woman standing guard at the staircase unfolded her arms. "You got a pass?"

Erin acted surprised but promptly pulled the laminated pass out from her shirt, where she wore it around her neck. It was a year-round VIP pass. The bouncer was new. Erin had never seen her before and counted her blessings. The woman gripped the pass and shone a small black light on it to verify its authenticity. She didn't seem to notice the name Erin McKenzie. Only the two intertwined female symbols seemed to be of importance.

She removed the velvet rope and nodded Erin through. Erin kept her head low and climbed the stairs, exhaling a sigh of relief. When she reached the top, she stood still for a moment, letting her eyes adjust to the low light. She crossed to the bar, but didn't let the bartender see her face. Instead she kept moving, making her way along the rail. She had no plan, had no idea what she was going to say. In fact, she felt a little crazy at being there. Liz had made it very clear that she no longer wanted anything to do with her, but the deep ache in her chest kept her moving. And the memory of their lovemaking, Liz calling out to her, drenched in sweat, her body blanched with moonlight. How would Liz look tonight? Would she take her back? Could they fall into each other's arms and…

Erin's hand slid to a stop along the rail. She focused in on the lone sofa at the very back of the VIP area. Liz sat with her arms outstretched along the back of it, staring straight ahead, as if a ghost stood before her, sharing in a heavy conversation. Erin moved closer, her heart nearly beating over itself. Liz's face was pale and drawn. She looked fragile, almost like porcelain, dark crescents below her eyes and her mouth set and tight. If not for the slight movement of her breasts, Erin would've wondered whether she was breathing.

The song changed. Stone Temple Pilots stirred up the crowd with "Sex Type Thing" and a woman exited Liz's private lair. Erin recognized her at once. Angie Hartman, the famous Hollywood actress who had often frequented the club when she wasn't filming. Erin hadn't seen her in over a year. She wondered if it was because of her absence that Angie was back.

Erin watched her saunter toward Liz. Red high heels and thigh-highs matched the red bra and panties seductively covering her lithe body. She moved like a supermodel on the catwalk, slinking to the beat, a walking, aching red rose, desperate to open and spread her velvet petals upon Liz. When she reached her she did just that, straddling Liz with her impossibly long legs.

Erin's breath hitched in her throat. Blood pounded in her ears and she worried that she wouldn't be able to hear any words spoken. But Liz remained still, arms along the back of the couch. Neither said a word. Angie began to gyrate against Liz's leg, dancing with her crotch rather than her feet. She moved as if she were one with the music. As if it played just for her.

She reached out for Liz's face, ensuring Liz's eyes were on her. Then she leaned in, her long tongue extended, exposing a small offering on the tip. She pushed the pill into Liz's mouth and licked Liz's lips, then tugged on them with her teeth. Her body kept moving, fucking Liz as she sat unmoving.

The song kept on, encouraging her, killing Erin. Angie unhooked her red bra and flung it to the ground. Hips gyrating to the beat, she reached for Liz's hands and pulled them to her exposed breasts. Liz blinked and her head moved a little, as if she wasn't sure exactly where she was. Angie rubbed their hands together over her own breasts, squeezing and lifting, her head thrown back in pleasure.

Liz's gaze was fixed on Angie's face, but her eyes seemed to stare right through her. Angie came as the song neared its end. Short cries escaped her as she rocked hard into Liz. Finally, her back stiffened and she stilled completely. She gave a laugh and leaned in to plant a kiss on Liz's mouth. Then she rose and stood before her. With Liz's hand still in her own, she placed it palm up under her crotch.

"That's how wet you get me," she said with another low laugh.

Erin stifled a cry. Her throat felt torn, like a cat had used it as a scratching post. She took a step closer, watching. Liz said nothing to Angie and the actress turned and strode confidently to the bar. Erin focused on herself. She didn't think she could move. She stood as still as the night, breathing like there wasn't enough air in the world for her lungs. Her legs moved before her mind reacted. Suddenly she was crossing the room. Suddenly she was standing before Liz.

Blue eyes liquid with the deep abyss of pain raised to scan her face. A glint of recognition preceded her voice. "What…what are you doing here?" Liz's voice seemed strained and tattered, like a rope that had been pulled too hard for too long. Unraveling.

"I need to talk to you."

Liz made a move like she was going to stand but her body went slack, as if she couldn't. "Who let you in?"

Erin took advantage of her lack of dominance. "I'm worried about you. Worried about Jay."

Liz stared at her. Her tongue licked at parched lips. "You need to go. I'll call Tyson."

Erin stood her ground. "Tyson isn't here. He must have the night off."

Liz blinked.

"What are you on?" Erin knelt to look closer into her eyes. "E?"

Liz didn't respond. Erin couldn't even remember the last time she'd seen her use drugs. Seeing her in that state only increased her heart rate.

"Liz listen to me. I need to know about Jay."

"My sister is no one's business but my own."

"The police are looking for her." Erin was near panicked with worry. If Jay was involved in any way, she needed to know. She had to protect Liz. "They released a composite sketch today. The hair and build was similar. Where is she? Do you even know?"

This time Liz forced herself to stand. Her hazy eyes bored into Erin's. "It's none of your business."

Erin touched her cheek and Liz flinched, but not before she warmed. Erin tried again, but Liz caught her hand. "Don't," she whispered.

"Why not?" Erin was dying to touch her, to hold her, to melt into her just like she'd done so many times before.

"You should go."

"I don't want to go. I want to be with you."

Liz swayed a little in her stance but then straightened with what seemed to be a sudden but rare jolt of strength. "No."

"Why not?"

Liz started to speak but then stopped. "I'm not going to do this."

Erin persisted, placing a hand on her upper arm. She felt Liz shudder. "Then please tell me where Jay is. For your safety, for hers."

Liz leaned into her. Slowly. Her cheek skimmed Erin's and then her mouth was at her ear. "Go, Erin. Go far and fast from me."

Erin's body continued reacting differently from her mind. She squeezed Liz's arm and said, "Then I'll find her on my own."

Liz pulled back to stare at her.

"Don't think I can? Well, I will. Because what you don't understand is that I'll do anything to protect you."

Liz didn't respond.

Erin released her grip. "Anything." She turned then and walked away, tears burning her eyes and her throat.

Liz watched her walk away. She squeezed her fists so hard she thought she'd break her hands. Shuddering from Erin's lingering scent, she whispered, "So would I."

❖

Patricia didn't bother with the doorbell, she went straight to knocking instead, rapping on the door so hard her knuckles felt like shattering beneath her skin. When there was no answer, she turned her fist and began pounding.

Still nothing.

"Hello?" she called out. "It's Detective Patricia Henderson. I need to speak with you."

Again she pounded. Her phone vibrated on her hip. It was a text from Gary. He wanted to know where she was. Whipping the phone off her belt, she quickly typed back. She hadn't told him of her plans. Purposely. He would've told her she was nuts, that it was unprofessional. And he would've been right, as always. But she was going with her gut on this. Her gut and her temper.

She stared at the screen, keying: Busy Will Call Later.

"Can I help you?"

Patricia nearly dropped her phone. She fumbled it as she took in the frustrated face of Detective Audrey Sinclair. "Yes, I uh…I…"

Sinclair was carrying a laptop briefcase and an armload of thick three-ring binders. Her biceps flexed and her face had taken on an edge of suspicion and confrontation. She held her keys defensively, one thrust forward between her knuckles, ready to be used as a weapon.

Patricia remembered her own anger and was able to find her words. "I had to come see for myself."

"What are you talking about?" Sinclair's voice was low and tight, a slingshot pulled all the way back.

"I came to see if you're really that stupid, or just completely and totally insane."

Sinclair tensed. Patricia didn't think there was any other muscle left to strain, but she seemed to be wrong. "You shouldn't have come to my home. Manners are something I'd hoped others were raised with as well." She stepped forward, as if Patricia wasn't there at all.

Patricia stood her ground, her temper flaring. "I will go where I please, Detective. Because I have a job to do, serial murders to solve. And no thanks to you, that job just became a lot more complicated."

"I suggested a meeting. You chose to avoid and ignore me." Sinclair stared into her with soft cinnamon-colored eyes.

It was amazing, Patricia noted, that something so soft could harden instantaneously, like the cracked crust of a desert plain. "You should've tried harder. Any good detective would have."

"I'm a professional. I don't play games. Political or otherwise."

"Then what do you do?"

"I solve murders."

"Ha!"

"I was hoping you did the same."

"I do my job, Detective Sinclair. Don't ever suggest otherwise."

Sinclair's eyes narrowed. "I *suggest* you move, Detective Henderson."

"I'm not going anywhere."

Sinclair took another step, raising her laptop case to push Patricia to the side. Even though Patricia had seen and even admired her muscles, she was still surprised at just how easily Sinclair was able to shove her aside. She stumbled a bit and embarrassment heated her cheeks. What was she planning to do? Box the woman?

She regained her stance as Sinclair forced the key in the lock and turned it. She marched into her apartment and slapped the binders and briefcase on the kitchen counter just inside the door. Then she turned, hands at her sides, face as hard as a rock.

They stared at each other for a heavy, slow minute. Patricia focused on Sinclair's hands, worried that they would ball into fists.

"Are you coming in, then?" Sinclair finally asked.

A bit surprised, Patricia hesitated, then stepped inside and eased the door closed. Sinclair moved around the counter to the kitchen, where she pulled out a glass and a full ice tray. After loading the glass with ice cubes, she poured from a pitcher of filtered cold water and drank heartily. She seemed to like her water cold, very cold.

Patricia felt awkward to suddenly be in the rival detective's space. Where she ate, where she slept, the place she chose as refuge. She hadn't expected Sinclair to let her in. She took advantage, though, and glanced around. The apartment was large, with a roomy living room across from the kitchen, den attached. A hallway was at the nucleus and held what appeared to be a bathroom. Beyond that were two other doors which she assumed belonged to bedrooms.

After catching another glimpse of Sinclair downing the ice water with the tendons in her neck showing every swallow, Patricia cleared her own throat and wondered why she was noticing. The past few days her mind had been on nothing other than the murders and Erin. Patricia had no idea how to solve either. Erin had grown increasingly distant and sad. She wouldn't talk and Patricia wasn't sure what they would say had Erin been willing. She knew deep in her gut that she'd lost Erin forever. That maybe she'd never even really had her to begin with.

It was more than obvious that Erin's heart was elsewhere.

Patricia forced the painful thought from her mind and busied herself observing Sinclair's home once more. The carpet was light brown and new-smelling, the couches a slate blue leather, the remaining furnishings light oak. She strolled into the living room. Numerous sculptures adorned the end tables next to the couches and the bookshelves in the den. All were white, and when she looked more closely she could see the detail of each piece. She wanted badly to touch them, to feel the rough coolness of the dried clay.

"Did you do these?" She couldn't help but ask. They must've taken hours of painstaking precision with small tools. She bent to examine an old man sitting on a bench, looking skyward, his face etched in wrinkles. She could feel his plight and sense his pain.

"It's a hobby." Sinclair moved from the kitchen and switched on the floor lamp, illuminating the room further.

"I'd say it's more than a hobby. You're really good." The idea of Sinclair molding clay into a life form with her hands made her seem more real. The thought sent an unexpected thrill up Patricia's spine.

"It keeps me sane," Sinclair said. She seemed to be relaxing a little.

Patricia offered a smile. "I know what you mean." Sometimes she felt that if she didn't write, she'd be certifiable. She wrote about what she was missing in her life, and doing so somehow helped her deal with her loneliness. Romances were her favorite, but recently she'd tried her hand at a mystery based on the Seductress Murders. That too had helped her to process her feelings.

"You too? What do you do…other than threaten with your physical presence?" A smile lifted one side of Sinclair's face, showing off a dimple. "Martial arts?"

"Used to."

"I figured."

"Am I that bad?"

"No. Just real confident in your movements." Sinclair switched on another lamp, this one on the large desk nestled in the den. "You know how to back up your words."

"Really? Never thought that about myself."

"Well, you've got it down pat." Sinclair paused. "Although I was surprised you let me knock you off balance back there."

"I wasn't expecting you to try. I guess I was thinking you had those manners you spoke so highly of." Patricia felt her own smile lifting the side of her face. "Anyhow, it won't happen twice."

Sinclair nodded, her smile full, her eyes alive. "So, do you work with your hands? I could easily imagine you doing so." Her gaze fell to Patricia's hands.

Patricia felt that thrill again and moved her focus to the desk. It held a flat-screen monitor and keyboard, a green shaded banker's lamp, and a few thick manila folders.

"I write." She ran her fingertips along the desk top and Sinclair's gaze followed.

"I would love to see your handwriting. You can tell a lot about a person based on their handwriting."

"I use the computer." She fought hard against a blush. "Most of the time."

"What do you write?"

Patricia purposely put off answering. She considered her writing a private matter and she grew angry at herself for even bringing it up. Why had she? Did some part of her want Sinclair to know that she wrote lesbian romances? Wouldn't that somehow be considered foreplay? Sinclair reading her words and knowing her thoughts and desires?

She stopped herself from going any further with such thoughts. Instead she continued to take in her surroundings.

The wall next to the desk caused her to stop in her tracks. She'd assumed, catching a glimpse of it in the dark, that it was covered with a large piece of art. But what she saw now was something only an artist in hell would create. She knew each victim, each wound, each macabre stare. She had the same images hanging by her desk at the precinct. A menagerie of death.

"How can you…" She could've never hung them at her home. To bring that evil into her home, her safe sanctuary.

Sinclair had followed her line of sight.

"I work from here. Think from here."

"I know, but how can you stare at them?" Patricia realized she brought the dead home with her too. But they remained flat on her desk and in the folders. Strictly confined.

"Not everyone can do it, I know." Sinclair faced the wall. Patricia came slowly to a stand next to her. "But I can't rest until I know something. How did it happen, and why? And if we're real lucky… who?" Her gaze ran across the reflecting photos. "They demand that of me. They deserve that. Only when most of the questions are answered can I take them down."

"Do you sleep?" Patricia asked quietly.

"Probably about as much as you do."

"Not well, then."

"No."

"I dream about them," Patricia said. "Their last moments. What they must've felt."

"Their fear," Sinclair whispered.

"Yes." Patricia had always felt that way. She knew it wasn't healthy, but she couldn't help it. She felt for each victim.

"How long have you been doing this?" Sinclair asked. "Most seasoned detectives are hard, shut off."

"Long enough." Patricia stole a quick, sidelong glance at her. "What about you?"

"I've been studying the criminal mind for a long time. And I've been chasing them for about seven years."

"Are you good?"

Sinclair gave a small laugh. "According to some." She met Patricia's eyes. Her irises were back to being soft cinnamon sand. "But according to *others*..."

"I'm sorry about that."

"Are you?" The smile remained.

"Yes."

"Those were your feelings, though."

"No, I guess I just don't understand."

"Ah, yes. The old saying, we fear what we don't understand."

Patricia started to argue but realized that she *was* a little afraid of Sinclair. Afraid of her ease and confidence, her tactics, and her unknown motives.

"Why did you do that? Say those things today?"

"You think I'm crazy."

Patricia had to be honest. "Yes."

"I can assure you when it comes to my job, I am far from crazy."

"But any other time you are admitting to being crazy."

A crooked grin teased Patricia. "When it comes to love, I can be."

"Oh." Patricia couldn't look at her. "I wasn't expecting that one."

"You asked."

"My mistake." She inwardly cursed herself for doing so. Why was she so reactive to everything this woman did and said?

Sinclair didn't seem the slightest bit embarrassed or fazed. But she did seem to sense that a change of topic was needed.

She pointed.

"Look at those photos. Tell me what you see."

"Are you serious?"

"As a heart attack."

"I see dead men. Murdered men." As her mind began to work and recall the facts she knew about the Highway Murders, the words seemed to fly from her mouth. "All of them middle aged, married, average incomes, stable home lives. Caucasian, of average to moderate build, well groomed, and well nourished. All strangled to death. The other, older bodies were also found with the hyoid bone crushed, confirming this."

"Tell me what you question most?" Sinclair probed. "What is it that has you pacing the floors at night. What doesn't make sense to you?"

Patricia began to relax a little, her mind firing in rapid response to the easy flow of the questions. This was what she lived, what she slept, and what she ate. "What were they doing? Who were they with? Why the condom, why the traces of lubricant?"

"Isn't it obvious?" Sinclair asked.

"Yes, sex was involved, but why? These men weren't risk takers, they had stable home lives, many of the wives went as far as to say that their husbands were passive."

Sinclair raised an eyebrow. "Detective Henderson, please. We both know that behind your average mild-mannered man beats the heart of a potential sexual sadist, a child molester, or even a killer."

Patricia scowled. "Yes, of course I know that."

"They're never the drooling scary monster everyone imagines them to be."

"No, they're not."

"Say it, then. Sex was involved. For whatever reason, these men took a risk. And they paid dearly."

"Okay. I still wouldn't make the leap that the killer is sexually motivated. He or she could be killing for something as trivial as the lunar cycle."

"Maybe so, but the lure was sex."

Patricia took a deep breath, her heart rate picking up again at being challenged. "Okay, I'll play along. But why tell everyone?"

"Why not?" Sinclair's eyes sparkled, each grain of cinnamon sand shimmering.

Patricia lost her train of thought for a moment, enraptured. "Because we aren't sure, and even if we were we should hold our information close. You know all this."

Sinclair sat down on the sofa and motioned for Patricia to do the same. "It'll smoke him out. Add some pressure. It worked in the Night Stalker case even though law enforcement was against sharing the information. Sometimes the public can be very helpful."

"It might pressure him, yes, but it might also enrage him, cause him to go on a killing spree. Or to hide the bodies."

"He may kill again, but he won't overdo it. He's smart. And we both know he won't hide the bodies."

Patricia said nothing. The bodies were how he showed off, how he got off. "What's the point, then?"

"To make him nervous. When one gets nervous, one tends to make mistakes or act before thinking."

"You're willing to give out valuable information on a mere roll of the dice, hoping it makes the killer *nervous*?"

"It's not invaluable information. Valuable, yes. It's obvious information."

"Then what about the composite drawing? Where did you get an eyewitness?"

"I interviewed countless truckers from the same list you had."

Patricia felt her body grow rigid. "We never had anyone report seeing anything or anyone."

Sinclair sat calmly. "One trucker changed her story and said she recalled seeing someone after all. At the time she thought it insignificant."

"I want her name."

"Okay."

"Now, please." Patricia needed to speak with the witness as soon as possible.

"Paige Daniels," Sinclair said. She stood and retrieved the details from one of the ring binders. "How are your recent murders coming along? The two young gay men?"

Was Sinclair reading her mind? Patricia couldn't help but think of those victims as they discussed the Highway Murders. "Fine." She accepted the slip of paper she was passed and slid it into her back pocket.

"For what it's worth, I think you're barking up the wrong tree."

Patricia laughed. "Is that so?"

Sinclair looked serious and unamused. "Yes."

"What tree exactly should we be looking up?"

"A gay male."

"A gay male?"

"Middle aged, Caucasian. Serious sexual issues."

"We have a good suspect, thank you."

"It's not her. It's not either Adams."

This time Patricia raised an eyebrow. She'd heard almost all she could handle. "Thank you for your concern, but we've got it under control."

"If you'd like to talk about it, call me anytime."

"Are you serious?"

"Why wouldn't I be?" Sinclair seemed genuinely puzzled.

"Because you just single-handedly compromised our investigation. Not to mention you withheld information regarding a witness."

"I offered a meeting and you blew me off," Sinclair reminded her again.

"I'm busy. You should've tried harder." Patricia headed for the door, beyond frustrated and something else…stirred.

Sinclair followed and held the door for her. "We're going in circles."

"I don't play games, Detective."

"Then next time call." Sinclair's face softened a bit. "Call anytime."

Patricia held her eyes for a long moment, her pride clashing with her growing curiosity. "I don't plan on needing to."

She walked out of the apartment and didn't look back.

CHAPTER SIXTEEN

Liz sank down onto the couch and ran her hands through her hair. Beyond the walls of her private lair, the club thumped like a rapid-fire heartbeat. She was thankful for its vibration in her chest. Her own heart had barely beat in weeks.

"Are you coming?" a female voice asked her from the bed not far away.

Liz tightened the grip on her hair in frustration. "No."

"Why not?" The voice was smooth and playful. The woman, who had a name Liz couldn't or wouldn't remember, got out of bed and approached the sitting area. "We were just getting started," she purred.

Liz avoided looking at the full, creamy breasts and long blond hair. She had allowed the woman into her private quarters, even showed her the way to her bed. But that was where she'd stopped. She'd watched as the woman undressed, slipped into the black satin sheets, and touched herself. The woman had beckoned her to join with her eyes, her hands, her sighs. But Liz was unaffected. And soon she'd grown bored.

"I'm so wet for you now." The woman slid her hand to her crotch, where she stroked up and down.

Liz clenched her jaw, no longer unaffected. Now she was annoyed. "Do me a favor."

"Anything."

"Get your shit and leave."

The woman's hand fell to her side and her mouth opened in surprise.

Liz eyed her coldly. "Do I need to say it again?"

The woman glared at her as she retrieved her clothes and got dressed. "What a major fucking disappointment." She gave a wicked smile. "Everyone is right, you know. The old Elizabeth Adams is gone."

Liz stood. "Get the fuck out of here."

The woman laughed as she headed for the door. Liz slammed it shut behind her. Returning to the couch, she collapsed once again, her head falling into her hands. She caught sight of her satellite phone and her stomach turned. It had been too long. It should've rung days ago.

She shoved it aside and focused on the short stack of bills. Something wasn't quite right with the books and the businesses. Two of her accounts seemed to be missing money. She didn't need the stress of a paperwork nightmare. That's what she employed Reggie to handle. Her hands froze as she came across a handwritten envelope addressed to her. With her gut churning, she tore it open and read.

She stood, read it again, and shoved it into her pocket. Grabbing her keys, she left the lair and hurried down the VIP staircase. Tyson spoke to her but she ignored him, brushing by him and countless others.

She had only one thing on her mind, and nothing was going to stop her.

She didn't have much time and the letters were getting stranger and stranger. This one was by far the most serious of all.

❖

Erin crept through the house, finding her way by the dim light of the tiny accent lamps Patricia kept on. It was after three a.m. and Patricia had been asleep for a couple of hours. Just to be sure, Erin peeked in on her. Next to the sleeping detective, Jack opened his eyes and lifted his head. Erin brought a finger up to her mouth, hoping he knew the sign for "Quiet."

He seemed to understand, jumping down from the bed without a sound. She bent to scratch his back and he followed her into the office, watching as she grabbed binder after binder from Patricia's desk.

Erin felt guilty, doubly so as the little dog stared. "I'm just going to borrow them." Although Jack couldn't hear her, she felt better offering an explanation. "I have no choice. She won't let me see them. And lives are at stake."

Jack's claws clicked on the hard floor as he followed to the front door. He sniffed the cool night air as she stepped out.

Telling him, "I'll be back," Erin locked the door and headed for her Toyota SUV.

The local Kinko's was bright and open twenty-four hours. She brought her bounty inside and set to work right away, politely declining when the young employee offered to do all the copying for her. She could trust no one with these documents and she couldn't risk the young man catching a glimpse of the gruesome victim photos.

As she copied page after page, various details caught her eye: There was no hit yet on the satellite phone number. Jay was still a prime suspect. The police had obtained more information from Arcane, Alabama, on both Liz and Jay. Liz had recently been arrested on assault charges. There was a crucifix drawn on Joe Gillette's body, and on Antwon's.

The whole way home Erin drummed her fingers nervously on the steering wheel, praying that Patricia would still be asleep. The house was dark and quiet as she stepped inside. Jack happily sniffed her feet as she crept inside and they both headed down the hallway. She dropped the large stacks of paper onto her bedside table, then hurried to the office and replaced the binders just as she'd found them. She was almost back to her room when she heard Patricia's voice.

"Mac, are you all right?" Patricia stood in the doorway in light cotton pajamas, hair askew.

Stiffening, Erin said, "Yes, I'm fine. Just thirsty is all."

Patricia didn't seem to notice her shoes or her blue jeans. Instead she yawned and cleared her throat. "Okay." Jack trotted up to her and she bent to lift him in her arms. "We should probably talk soon. About things."

Erin stood very still. "I agree. How about tomorrow?" Her heart thudded like mad.

Patricia nodded. "Good night, then."

Erin produced a smile. She hoped it looked normal. "Sleep well."

She stripped off her clothes as soon as she closed the door. For the next two hours, she pored over the case files she'd waited so long to read.

❖

The ringing phone seemed to bang against her skull. Patricia reached for the receiver.

It was Gary Jacobs, and he sounded worked up. "Get up and get down here."

"What's going on?" She kicked the covers off and walked into the bathroom.

"We got the hair and fiber analysis back on De Maro."

"Yeah?" She covered the phone as she sat to pee.

"Are you ready for this?"

Her heart rate kicked up. "Lay it on me."

"We've got DNA. From his underwear. A small bloodstain that isn't his own."

She grinned so hard it hurt. "I couldn't have woken to better news. Don't tell me there's more, I might have to pinch myself."

"Pinch away. The sample wasn't great but it was enough to get mitochondrial." He paused to catch his breath. "Guess who it matches?"

She sat in silence, her heart now thudding in her ears.

"Elizabeth Adams."

Patricia stood, pajamas around her ankles. She flushed. "No fucking way."

"Yes way." He laughed, overcome with joy, something Gary rarely seemed to feel. "We've got her. We've really got her this time."

Patricia stepped out of her pants and hurried over to her closet. "Where is she?"

"We sent a few squad cars over to her place about five minutes ago."

"I'll meet you at the station." Patricia hung up in near disbelief. She tossed a shirt and chinos on the bed and found underwear. She was still fastening her belt as she rushed out into the hallway and ran head-on into Erin.

"Leaving already?"

"Yeah."

Erin studied her. "Something big going down?"

She had a way with her eyes, an ability to somehow see right through her. And Patricia couldn't risk that scrutiny at the moment.

"You could say that," she answered cagily. She knew she couldn't tell her. Even if she could, she wouldn't want to. It would devastate her. "I've got to go."

"We'll have that talk later, then?" Erin called out after her.

Patricia looked over her shoulder. "Yep. Later. Promise."

She grabbed her keys and headed out into the garage. As she started her Blazer, she knew in her gut that all of their lives were about to change forever.

CHAPTER SEVENTEEN

"Where the hell is she?" Sergeant Ruiz screamed.

Patricia held the phone away from her ear. "We're not sure." She and Gary were standing inside Erotique Studios. A dozen or so employees milled around, eavesdropping and whispering among themselves.

"We've checked her house and the nightclub," she reported, "and the staff here say she didn't come into work today."

"God damn it, good God damn it! Find her!"

Patricia hung up and Gary shook his head as if apologizing to her. No one liked to be on the end of Ruiz's very short fuse.

"Even if we do find her…" he started.

"Doesn't mean it's her," she finished. Mitochondrial DNA came from the mother. So the sample could be from Liz, or it could be from Jay.

At the moment Ruiz and the department were betting on Liz. If they found Liz, they'd most likely find their answers. No one could dispute DNA, and Liz had left an ample amount of blood on Patricia's carpet the year before. Plenty for comparison.

Patricia wished she could remember more about that night. What really had happened? Had Liz really come to save her and Erin? Could Liz really kill someone? Her mind clouded over with dark, confusing thoughts. How could Erin love a killer? Was it possible? Even if Liz had everyone else fooled, would Erin really be able to fall in love with someone like her? Patricia didn't think so. If there was one thing she knew, it was that Erin McKenzie was a good person with a good heart and good instincts. Patricia desperately wanted to trust those instincts.

"Is there anything we can help you with?" a nice-looking man approached and asked her quietly.

Patricia had been introduced to them all an hour before when they'd first arrived. "Reggie, right?" At his nod, she asked, "Who worked the closest with her?"

Reggie seemed to think for a moment. "Next to Ms. McKenzie, me, I suppose."

"How's she been acting lately?"

He blew out a hiss of air. "Distant. Bothered. Sad." He met her eyes. "We've been worried about her for a long while now. Since Ms. McKenzie left."

"Have you seen anything out of the norm?"

He shook his head but then stopped, his eyes returning to hold hers for a few seconds. "You know there was that one night."

"Go on."

"I was here working late and I heard something. Ms. Adams and I nearly ran into one another. The halls were dark. She had someone with her, and the woman looked so much like her, I thought I was seeing things."

"Did she say who it was?" Patricia swallowed against a dry throat, her pulse doubling.

"No. She just got pissed and said I should turn the lights on if I was going to stay late. They left in a hurry."

"Why did this seem so strange to you?" Gary interrupted.

"Ms. Adams is never here that late. It was past eleven."

Gary gave Patricia a telling glance. The other woman was Jay. It had to be. "Would you excuse us for a moment?" He drew her aside, out of earshot. "Have you asked Erin where Adams is?"

"I left her at the house. She doesn't know where she is." Patricia grimaced. She was positive Erin wasn't even speaking to Adams. Still, what if she knew about a hideaway? Damn it, why hadn't she thought to ask? Was she losing her mind?

Gary's face hardened. "You're letting your relationship with her get in the way."

"Oh, I am not." She looked away, angry.

A younger, somewhat effeminate man caught her eye and immediately approached. "How much longer are you all going to be hanging around? You're kind of scaring everyone."

Patricia snapped at him. "We're here trying to apprehend a possible killer. I'm sorry if that's an inconvenience."

His face dropped. "That's what I mean." He looked to Gary. "This is all very scary to us. We've lost two coworkers and now you're telling us our boss is a suspect." He inclined his head toward Patricia. "And she's not being very nice."

"Blake, is it?" Patricia said. "Please forgive my rudeness, but I think apprehending a killer is far more important than worrying about tact right now."

"Ms. Adams isn't a killer," he replied softly. "A bitch most of the time, yes. But not a killer."

"You're sure of that, are you?" Patricia had known Adams far longer than any of these people and she wasn't sure of a damn thing.

"We've all been kind of sticking together lately, sharing rides, leaving together," Blake said. "Looking out for each other, you know."

"That's great. What's your point?"

Patricia glanced past him, toward Reggie. The accountant still stood where they'd left him, nervously watching the proceedings. His constant darting stares annoyed her, and she guessed he was trying to pluck up the nerve to say something more. She wondered just what all he'd seen working on a daily basis with Elizabeth Adams.

"It was all Ms. Adam's idea," Blake informed her and Patricia realized she hadn't heard a word he'd just said.

"What was?" she asked.

He sighed loudly, obviously displeased with her inattention. "Partnering up. She told all of us to never be alone unless we were at home with all the doors locked. She even gave us her private number in case we ever need anything."

Patricia didn't respond. She was surprised. The Adams she knew didn't give a fuck about anyone, much less their safety. Even when they'd dated, she didn't give her the private number to her home or her lair. Patricia had been lucky to get her cell phone number and luckier still if she ever answered.

"Thank you for the information, Blake," Gary said. "Here's my card. Call me anytime if you think of anything else."

As Blake slid the card into his pocket, Patricia said, "Keep doing what you're doing. For safety. It's better for you not to be alone."

He said nothing, lowered his eyes, and walked away.

"Are you all right?" Gary asked.

Patricia stared after Blake, lost in thought. "Not exactly."

Things she thought she knew for certain seemed to be melting away. People she thought she knew well seemed to have changed, or perhaps she was the one who'd changed. Erin. Elizabeth Adams. The murders. Her life. Her feelings. All of it spun together and warped into a heavy swirling mist that clouded her mind and made her dizzy.

Behind her, she heard Stewart cursing. He and Hernandez had shown up to help with the interviews. Stewart was gripping a doorknob, shaking it furiously. "Why does this bitch keep everything locked!"

Hernandez laughed. "To keep you out."

The door led into Liz's private office. When Stewart dug in his pockets and retrieved a folding knife, Gary called, "Hey, pal. We can't pick the lock. Not yet."

Stewart grimaced. "We got the bitch's DNA. Ten minutes from now we'll have the warrants to ransack every dyke pad she owns."

"I know." Gary glanced toward Liz's employees. They were watching every move the detectives made. "But we need to wait for those warrants. We have to do this exactly by the book. Ruiz and the department want to put her away for good this time. No fuckups. Nothing for her elaborate defense team to have fun with."

Stewart grumbled and put his knife away. "I really hate this Adams bitch. If you ask me, she's with her sister. Whacking more men." He looked around the studio with distaste. "They really film fruity porn in here?" He didn't wait for an answer.

"What about that phone number? Any luck yet?" Hernandez was referring to the satellite phone number Patricia had gotten from Erin.

"Not so far," she said. "We confirmed it was a satellite number, and they were waiting for some calls to come in on it in order to try a trace. But we all know those phones are damn near impossible to get a fix on."

"Last word we got on it," Gary added, "was that the phone was in the Valle Luna area."

"I'm telling ya, they're out whacking together." Stewart shared his thoughts again. "One strangles, one stabs."

"But why?" Patricia murmured, surprised when she realized she'd spoken aloud.

Stewart's eyes nearly popped out of his head. "Why?" He looked to Gary. "Did you hit her in the head this morning or something?"

She didn't respond. Which also surprised her. Normally she'd have bitten back, but she was too confused and disoriented.

Stewart took advantage and continued. "They're fucked-up fruitcakes, that's why. Man-hating dykes with a vengeance. Adams is borderline sociopathic, and the sister's a loony. Any of this ringing a bell?"

"Don't forget what Henderson found digging around in Alabama," Hernandez said.

Stewart shoved in a mouthful of gum and nodded adamantly. "Yeah, if the sister really was sexually assaulted, that's all the motive we need, right there."

Patricia agreed but thought back to the old woman she'd interviewed a few months before. In search of more on Jay Adams, she'd gone back to Arcane, Alabama. She hadn't been able to find much, but what she did find was a story she'd never forget.

"I'm going to run home for a bit," she told Gary. "I need to talk to Erin."

"I'll call the second we hear something," he said and escorted her to the door.

As she stepped out into the piercing sun and walked to her vehicle, she thought back to the woman who'd told her that story. Lema Thorpe.

The cicadas were so loud Patricia had asked the eighty-eight-year-old woman if they could speak inside. The rickety old screen door without a screen slammed shut behind her, causing Patricia to jump. Lema paid no mind, feet scooting along the worn wood floor, leading the way. Her house shoes were old, covered in tiny holes, and the once-white bottoms made a whooshing noise as her feet scooted.

From deeper in the house Patricia heard the chirps of caged parakeets. Two cats caught her eye, one sprawled on the old kitchen table and the other crouched in a dark corner, watching her. The sound of claws clicking brought her gaze to Lema's feet, where a fat little Chihuahua waddled in excitement.

Patricia bent to pet him and he peed a little puddle while his tail went a mile a minute.

"He does that," Lema explained. *"Means he likes you."*

The overstuffed dog followed them into a tiny living room with walls completely covered in dusty-framed photos. Patricia thought the walls were all leaning inward, the weight from the frames too much to bear. There were school pictures of at least a dozen different kids.

"Those are my great grand youngins," Lema offered on a grunt, lowering her hefty frame into a creaking vinyl recliner.

"That's quite a bunch."

"Fourteen of 'em so far." She was about to prop her feet up, but hesitated. *"You don't want nuthin' to drink, do ya?"*

"No, I'm fine, thank you."

Lema grunted again as she reclined. *"Chi Chi, come."* The dog scurried over but couldn't jump up. She grabbed him by the collar and popped him up onto her lap.

Patricia eased herself down onto a very comfortable couch covered in an old Pound Puppy bedsheet. Lema's love for animals was evident everywhere.

Lema scratched on Chi Chi's head for a while, then reached for a Hill's Brothers coffee can. She spat so hard Patricia swore she heard an echoing *"ding"* from the metallic bottom.

"Now then." Lema exchanged that can for a smaller one, stuffing snuff into her bottom lip. *"What can I do for you, young lady?"* Her eyes were so light blue that Patricia had wondered at first if she was blind. Combined with a short shock of messy white hair, they almost made Patricia lose her train of thought entirely.

"I'm looking for information on Jay Adams."

Lema stared. Patricia had gotten access to the house asking about a neighbor who lived nearby. Now that her real intentions had come to light, Lema Thorpe no longer seemed so welcoming.

"How do you know Jay?"

"I know her sister, Elizabeth."

"Why did you come to me?"

Patricia hesitated. She'd sworn to the deputy that she wouldn't tell anyone where he'd pointed her. *"A friend told me you were the one to see."*

Lema seemed to take that in for a moment. *"Who was Jay's father?"*

It seemed Patricia was in for a quiz.

"That's a secret."

"You don't know." Lema spat.

"How do I know you do?"

Again the stare.

"If Dayne and Jerry were alive I wouldn't be here bothering you," Patricia said smoothly. *"But Elizabeth is ill and we need to find Jay. You're my only hope."*

The names seemed to help melt Lema's resolve. *"Lizzie is sick? Out there in New Mexico? I told that child not to run off. You can run from demons but you can't run from the devil."* She fixed her stare on the nearby wall. *"Jay and Lizzie Adams,"* she said, almost to herself, *"Those were the two biggest tomboys I ever did see."*

"Do you happen to know where Jay is now?" Patricia tried to keep her on topic.

"No, ma'am. Heard about her being around, but I hadn't seen her in years."

"Can you tell me about her childhood?"

Lema grew quiet. *"You don't want to know about that."*

"Actually, I do. I need to know. In order to help find her."

Lema spit in the can and Patricia caught a whiff of the sticky-smelling tobacco mixed with old coffee. Somehow it soothed her. The birds chirped from the next room.

"Jay didn't have no normal childhood. Laws, no." Lema seemed to grow sad, working her lower lip. *"That poor child."*

"Why is that?"

"If you know Lizzie, you should know this."

Patricia squeezed her hands together. *"Liz refuses to say. And no one else will tell me. Did something happen to her? Did someone hurt her?"*

Lema's eyes drifted back to hers. *"They didn't want no one to know. Something like that happens, it's best if folks don't know. And around these parts, your word is your word."*

"Mrs. Thorpe, please. I need to know. She and Liz, they're in trouble and I'm afraid someone will get hurt, Liz is sick. Please." She was having trouble keeping her stories straight, but she was so close to the truth she could feel it vibrating her bones.

"You ain't the law, are you?"

"No. Of course not."

"So she ain't done nuthin' bad?"

Patricia lied again. "No."

"'Cuz if she did, it wouldn't been all her fault. After what happened to her, she just wuldn't right after that."

"Mrs. Thorpe, what happened?"

Lema worked on her snuff a bit as she thought. "When them girls was about eleven, they came upon a man in the woods. He got to Jay. Lizzie ran off to tell. My boys was Jerry's friends. They went with him that day. By the time they found her, she'd been violated and beat to tarnation." She met Patricia's eyes. "What that man done to her, no human should have to suffer."

Patricia's heart rose to thud in her throat. "Did she see a doctor?" Her first thought was of Jay's well-being, but then she wondered if there was medical record somewhere from a hospital.

Lema stroked Chi Chi. "Yes. And he told Jerry what the man had did."

"What happened to the man?"

"I can't say."

Patricia wasn't sure if she didn't know or if she really couldn't say. Whatever the reason, Lema had stopped with her tale and her constant stroking. Chi Chi gazed up at her, offering his belly if she would continue.

"What happened to Jay? Did she stay in the hospital?"

"No, the doc looked her over, cleaned her up the best he could. Jerry didn't want her in no hospital after he heard what all had been done to her." She paused again, staring off at the wall. "But she wuldn't right after that. In the head. Never was the same."

"Well, this certainly explains a lot."

"How's that?"

Patricia rose, having said too much. "Thank you for your time, Mrs. Thorpe. I really appreciate it."

Lema looked surprised. "You leaving so soon?"

"Do you have more you can tell me?"

Lema stroked the dog. Her light eyes seemed to cloud over with sadness. "No, I can't say no more." She started to pet Chi Chi again. "Those two girls. What all they went through. They was attached at the hip. Before and after. Seen things, and been through things no child should have to go through."

"Mrs. Thorpe, is there anyone else I might be able to talk to about this? Someone who might know more?"

"Heavens no. Ain't no one around here gonna talk. I didn't ever give anyone my word, but I've already said too much."

"Is there anywhere I could look for Jay?"

Lema wagged a finger at her. "Child, the one and only place that holds Jay Adams is them woods."

"She's in the woods?"

"She'll always be in them woods. They know all. They hold all." Lema spat. *"Can you see yourself out?"*

Patricia nodded, thanked her again, and walked out.

Chapter Eighteen

Jack greeted Patricia at the door. He wagged his tail and danced on his hind legs until she plucked him up and kissed him. She sighed as she punched in the code to turn off the alarm. Erin wasn't home. Nothing seemed to be going right. She picked up the phone and called her. Erin's voice mail answered. Patricia hung up. She was about to call back and leave a message when the doorbell rang. Surprised and thinking maybe Erin forgot her key, she quickly answered.

This time true surprise formed a gasp that escaped her throat.

Sinclair thrust out a small cake and smiled so the one dimple showed. "I came offering peace."

Patricia just stared.

"I was wrong about Adams. We heard this morning." Sinclair withdrew the cake by a few inches when it was not accepted. She shook her head. "This was a bad idea. I never do stuff like this. I should go."

"No. Please. Come in." The words rushed out and Patricia stepped to one side.

"Are you sure?" Sinclair palmed the back of her neck, looking nervous.

Up until that point Patricia hadn't thought the woman could ever get nervous. She always seemed so poised and confident. Patricia smiled and took the cake from her. As Sinclair stepped inside, Patricia caught the freshly scrubbed spicy scent of her. Her heart fluttered like a hummingbird's wings.

"I'm sorry about showing up like this," Sinclair said.

"Don't worry about it." Patricia smiled again at her. "At least you were polite enough to bring cake. I didn't bring you anything but attitude when I showed up on your doorstep."

Sinclair laughed and lowered her hand. She looked to the cake. "It's a pineapple upside-down cake. My brother-in-law made it. He uses a good recipe, Hawaiian."

"Oh." Patricia moved into the kitchen. "Should we cut it now?"

"Sure."

Patricia set the cake on the counter, peeled off the saran wrap, and pulled a large knife from the block next to the stove. "So how did you find me?"

"It wasn't hard." Sinclair was looking around at the house. "It's funny, but this is just how I pictured it." She was in baggy jeans and a white long-sleeved soft flannel shirt. She rolled up the cuffs with long nimble fingers.

"You pictured my house?" Just the thought threatened to color her cheeks so she focused on the cake, cutting two thick slices and placing them on plates.

"Yeah. Well, you know, you meet someone and wonder about things."

Patricia didn't say anything. *Has she wondered about me as I have her?* She handed her a plate and then remembered the forks. Turning toward the drawers so her face couldn't be seen, she asked, "And how is that?"

As she plucked out two forks she felt her ears redden. Sinclair was behind her saying words like "warm" and "lots of reds and earth tones." The word "fiery" made her skin burn, and she turned around slowly. Their eyes met. Sinclair's skin had darkened as well, at the base of her jaw.

They sat at the table in silence until Jack rocketed back in through the doggie door. His whole body shook with excitement as Sinclair leaned over to pet him.

"You like animals?" Patricia asked.

"Of course. I just haven't decided on one yet. With my hours sometimes it seems unfair." She straightened and looked back down at Jack. "He seems to be fine, though. The dog door probably helps."

"I try to come home frequently during long hours. To check on him and stuff." Patricia finally took a bite of the cake because she couldn't seem to form any more words. It was so good it made her mouth water. "God, this is delicious."

Sinclair smiled. "I'll tell Denny you like it. I'm sure he'll send some more my way for you. He and my sister just moved here from Hawaii. I followed."

"Wanted to be close to family?"

"Yes, and they're pregnant."

"How exciting."

"It is. I can't wait."

Their eyes met again. Patricia looked away first. She thought of a question. "So where were you before, D.C.?"

Sinclair blinked. "How did you know?"

"It wasn't hard."

Sinclair took another bite, chuckling softly. "Yes, I was with the Bureau."

"Must've been quite a change. The Bureau to Valle Luna."

"It was. But it was needed. My relationship had ended, I was tired of D.C. and I wanted the chance to physically chase criminals rather than just chasing them on paper."

Patricia assumed she was referring to the profiling work she'd done. But her mind focused in on the word *relationship*. "I'm sorry about your relationship."

Sinclair swallowed. "Do you mind if I get something to drink?"

"Of course, I'm sorry."

Patricia stood, embarrassed. Sinclair did as well and they bumped into one another. They were eye to eye. She could smell the pineapple and spice coming from Sinclair. Her eyes were that warm, soft cinnamon again.

Sinclair squeezed her forearm, as if trying to comfort her. "I can get it." The smile was back and Patricia wanted so badly to reach out and touch the dimple. Sinclair pointed to the cabinet next to the fridge. "In here?"

"Yes."

She got down two glasses and opened the fridge. "Milk okay?"

"Yes." Patricia stared at the thick muscled legs and ass under Sinclair's jeans.

Oblivious, Sinclair continued speaking as she poured the milk. "My relationship ending was a good thing. I'd been in it for almost ten years. The last few weren't good." She set the milk on its shelf in the fridge and handed Patricia a full glass. "My partner started drinking about five years ago. She'd seen something really bad, something she couldn't handle."

"That's terrible."

"It was, yes. She worked in missing children."

"Oh." Patricia could only imagine the horror.

Sinclair nodded. "Anyway, I got her into therapy, but nothing helped. The drinking worsened. Then it became less about the pain and more about the drinking. She lost her job. Hated me and all I stood for. Eventually, I came home one day and she was gone."

"She just left?"

"Uh-huh. She went off with her new friends. She'd started hanging around with some pretty scary people. Drug addicts and the like. I found her at a run-down duplex, living there with two other women and a man." She paused, staring into her glass of milk. "I asked her to come home, offered again to get serious help. She told me to fuck off. Slammed the door in my face."

The pain on Sinclair's face was heart wrenching. "I'm so sorry." Patricia covered her hand and squeezed.

Sinclair snapped out of her daze. "It's okay. I got through it. Realized it wasn't me. And that it really wasn't even her. It was the alcohol. So when my sister called with the news of the baby and the move to Valle Luna, I made my move."

"She hasn't tried to contact you?"

"No."

"Do you want her to?"

Sinclair lowered the glass. "No. I've moved on. She has too. She'll never call for money or anything like that. Her folks are wealthy and they won't cut her off."

"Have you dated?" Patricia couldn't believe she'd even asked. She fought off the urge to smack herself in the head.

Sinclair merely smiled. "Not yet. I needed to redefine me first. Find my happiness, my core."

"And have you?"

"Yes."

They both ate after that, sitting comfortably in silence.

"Thank you for coming over," Patricia said after a while.

Sinclair seemed surprised by her words. "Thanks for having me."

"Anytime."

"I can't believe I just told you all that."

Patricia formed a half smile, one of amusement. "I can't either."

"I'm just going to eat my cake now and try to forget how crazy my life must sound."

Patricia laughed. As far as strange went, Sinclair's life had nothing on her own. She and her department were hunting down Elizabeth Adams, her own former lover, on murder charges. As if that weren't enough, Erin, whom she'd also slept with, could be obstructing justice if she knew where Adams was hiding out. Yet with all that going on, the last place Patricia expected to be was sitting there at her kitchen table eating pineapple upside-down cake with the rival, yet very intriguing Detective Audrey Sinclair.

"So why didn't you tell me you were a published author?" Sinclair pushed her plate aside. "It's all over the sheriff's department. Everyone's got your new book."

"Oh, God. I was hoping it wouldn't cause a ruckus." Patricia stared down at her plate. The cake suddenly seemed way too heavy on her stomach. "How did the sheriff's department even find out about it?"

She'd used false names and the book was written as fiction. But the storyline was very real.

Sinclair laughed. "The departments may be rivals, but rumors spread freely and often across the border."

"Great." She could already hear Ruiz thundering down on her like God himself.

"It's a great book," Sinclair said.

"You've read it?" Her publisher had called to say the early reviews were good and the book was selling.

"Sure. As soon as I heard about it, I picked it up."

"And you were worried I would think *your* life is crazy?"

"Reading your story helped. I probably wouldn't have shared mine otherwise."

Patricia grimaced. "It's supposed to be fiction." She thought of the romance she'd also written, the one about Erin, and how quickly she was called out on that one.

"Everyone else in America will see it as fiction," Sinclair said. "Good fiction."

"Yet your colleagues are talking about it like frat-house boys discussing an easy lay."

Sinclair laughed. "Well, the sheriff *is* using it as an example as to why we should steer clear of the Valle Luna P.D."

"Wonderful." Patricia had heard enough to light an unpleasant fire under her ass. She rose and took their plates, heading for the sink, needing to do something other than sit.

"I won't hold it against you." Sinclair followed, carrying their glasses. "You're the one who saved the day, solved the case."

She stood next to Patricia, waiting as she turned on the faucet. Patricia sank her hands gratefully into the hot water. When Sinclair added her dishes, their hands collided and Sinclair's fingers slipped into hers. A breath of air escaped Patricia at the contact. The baked-cinnamon eyes moved from Patricia's face to her lips. When they came back up they were full of shimmering flames.

The scent of pineapple and sugary rum sauce mixed with the lemony fragrance of the hot suds. They floated into her head like a dream. Feeling pleasantly dizzy, she lingered under Audrey Sinclair's warm, hazy gaze the way she would face-up to the sun. Her skin felt caressed, and she seemed fixed to the ground like she never wanted to move out from the rays.

When Sinclair kissed her, she moaned and pressed back. Full and agile, Sinclair's lips framed hers, first the top, then the bottom. Pressing and holding and tasting. The soft warmth of her lips gave way to the soft, hot wetness of her mouth. Again Patricia moaned, loving the taste and feel of her. Sweet like sugar, liquid sugar.

A cough came, loud and excusing. It didn't come from Sinclair. Patricia heard the cough again and the lips left hers. She opened her eyes, feeling empty. Sinclair squeezed her forearm and followed her gaze to the woman standing in the kitchen entryway. Erin looked ashen and a little angry.

"Mac, hi." Patricia wiped her hands on a dishtowel and passed it to Sinclair. "This is—"

"Sinclair. With the sheriff's office," Erin snapped. "I saw you on television."

Sinclair dried her hands and offered a small smile. "I should get going."

Patricia was tempted to ask her to stay, but she remembered her promise to Erin. They had a lot to discuss. She felt her face fall with disappointment. "I'm sorry," she said with a regretful smile.

"No, I'm sorry," Erin let out. "Please don't leave on account of me. I can just go back out the way I came."

"Mac, wait." Patricia moved toward her. "I need to talk to you."

"You can say that again."

"What do you mean?"

Erin looked past her to Sinclair. "Obviously this was what you meant when you said we needed to talk."

"No." Patricia hated the hurt she saw in her friend's eyes. "It's something else."

"I'll see you later," Sinclair said gently, excusing herself.

Erin stepped to the side to let her by.

"Nice meeting you," Sinclair said politely.

Erin made a noise and nodded.

Patricia felt torn and panicked. She told Erin to wait, then quickly followed Sinclair outside for some privacy. "I'm sorry about that."

Sinclair sank her hands into her jeans pockets. "I understand."

"She's staying with me for a while, until…" But she didn't have any answer.

"That's the one from the book?"

Patricia suddenly grew angry with herself and swore she'd never write another word unless it was about someone completely made up. "Yes."

"You're a good friend." Sinclair sounded sincere but her gaze was elsewhere.

"I try to be. Unfortunately, I have to go back in there and tell her we are pursuing her lover on murder charges and that we found DNA."

"I was wrong about what I said. About Adams."

Patricia studied her. "Is that why you came tonight?"

"Yes." Sinclair's voice softened with sincerity. "I'm not wrong very often, but when I am I own up to it."

"I'm glad you came." Patricia smiled. "I'm glad I got to know you better."

Sinclair fished out her car keys. "Me too." She gave her a wink. "Call me if you need anything. The case…anything. Call me."

Patricia nodded and this time said, "I plan on it."

She waited until Sinclair drove away before heading back inside. She didn't like what she was about to do or what she was about to face. Erin sat waiting on the couch, one leg crossed over the other, swaying casually. Jack was in her lap, eating up the affection. Patricia sat down on the opposite end of the couch, her insides churning.

"She seems nice," Erin said. "Very professional at that press conference."

Patricia looked at her in amazement. "She is. And yes, she was." *Why do I feel like I just got caught coming in late from a date?*

"How long have you been fucking her?"

"What?"

Erin turned sharply and nailed her to the couch with her eyes. "You should've told me." Patricia couldn't keep up as Erin continued, "Had I known you were seeing her, I wouldn't have had sex with you and I probably wouldn't have even stayed here."

"Mac, slow down."

"Slow down? Why would I want to do that when I'm just catching up?"

"I'm not sleeping with her."

"She's with the sheriff's department, you know. Ruiz will spontaneously combust when he finds out."

"Mac, I'm not sleeping with her."

Erin shut up suddenly, finally hearing her.

"She came over tonight to talk. As friends. She's nice." Her words drifted off as she recalled the kiss. "What you walked in on, that was a first-time thing."

Erin uncrossed her legs as if she were uncomfortable. "Then if she wasn't the reason you want to talk, what is it?" She rubbed her hands on her denim-covered thighs, something Patricia had noticed she did when she got nervous.

"You and I need to talk about what happened between us. It has nothing to do with anyone else."

"Okay." Erin breathed deep, as if readying herself.

"I know you're unhappy," Patricia said gently. "And I know what happened between us will never happen again. Not because I don't want it to, but because I know you don't want it to." Erin started to shake her head but Patricia held up a hand. "Be honest, Mac. With me, with yourself."

Erin clasped her hands together in her lap, causing Jack to paw at them. When she wouldn't pet him, he trotted over to Patricia and curled up against her instead.

"I know you love Liz."

"Yes," Erin whispered. "But she doesn't want me."

Silence.

"Do you love me?" Patricia needed to ask, she needed to hear. She'd hoped for so long that Erin would come to her and love her, but now she feared hearing what she already knew.

"I do." Erin's eyes were full of tears. "But not like I love Liz."

"I know." Patricia could feel her own eyes filling. "That's okay."

"I'm sorry."

Patricia shook her head. "Don't be."

"Do you want me gone now?" She seemed so very fragile at that moment.

"Of course not." Patricia didn't say what she didn't mean. "You can stay as long as you like."

"But we can't have sex again." Erin laughed a little as she wiped her eyes.

"I don't think it's a good idea."

"Do you still want me?"

Patricia studied her, taking in the delicateness of her face, the honesty of her eyes. She saw a new maturity there as well. "I'll always wish for that something we could've had. But reality is what it is. Your heart belongs to someone else. I want my heart to belong to someone too."

She thought of Sinclair again, and warmed all over. She could just about kill Adams for hurting Erin so badly, for turning her away when she'd accepted things no other person would. When she'd risked so much and sacrificed so much to be with her. Erin's question stuck in her mind: *Do you still want me?* That was really all Erin wanted, for someone to want her. Patricia was suddenly thankful Adams had turned her away. If she was involved in all this, in murder and God only knew what else, maybe she did care about Erin after all. Enough to push her away so she wouldn't get caught up in the fallout.

"Erin, there's something else we need to talk about."

Erin looked at her. Waiting.

"We found something on Antwon De Maro's underwear. A bloodstain. We got mitochondrial DNA from it." Patricia reached out and squeezed her hand. "It matches Liz."

Erin began shaking her head. "No." She stood and pointed at Patricia like she was the devil himself. "No. It's a mistake. You made a mistake!"

"There's no mistake, Mac. DNA doesn't lie."

Erin paced, mumbling to herself. "It's not her. Liz couldn't do something like that. She couldn't." She froze. Her head whipped around to Patricia. "It's a mitochondrial match?"

"Yes."

"It's Jay."

Patricia sighed. "It very well could be, yes."

"It is. I know it is."

"Then we need to find Liz so we can figure this all out and clear her if she's innocent."

"You mean she's not in jail?"

"We can't find her. I was hoping you might know where she is."

Erin shook her head. "I have no idea."

"Is there someplace she may have mentioned before? A place she might like to go?"

Erin's eyes flew up to her. "She did tell me that she went to Mexico last year, to hide for a while."

"Which part?"

"Cabo."

Patricia was about to ask more when her cell phone rang. She plucked it from her hip. Gary spoke as soon as she picked up.

"We just got a call."

"Adams?"

Erin's eyes were fastened to her.

"Yeah."

"Where?"

"The desert, close to where De Maro was found."

"They have her in custody yet?"

Gary grew quiet.

"Hello?"

"Yeah, they have her."

"Great."

"No, not so great," he said without expression.

"Why?"

"She's dead."

CHAPTER NINETEEN

"What is it?" Erin's bones felt like dry twigs, ready to snap at any sudden movement. Her blood thudded in her ears. Patricia wasn't talking fast enough. "Is it Liz? Do they have Liz?"

Patricia's face had clouded over with fear, the blood draining down into her neck where the skin started to flush crimson. "I need to go." She walked into the kitchen to retrieve her keys.

Erin followed. "Tell me. I have to know."

"I can't, Mac."

"You have to!"

Patricia wouldn't hold her eyes.

"Why won't you tell me?" Erin stepped in front of her, forcing her to stop. "Just tell me. All I want to know is if they have her."

Patricia finally looked at her. Her eyes were soft with sadness. "They think they do, yes."

"Okay, well, I'm coming with you, then."

"You can't."

"I'm coming. Either in your car or behind you in mine."

"Mac, I want you to wait until I call you."

"No. I want to see her. And you know damn well she won't talk to any of you."

Patricia's face fell, her eyes so frightened and serious Erin's skin pricked. "Mac, they've found a body."

Erin shook her head. A body? "What are you talking about? Did they find Liz with another victim?" Please God, no. It couldn't be true. Liz wasn't a murderer.

Patricia was silent for several long, excruciating seconds. When she spoke again, her voice was so soft Erin barely heard. "They found a body. They think it might be Liz."

"No. No, no, no, no." Erin swayed. Her head felt heavy and light at the same time. Her body seemed to have drained of everything, bones, blood, soul. All of it had rushed downward in a flash of heat and was gone. Patricia propped her up with an arm around her waist. She was holding her tight, Erin knew that, but she couldn't feel it.

Patricia led her to the couch. "I need to go, Mac. To make sure. I'll call you as soon as I know."

"Patricia, it's not her." The words hardly emerged from her dry, useless mouth. Images began to fill her head. Ones of Liz lying dumped on the desert ground, pale blue eyes fixed to the sky, wide open in terror.

"Stay here," Patricia said gently. "I'll be in touch soon."

Suddenly Erin snapped back from the fog and weight of the thought of death. "No. I'm coming with you."

Patricia sighed. "Mac, you know that's impossible. Ruiz would shit, and you don't need to be seeing…that."

Erin stood. "One way or another, I'm going to that scene. You can take me, or I'll go by myself."

❖

They rode in silence. Erin stared out the windshield, wringing her hands in her lap. Nothing had ever felt this way before. Her fear was so intense and reality so sharp, she felt certain every cell in her body would self-destruct at the moment of confirmation. She knew it would hurt like nothing had ever hurt before. She would feel every last cell as it was sliced apart and shredded.

"It can't be her. It can't be her." She kept saying it over and over. She wouldn't let it be her. If she wouldn't let it, then it just couldn't be.

When she saw the tall, piercing portable lights, she started to cry, and suddenly she didn't want to see. She wanted the lights to stop shining into the blackness, to stop spotlighting the reality. She wanted everyone to leave. Liz wasn't here.

Patricia pulled the Blazer onto the rough terrain, a big black moth heading toward the lights. Erin cried softly, wringing her hands harder and harder. Patricia offered words of comfort but she couldn't hear over the loud throbbing fuzz in her ears. When they parked, Erin looked out in the distance and saw the yellow tarp over the hump of a body. She started to hyperventilate as she imagined Liz lying under it.

Patricia climbed hurriedly from the truck. She rounded the front and opened Erin's door. She hugged her fiercely, whispering roughly in her ear. "I'm going to go see. I'm going to go see. Wait here. Just wait here and breathe."

Erin didn't want to let her go. She didn't want to know. "No. Let's just go. I don't want to be here anymore. I can't do this."

Patricia pried away from her as a few others hurried over.

Gary Jacobs's face contorted in shock and disbelief. "Jesus Christ, Henderson. You brought her here?"

"She insisted. What was I supposed to do?"

Erin swallowed, trying to control herself. "I made her bring me."

Jeff Hernandez walked up and grabbed her hands. Erin started to cry again.

"Stay with her. I'm going to go look at the body," Patricia said.

Jacobs went with her.

Erin shook all over. She took off her seat belt and slid down into Jeff's arms. He'd been a longtime friend and she couldn't be more thankful for his friendship at that moment. He soothed her as she clung to him. Over his shoulder, she watched Patricia approach the body. Part of her wanted to look away, but another part insisted she watch.

Cops and forensic specialists milled around them. Radios went off. More lights surged on. Erin inhaled deeply, taking it all in, eyes still on Patricia. Jacobs knelt first as Patricia spoke to two forensics people. Then she knelt beside him and he lifted the tarp.

Erin doubled over as some midnight hair caught the light. She collapsed onto the hard-packed earth and wept. Hernandez bent with her and held her. He smelled like aftershave and felt so strong she wished she could melt into him so she could use his strength. She started to hyperventilate again, saying "no, no, no."

When she heard Patricia say her name, she buried herself farther into Hernandez. "No, I don't want to know. Go away."

Patricia knelt next to them, the ground crunching beneath her. "Mac, it's not her. Mac?"

Erin felt Hernandez stiffen first. He drew back. They both stared at Patricia.

"What?" Hernandez sounded stunned.

"It's not Elizabeth Adams."

Erin scrambled up on wobbly legs. Patricia offered a steadying arm and Erin fell into her. She cried, noisy cracked sobs of relief. Patricia stroked her hair. Erin laughed and trembled at the same time.

"It's not Liz," she gasped.

"No." Patricia wiped Erin's cheeks softly. She smiled, but the smile was still sad. She gripped Erin's hand. "I think it may be her sister."

Panicked, Erin asked, "What?"

Dread settled against her ribs, crushing the breath from her lungs. Liz was about to experience the same thing she'd just gone through. The pain, the sorrow, the shock. Liz might not be dead, but this surely would kill her.

"I need you to come look," Patricia said. "You and I are the only ones who've ever seen her."

"I don't think I can." Erin's system was shocked. She could hardly stay standing.

She glanced out over to the body. Hernandez and Stewart stood a few feet from it, shouting about something.

"We need to be sure. So we can let Liz know when we find her."

Dear God, how would she get through it? Erin focused. She would have to help her. She would have to be strong for her. She breathed. "Okay."

Patricia gripped her arm, helping her along. As they approached the yellow hump, the other detectives stopped arguing and backed away. Erin felt her throat burn, and she began to cry deep in her chest when she first caught sight of the dead woman. She jerked and stiffened at the shock of the resemblance.

"Are you all right?" Patricia asked from the end of a long-sounding tunnel.

Erin nodded and looked down at the body. At Jay's face. Her hair was thick and tousled, a dark shadow next to the brown earth. It was still short, but longer than the last time she'd seen it. Her head was turned away from them at a slight angle, her mouth open as if someone had lightly tugged on her chin with their thumb. Her eyes stared up into the night. Pale blue and stark, as if she'd just learned the secret of the universe a second before she died. The blood at her temple had darkened and matted in her hair. Her skin was white, her lips a bruised blue.

Erin took in her face for as long as she could, branding on her mind the fact that it was Jay and not Liz. She stared into the far-off glaze of her eyes and thought about her horrible childhood, her confused mind, and her love for her sister. She wiped away an abundance of tears.

"She was shot?" Erin hugged herself, feeling very cold.

"Yes." Patricia escorted her back to the Blazer. "Looks like a suicide."

"The gun was in her right hand, and a note was found in her pocket all but confessing to the murders."

They both looked back. The tarp was pulled up to her neck as if it were a blanket warming her.

"There was also a cross on the back of her hand." Patricia clamped her mouth shut and cleared her throat.

"The same one?" Erin shut her own mouth, but not before Patricia heard.

Patricia narrowed her eyes at her. "I'm going to kill Hernandez."

Erin didn't know how to respond. Patricia obviously thought Hernandez had shared private information about the murders with her. She was thinking about how to correct the wrong impression when someone shouted and a uniformed officer ran toward them from the darkened brush beyond. When he reached the light he lowered his flashlight and bent to catch his breath. He pointed back behind him with the black Maglite.

"There's another body. Back there a ways," he rasped. "Get a bus. This one's still alive."

Immediately everyone scrambled. Patricia reached in the Blazer for her flashlight, then hurried away. Erin followed. Hernandez, Stewart, and Jacobs were out ahead, their flashlights flickering over the shrouded desert. Voices called and Erin heard the radios crackling again, this time with an urgent request for an ambulance. Someone had turned two of the large lights and Erin squinted, disoriented by the white light and the new shadows it cast. She tripped over something as she followed the dark figures. Catching herself, she straightened and slowed her pace. Her heart felt huge in her chest. Panic seized every cell.

What if it was Liz? The thought slammed into her and she nearly stopped walking. Ahead of her, the group formed a circle. The sense of urgency was like thick static in the air. Everyone worked together, talking, moving large branches, giving and taking orders.

"Jesus H. Christ," Jacobs said.

"He's breathing." Hernandez leaned over the victim. "Where's that bus?"

"Careful, don't move him."

"Lucky motherfucker."

"Look at his face. This ain't no lucky motherfucker." Stewart looked distraught.

"Serious head trauma."

"Jesus H. Christ. How is he alive?"

Erin inched closer. Patricia snapped on gloves and felt for a pulse. Erin caught a glimpse of a sock-covered foot covered with dirt. As she moved closer she could see that the body had been partially buried in a groove in the hard earth. It had then been covered with large branches from a mesquite tree.

"Pulse is low. Real low," Patricia said.

"Any ID on him?" Hernandez asked.

Someone felt around very carefully for a wallet. Erin saw dirty denim and the nude torso of a man. She breathed out a long, shaky breath. She wanted to thank God above that it wasn't Liz, but she winced when she moved her gaze from his chest to his face. It was severely beaten and swollen. When she saw the ligature marks around his purpling neck she turned away.

"God damn, how is he even breathing?" Jacobs said.

Erin walked slowly back to the Blazer. When she reached it, she crawled inside and cried herself to sleep.

❖

Liz wasn't going anywhere. That fact was clear in just the way they were behaving. Every cop she saw either stared directly into her eyes or wouldn't look at her at all. They were angry, yet they were anxious. She couldn't figure it out. Her last encounter had been a particularly bad one, so anger she expected; the anxiousness and all-out avoidance she didn't quite understand. Maybe their hate for her had reached an all-time high.

The feeling was more than mutual.

The door to the interrogation room opened and she sat up straighter. Her wrists stung in protest, reminding her that she still had on handcuffs. She'd been a bad girl last time and lunged after the asshole who'd made remarks about Erin. She wondered if she would see him tonight and whether or not he would look her in the eyes.

For the moment it seemed she was stuck with Patricia Henderson. The detective walked in carrying two small cups of coffee. She offered a smile and right away Liz stiffened with alert. A smile from Patricia was like a rattler giving you a wink. She readied herself for the strike.

"Thanks, but no thanks," she said as Patricia lowered the steaming cups. It was probably poisoned. That explained the smile.

Patricia sat. "You might change your mind."

She looked as though she'd probably been up most of the night. Her thick auburn hair was tied back in a loose ponytail. She had on chinos and a polo shirt. Both looked as if she'd been playing in the dirt with a shovel and bucket. Liz wasn't in the mood to see her castle.

She'd called Cynthia an hour ago, waking her up. She then had to listen to a minute of grumbling and then another minute of instruction on how to keep her mouth shut until she got there.

"When can I go?" she asked.

"That's up to you."

Liz grimaced. "Spare me the bullshit, Patricia." She stared hard into her eyes. "What is it that you want tonight?"

She'd been pulled over about a half mile from her destination. She only hoped she hadn't led them directly to Jay. It had been close, way too close. On the ride to the station she'd wondered why there was an APB out on her this time. When she was being cuffed the young cop had said something about murder. But she'd rolled her eyes. How many times had she heard that before?

"Well, there's quite a bit we need to discuss."

"Not without Cynthia." She didn't feel like talking. She was keyed up, worried about what Jay would do when she didn't show.

"Hear me out. You might change your mind."

"Don't waste your time. I don't like coffee and I don't like you. That won't change." Her hatred for the Valle Luna PD was growing, just when she thought it could grow no more.

Again Patricia offered a smile. This time Liz studied it closely. It wasn't the condescending smile she usually gave, it was different, more…sad.

Patricia cleared her throat. "Liz, I'm afraid I have some bad news."

Liz hid her confusion and clenched her jaw. "What?" They were throwing her in jail for something she didn't do? What else was new?

"There's no easy way to say this."

"Please spare me the drama, Detective." It was fucking four o'clock in the morning, she'd been driving all damn day, and she'd missed her meeting with Jay, and—

"Your sister, Jay. She's dead."

Liz reared back. "What did you say?"

Patricia held her stare. "I'm sorry. We found Jay's body this evening about a half mile from where you were picked up."

Heavy blood surged up to Liz's head and began thudding like an angry mob in her ears. She leaned forward, unable to hear. "What?"

"Jay's dead."

Liz laughed. She laughed so hard she pounded her cuffed fists on the table. "Fuck you, Patricia." She sat back in her chair. Where the hell was Cynthia? "Fuck you and your entire department. I'll sue you all for this shit. Bury you."

She couldn't believe this. She looked around the room, expecting the walls to melt away to reveal some wicked sort of sideshow where all the cops were dressed as evil clowns and the eternal joke was on her.

"I've hated a lot in my life. I've had good reason to. But this?" Her body stiffened as every last muscle flexed to its max. "This goes beyond any hate I've ever felt before."

Patricia watched her, listened without remark. Then she reached in her back pocket and pulled out a Polaroid photo. She laid it face up on the table and slid it across to her. Liz looked at it briefly and looked away. It looked like Jay. Blood on the temple. She felt her face harden and contort in anger.

"This isn't funny. You can't fucking do this to people." Patricia still didn't move.

She eased the photo closer, urging softly, "Look at it, Liz. It's Jay."

Liz stood, chest heaving in anger. She looked to the door expecting the entire squad to come running in, ready to tase her. But no one came. She glanced down at the picture again. "It's not her. It's someone you made to look like her."

"We found her out in the desert. She had a gunshot wound to the temple. We think it was suicide."

Liz sat back down but didn't remember telling her body to do so. She picked up the photo, and again the angry mob throbbed in her ears. Her breath hitched in recognition. She threw the photo across the table. "Fucking liar. That's not my sister. She's not dead."

"Were you going to meet her tonight?"

Liz whipped her eyes up. How could she know? Was the world tilting? She held the table, trying to right the balance of things as her brain swam in her head.

"We found a note in her back pocket," Patricia continued. "It had directions on how to get to the location and it also spoke about the recent murders. We think maybe she arrived before you, and then killed herself knowing you'd find her." She paused. "Did you know she was killing, Liz?"

Liz didn't speak. Her mind raced but nothing made sense.

There was a brisk knock at the door and Cynthia Carmichael stepped in. Patricia whispered with her and then led her to another chair. Both women sat.

Cynthia gave her a smile, the same kind Patricia had moments ago, a soft, sad smile. "Liz, I'm so sorry."

"Don't." Liz ground her teeth and shook her head, fighting the rising emotion. "Don't. Not you."

"They wouldn't lie to you about this."

"Yes, they would. They are. It isn't her."

Patricia handed the photo to Cynthia. "If Liz agrees that it's Jay, then it is her. We have more photos, one of her abdomen where there's a scar—"

"Stop it!" Liz stood. She couldn't take it. Couldn't take any more.

Patricia froze. She and Cynthia looked up at her in surprise.

"Detective Henderson, will you give us a moment, please?" Cynthia asked.

After Patricia left them alone, Cynthia moved alongside Liz and placed an arm around her waist but Liz stepped away. "Liz, I'm so sorry. I'm so sorry this has happened. Come on, come sit down."

Liz didn't want to sit. Didn't want to hear the words of comfort. Didn't want to hear any fucking apologies. She screamed as she charged the table, lifting it up off the floor, breaking the hinges that secured it. The coffee cups slid and spilled, the strong scent egging her on. She pushed as hard as she could, forcing the table up and back, slamming it down on its top. It wasn't enough. The closest thing was a chair. She threw it across the room and went for the next one.

Cynthia cried out, begging her to stop.

The chair bent and one of the legs got stuck in the wall. Liz yanked it out and threw it. She heard the door open as she rammed the second chair against the wall. Patricia was calling to her, along with Cynthia. Then there were other shouts as the little guy with the glasses came in. The voices became a series of blurred noises. The room spun. The image of Jay went around and around in her mind. Dead. Shot. Gone.

She should've been there. It was her fault. She'd let it happen.

Jay had been there waiting for her.

Jay.

Oh, God. Oh God, no.

She went for the wall again. This time with her fists. She beat at it over and over, loud wails coming from deep in her chest. She pounded harder. She tore at the holes with her fingers. If she could just get through. If she could just escape, it all would be better. The real world was on the other side. This was just a nightmare. This room was a stage in a wicked, wicked play. She had to get through to the other side.

Hands clamped down on her back but she stood her ground and beat at the wall until it turned pink with her blood. Her arms and hands burned. But nothing hurt as bad as the pain inside. It scorched her heart, blackening it to a crisp. Then it churned in her gut and sent shooting flames up her chest to her throat. Oh, God, how it hurt. When she was dragged away from the wall, she collapsed and pounded the floor as the sobs came.

Uniformed officers were now in the room. She heard Patricia telling them to back off. No spray. Leave her alone. She gave in completely then, too exhausted to continue. She lay on the floor, the smell of the worn gray carpet somehow soothing her.

Patricia herded the men out of the room. Cynthia carried over a salvaged chair. A paramedic knelt down beside her. He spoke gently, encouraging her to sit up. She did so slowly but the room turned evilly and she retched. He held her arms and helped her straighten. He told her to breathe deeply as he shined a pen light in her eyes. He held her wrist for a pulse and examined her hands.

Patricia stooped to unlock the cuffs.

"Is she okay?" Cynthia asked the paramedic. She sounded very worried and looked even worse.

"She needs to go to the hospital. A few fingers look broken and her wounds need to be cleaned, and possibly stitched." He spoke into the mic. Then he covered the wounds as best he could and wrapped her hands in gauze, winding and winding.

"I want to see her," Liz said, barely able to get the words out.

Cynthia spoke calmly. "You need to be tended to first."

Liz wanted to argue but couldn't. A gurney was wheeled in. She stared at the ceiling tiles as they strapped her in and started an IV.

Cynthia's face appeared over her. "Just try to relax."

The ceiling started to move.

"Erin?" Where was Erin? She wanted to see Erin. Needed her.

"Jay," she whispered, seeing her sister's face floating above her. But darkness moved in from the sides, covering the ceiling, covering her sister. Her eyes grew heavy. Then there was nothing.

· CHAPTER TWENTY

When Liz woke she was staring at the ceiling again. She lifted her head and tried to move, but her right hand was covered in gauze and handcuffed to the bed. She tried to curse but her mouth felt like cotton. A curtain was pulled back, the metal rings scraping the rod. Cynthia stepped into the light. She had on a different outfit.

"How long have I been here?" Liz asked.

"They kept you through the night." Cynthia's smile was genuine but guarded, as if Liz were a child about to have a tantrum.

"They drugged me." Liz wished she was still unconscious, anything to kill the pain. She ached at the horrible realization that her sister was gone. Forever. Her head was like a boulder on her shoulders. She laid it back against the pillow.

"They gave you something to help calm you and they thought it best for you to stay here to sleep it off." Cynthia sat down on a vinyl chair next to the bed. The shadows under her eyes told of her lack of sleep.

"Why am I handcuffed?" Liz couldn't run away if she tried. Her bones were lead pipes.

"You're still a suspect." Cynthia pressed the button to raise the back of the bed. "They think you knew or may have even helped Jay in the killings."

Liz took in the room, noting how quiet it was. Sunlight sliced in through the vertical blinds, stabbing behind her sensitive eyes. Squinting, she saw the curtain to her right behind Cynthia. Shadows loomed beneath it.

Cynthia followed her line of sight. "We're alone. They removed the other bed."

"I'm a criminal." She cringed.

"For now. There's an armed guard too."

Liz tried to laugh but it hurt. Cynthia missed the humor in the situation.

Liz grew serious in a split second. "Jay didn't kill anyone."

"How can you be so sure?"

"Because she was trying to solve the murders herself." The ridiculousness of it got to her. "She came back to Valle Luna to find out who was responsible. I tried to stop her but she wouldn't listen. She was just trying to help me."

"So you knew she was here."

"Yes. We'd meet up and I'd try to talk sense into her. I knew the cops were after her, so we had to be careful. She started writing me letters."

"About what?"

"At first there were instructions about when to meet her. Then they came almost every day. They grew longer and stranger."

"Were they suicidal?"

"No."

"Then how did she end up dead?" Cynthia asked the question gently, obviously trying to keep her calm.

"He killed her." Liz stared into the wall in front her. Thoughts of what Jays last moments must've been like cut like razor blades through her veins. "Jay had a suspect. Her last letter said she was getting close. She was going to tell me that night."

"But you think he got to her first?"

"He must've. She's dead." The words were painful. But the thoughts were worse. She felt woozy all of a sudden and breathed deep. "I would like to go home."

But then she remembered her empty house, sitting dead itself without Erin. The only other remaining love in her life had gone as well.

"Are you in pain? I'll get the nurse."

"No, although more drugs would possibly help." Liz licked her lips. "Listen, Jay didn't kill herself, Cynthia. She wouldn't kill herself."

"Why not?"

Liz met her eyes and held them. "Because it would hurt me."

❖

Patricia took a deep breath. Liz was getting worked up and they were losing precious time.

"She never killed anyone," Liz insisted. "Ever. She never would."

"Unless they were hurting you." Patricia was back to her old self as well, the ultimate professional. "Ms. Adams, do you have any idea who the last victim is? The man found near Jay?"

"I have no idea." Liz's gaze traveled over to the wall. "Unless he's the killer."

"We have reason to doubt that," Patricia said.

"What if he shot my sister? What if she found him out and he killed her?"

"He was beaten too severely, and he was buried. There's no way he could've shot her."

Liz fell silent.

"Was Jay a religious person?" Gary asked.

"No. Not at all."

"You guys didn't go to church, growing up in the South?"

"No."

"Not ever?"

Liz looked to Patricia as if Gary were a complete idiot. "What's this about?"

"Was she fond of crosses?"

"Crosses?"

"Crucifixes," Patricia clarified.

Liz shook her head. "No. Why are you asking?"

"Could she draw?"

"What?" Liz looked completely confused.

"Was she artistic at all? Could she draw or sketch well?" Patricia asked in a softer tone.

"No. She had trouble with writing ever since she was a kid. Now, tell me what this is about."

"It's about murder, Ms. Adams. These questions pertain to the case," Gary made some notes.

The room grew quiet again. When Patricia glanced up, Liz was watching her.

"How's Erin?"

The question sounded sincere but Patricia wasn't sure how to answer. Liz looked to be in bad enough shape. Hearing that Erin was miserable might make things worse. And for some unknown reason, Patricia felt empathetic toward her.

Liz sensed her hesitation. "Is she still staying with you?"

Patricia lowered her notebook and pen. "Yes."

Liz stared at her gauzed hands. When she looked back up her face had hardened again and Patricia knew the topic was closed. Cynthia rose and brought her client a cup of water. Liz shook her head, too proud to be assisted in front of them. Patricia studied the woman she'd spent years hating. She was beaten now, and in physical and mental anguish. The sight was something Patricia thought she'd never see. There was no satisfaction in it, though. Just the understanding that Elizabeth Adams was indeed human after all.

Her vulnerability didn't change anything. Ruiz wanted Liz officially charged. He was practically drooling down their necks to get her, a rabid dog chewing through the last link of the chain.

But Patricia still wasn't comfortable with the facts. The blood found in De Maro's underwear could belong to Liz, yes. But Liz's alibi was panning out. She'd stopped for gas around eleven p.m., which was the estimated time of death for Jay. They found the receipt in her Range Rover and were reviewing the surveillance tapes from the station. Then she'd been stopped driving toward the scene a short time later. Liz wasn't their killer. Patricia was pretty sure of that. But still things weren't adding up.

"We found blood in the second victim's underwear," Gary said. "Antwon De Maro. The DNA was a match for you or for Jay. How do you explain that, Ms. Adams?"

Gary was overtired and had reached the point where his body was firing on one last cylinder of energy. Patricia knew he was good for about another hour, then he'd be toast.

Liz didn't seem to have an answer. She clenched her jaw in obvious frustration. "I don't know."

"If neither one of you were involved…" Gary added.

"Look, I said I don't know." A tiny vessel in her temple throbbed. "I can't tell you what I don't know." She looked to her lawyer. "Someone is framing me."

"Who?"

"If I knew, don't you think I'd tell you?"

"Up to this point you haven't been very forthcoming," Gary said.

Liz tried to move again. Her anger was palpable. "You're lucky I'm telling you anything at all, asshole."

"Detectives, I think that's quite enough," Cynthia said. "She's told you all that she knows."

But Liz had more to say. "Jay did what you couldn't. She found him and he killed her. He made it look like she killed herself. Then he tried to kill one more, just to make it seem convincing."

Patricia listened without reservation. She wasn't sure what to think. She nodded at Gary and he stopped the recorder and tucked it into his pocket. They stood to leave.

"Am I still under arrest?" Liz asked.

"Yes."

"On what grounds?"

"For starters, the DNA match," Gary said. "Then there's the connection between you and three of the deceased. You've been harboring a wanted person. A person who was wanted in connection to another string of murders. Shall I go on?"

Cynthia spoke, trying to head off further confrontation. "I've arranged to meet the bail."

"How much was it? A million?" Liz's sarcasm was tinged with anger.

Cynthia cleared her throat. "Five hundred thousand."

Liz glared at the detectives. "Get out."

Patricia followed Gary out the door. She could hear Liz cursing behind them as the door eased shut.

"Wait till she hears about the monitoring bracelet she'll have to wear," Gary said.

Patricia shook her head, glad for about the tenth time that day that she wasn't Cynthia Carmichael.

CHAPTER TWENTY-ONE

Erin approached slowly, her black pumps sinking in the thick Bermuda grass. A cool breeze blew against her face. Patricia walked next to her as they wove a silent path between dozens of head stone markers. The majority were flat and flush with the ground; only the older ones stood vertical. She read the names absently as she passed by. *Lesnick. Raphael. Shepard.*

When she saw *Elizabeth* she sucked in a quick, panicky breath. Glancing skyward, she thanked any and all that Liz was still alive. The sun broke through the clouds, as if answering. Thick angled beams shot through the clouds, five of them, fingers of the heavens. She inhaled deeply at their caress. The sharp scent of fresh grass clippings lingered in the air. In the distance a caretaker's weed eater buzzed.

"You sure you want to do this?" Patricia asked.

"Yes." Erin smoothed down her simple black dress and focused through her sunglasses.

Ahead several people were gathered around a shiny black casket adorned with a mountain of wildflowers. Liz and Tyson stood next to the robed minister. A few feet from them, two men in suits looked on with stoic professionalism, obviously the funeral directors. Tyson stepped forward to lay a single white rose next to the wildflowers on the casket before returning to Liz's side and placing an arm around her.

Erin stopped walking. Her breath hitched in her chest. Liz wore a dark suit. White bandages covered her hands. But Erin's eyes fixed on her hair. It was gone...the long, black-as-midnight strands. Cut completely off. Shorn as Jay's once had been. And the similarity in their appearance was overwhelming. Erin couldn't get over it. Beside her, Patricia drew a sharp, unsteady breath. She saw the same picture. It looked like Jay was standing at her own funeral.

Patricia took Erin's hand and squeezed it gently. They stayed where they were, on the perimeter. The minister kept reading, talking about heaven and earth. Liz stepped up to the casket and held up a dandelion. She blew it into the wind and then bent to kiss the casket. Erin could see her struggling to keep her composure. Her strong body seemed frail. When she straightened, she caught sight of them. Erin instantly released Patricia's hand, but not before a flash of hurt and anger slashed across the fierce blue eyes. Liz stepped away and hurried toward them. Her gait was determined, her face thin and contorted in venomous anger.

"Get the fuck out of here," she hissed, glaring at them both.

"Liz, I…" Erin said.

"I don't want to hear it." Liz stared at Patricia. "My sister is dead. Isn't that enough for you? Isn't it enough that it's killing me?" She looked around in a fury. "Are you staking out her funeral? Watching as I put her into the ground? Is it funny for you?" Her entire body trembled with her words.

"I didn't mean to upset you," Patricia said softly. "Erin didn't want to come alone."

Liz tore her gaze over to Erin. Her face twisted with hurt. "How could you?"

"I came for you," Erin said.

"For me? What for? To shove it in my face?"

Erin looked to Patricia. "Will you excuse us for a moment?"

"Sure." Patricia hesitated. She seemed to sense what Liz was thinking and said, "There's nothing going on with Erin and me. We're friends."

As she walked away, Liz turned to Erin and said bitterly, "What are you waiting for? Go."

"I'm not leaving." Erin grabbed Liz by the forearm before she could turn back toward the funeral service. "You're not going to push me away this time."

"I don't need you, or anyone else," Liz said, her voice cracking. "They all leave. Everyone leaves. No one stays forever. No one."

Erin was pained at the words. Tears slipped down her cheeks as she examined the thick bandages on Liz's hands. Patricia had told her about the outburst, about the broken fingers and lacerations. It hurt her terribly to see Liz like this, to know that she was hurting so badly.

"I won't leave," she whispered.

"You already have."

"No, I haven't. I'm here. I'll always be here."

"You can't guarantee that. Jay's gone, and she was always there."

Erin rubbed the bandages carefully, wishing she could unwrap them and lightly kiss her skin, tend to her wounds. "You don't have to push me away, Liz. You don't have to keep stuff from me. I can handle it."

When they'd found Jay it became clear to Erin why Liz had rejected her. She hadn't wanted to tell her about Jay, she hadn't wanted her involved.

Liz didn't respond. Behind her, Tyson approached. His suit was tailor-made, his tie slate gray. He looked enormous and kind, his brown eyes tired.

"Is everything okay?" He seemed relieved to see Erin, but it was short lived.

"Ms. McKenzie was just leaving," Liz said.

Erin squeezed her arm and held her eyes. "Tyson, I'm not going anywhere."

He appeared confused, looking from Erin to Liz. "Ma'am?"

Liz jerked her arm away.

"I love you," Erin declared.

"Get her out of here." Liz turned away as she began to shake with sobs.

Erin rounded her quickly and enveloped her in a hug. She held her tight, not caring that Liz didn't return the embrace. The pain came out of Liz in short, sharp gasps and sobs, each one piercing Erin's heart. Erin held tight, inhaling the scent of her, relishing the feel of her. It was so right.

"I love you," she said again, crying with her.

Liz was hurting so badly. So very, very badly.

They cried into one another for a long while before Erin felt Liz stiffen. Pushing away from Erin, Liz attempted to wipe her eyes with her bandaged hands. Erin did it for her, smoothing the tears away, holding Liz's face in her hands. She was so thin and fragile, all dried out from the oozing pain, a dead fall leaf scraping along the sidewalk, aimless, waiting for the wind. Erin feared that wind, knowing it would whisk her up and carry her away forever.

"Please, Liz, let me in. Let me love you."

Liz looked at her with eyes the color of a melting glacier. "Go." The word came out on a strangle. She turned and walked back toward the service.

Tyson gave Erin an apologetic look and followed.

The clouds swallowed the sun then, leaving them all in shadows.

❖

Tyson held on to his longtime boss as the casket descended slowly into the ground. Her body felt like bones under the suit. Tears of his own fell as the minister sprinkled dirt into the air, intoning, "Ashes to ashes, dust to dust." As the dirt hit the casket, Liz nearly collapsed in his arms.

They turned away and he held her tightly as she cried. The past few days had been hard and he'd worried that she wouldn't make it through. She'd always been a rock, a pillar of grace and strength. But this, this had killed her. She wouldn't eat and would only sleep when drugged. He'd brought the Xanax to her late last night, insisting she take them to rest. When she took them without argument, he figured it was only because she was too exhausted to fight.

"It's all right now," he whispered.

"I don't want to leave her. She'll be alone. All alone in the ground."

He knew she was worried about that. It was why she'd had her buried here rather than where they were from. So she could watch over her.

"She's gone now, Ms. Adams. She's not really in there."

"Then where is she, Tyson? Because I need to find her."

He placed his hand on her chest. "She's in here. And you don't need to look no further."

He hadn't ever known Jay Adams, but he knew enough. To see his boss like this told him what kind of a person Jay was.

She placed a heavily bandaged hand over his. "I love you, Tyson."

He was surprised but he nodded. "I know. I love you too."

She inhaled and her breath shook. "You've been very good to me."

Again he nodded. "And you've been good to me."

He took good care of her and she took good care of him. Recently she'd given him a large bonus to help with the purchase of his house. A couple of years earlier she'd paid the medical expenses when his youngest daughter fell ill with pneumonia. No one would know these things and few would ever believe them. But he knew who Elizabeth Adams really was. He wouldn't put in the long hours or remain so loyal otherwise. Over the years their business relationship had evolved into friendship and an unspoken understanding of unconditional support. They could count on one another, no matter what.

"We should go," he said gently.

Two grave diggers had arrived, shovels in hand. They lit smokes and lingered against a tree as they waited. The men in the suits had gone for the limousine, which sat idling against the curb.

Tyson helped her walk, cupping her elbow and supporting her waist. He glanced to his left and saw Erin McKenzie crying onto the shoulder of the detective. It had been a punch to his gut the way his boss had spoken to her. The happiest he'd ever seen her was when she was with Erin McKenzie. And she'd been the unhappiest he'd ever seen her without her. That unhappiness, coupled with the loss of Jay, caused him a great deal of concern.

"That woman loves you," he said. "And you can say what you want, but I know you love her too."

For a second he thought she was going to lay into him. But the flash of anger never glinted in her eyes. Only sadness. "I can't, Tyson. It's not safe and I just can't."

He thought on that a moment. He thought of his wife and his children. If their safety was ever an issue, he'd figure out a way to protect them, but he would never leave them. *If you love someone enough you do what you have to do.* She might be worried about Erin's safety, but forcing her to leave was no solution. It was just an excuse because Erin had obviously gotten under his boss's skin.

Since no one else ever had, he figured that probably scared her pretty good.

He looked her in the eye and told her point-blank, "Then you better figure out a way so you can be with her."

CHAPTER TWENTY-TWO

How is he?" Patricia studied the unidentified male from behind a pane of glass.

The doctor popped a white Tic Tac in his mouth and crunched. He slid a thick pair of eyeglasses over his ears and opened a binder. He had three other pairs of glasses around his neck as well. Patricia wondered what they were all for.

"He's still unconscious. Unable to breathe on his own. His brain scans look promising, though."

"So, you think he'll wake up?"

"Hard to say. One never knows for sure. Some do, some don't."

"But he isn't brain dead?" Patricia looked back through the window at all the tubes running into him, each one keeping him alive. His head was completely wrapped up with only slits for eyes. He looked like an alien mummy. She shivered.

The doctor closed the book and exchanged the thick glasses for another pair. "No, the head trauma was the worst of it. He was beaten pretty badly. There was some swelling of the brain, which we had to drain. But his initial scans look good. It's up to him now."

Patricia looked back at the sole surviving victim. His hands were also bandaged. They couldn't lift good prints because of his self-defense injuries. He'd fought hard, tearing up his fingers, fingernails, and neck in the process. Patricia wondered why he'd fought when the other two hadn't. Why he was buried and hidden under brush when the others had been left out on display.

"What about his toxicology?" she asked.

Again the doctor switched glasses and flipped through the binder. "Alcohol was below legal limit and he was clean."

That could explain why he fought back. He wasn't drugged. Both De Maro and Gillette had ecstasy in their systems.

She checked to be certain. "No ecstasy?"

"No, nothing like that."

"How much would one have to take to be rendered helpless?"

He closed the book and dropped the glasses to rest around his neck. This time he stared through the window without any aid. "Helpless? I'd say one would have to be pretty well impaired. Unconscious or close to it. Ecstasy affects people in different ways depending upon height and weight. Some can handle more than others."

"If someone on ecstasy was being strangled to death, would they fight back?"

He frowned at her, obviously disturbed at the thought. "Yes."

"Unless they were completely out of it, nearly unconscious?"

"In my opinion, yes."

His answers only confused her more. They stared at the unidentified man. She needed him to wake up. She needed to know who he was.

"When do you think his hands will be healed enough for us to lift prints?"

"Another week or so. I'll call with any news." He slid on another pair of specs and walked away.

Patricia glanced at her wristwatch. The truck driver she'd called for an interview was probably waiting. She hurried to her Blazer and climbed in. The alarm hadn't been set and it was unlocked. Again she wondered if she was losing her mind.

"Hi," a voice said softly.

"Holy shit." Patricia grasped her chest. "Mac, what the hell?"

Erin was slumped in the passenger seat. "I'm sorry. I don't know what to do anymore."

Patricia didn't know what to say. She couldn't understand why Adams had been so stubborn when Erin reached out to her at the funeral. If she didn't love Erin that would be one thing, but it was pretty obvious that she did, as much as a woman like that could love anyone.

"How did you get here?" It seemed as though Erin had appeared from nowhere.

"I drove. I was going crazy at the house. I don't want to go back there. Can we just drive around or something?"

Patricia eyed the clock. She didn't have time for this now. "Sally Trucker," as Gary called her, wasn't going to wait all day to make her statement. She started the Blazer and sped out of the parking lot.

Erin was silent for a few minutes, staring down at her hands, then she said, "I haven't been honest with you."

Patricia glanced over at her.

"I took your paperwork on the serial cases and copied it. I've been reading it. I know everything." She sniffled. "Well, everything up until Jay was found."

Patricia braked hard at a red light. "Why would you do that?" Her body tensed and her heart rate kicked up in betrayal. "You knew how I felt about you getting involved. You aren't a member of the force anymore, you're a civilian."

"I know, I know. I just…" Erin began to cry. "I did it for Liz. I wanted to help. I wanted to find the killer."

Patricia smacked the heel of her hand on the steering wheel as the light turned green. "Damn it, I trusted you. I should've locked my office door." She glared at her, the woman she thought was a friend. "You betrayed me, Mac."

Erin wrung her hands. "I'm sorry. I know you'll probably never forgive me."

"You should've just asked." Patricia stared ahead.

"I did ask. You told me no."

"Well, you should've asked again. I would've done something."

"No, you wouldn't have," Erin said softly. "Because you're a good cop, Patricia. The best. This is my fault. And I don't like keeping things from people, especially you, especially after all that's happened. You're a good friend and I don't ever want to lose you."

Patricia drove on, nearing the station. As mad as she was, she couldn't hate Erin. She still loved her. Erin was a good person. Just confused and in love. Lost and in love. "Did you share the information with anyone else?"

"No, I swear. No one else laid eyes on those files."

"When did you do it?" Her mind flew as she tried to put what Erin was telling her together.

"One night when you were asleep."

Patricia rubbed her forehead. "Damn it, Mac." But she was more frustrated than she was angry. "Well, what's your opinion? I might as well ask." God knew, she wasn't getting anywhere.

"The crosses bother me."

Patricia drove on. "Yeah, me too."

"I think they're very significant. A message from the killer."

"What kind of message?"

"I'm not sure. But they mean something. It could be a religious statement."

Patricia needed to do more research. Erin was on the right path; she agreed with everything she'd said so far. "Has Liz ever talked about religion?" she asked.

"No. It never came up. And she never spoke about it in regard to Jay either."

"What about the DNA? How do you explain that?"

"I can't explain it," Erin said. "How does blood from Jay or Liz end up on De Maro? It's one thing if it was on his clothes, because Liz is in daily contact with him. But for it to be on his underwear?"

"Yeah, I can't figure it out either. It just seems to say that one of them was there at an intimate time with him." An idea flashed in Patricia's mind. "What about the restrooms at the studio? Are they unisex?"

"Yes."

"Maybe he somehow came into contact with Liz's blood in there?" Patricia tapped her hand on the steering wheel. "Although that's awfully coincidental, don't you think?"

"Stranger things have happened."

"So, what now?" Patricia asked, referring to everything.

Erin wiped her eyes, the tears no longer falling. "I give every last piece of paper back to you and move on."

"Where are you going to go?"

"I don't know."

"You can still stay with me. For as long as you need to." Patricia glanced sideways again. "I'll just lock my office."

They both laughed a little. The sunlight reflected off Erin's watery eyes.

"No, you shouldn't have to do that. I'll be fine. It's time for me to go." Erin stared out the passenger window. "I couldn't solve the case. And it doesn't matter because Liz doesn't want to work things out with me. I'm beginning to think it's because Jay really was involved in the whole thing. And maybe Liz knows that."

"I'm not sure. Things still aren't adding up. I honestly don't know what to tell you." Patricia slowed and swung into a parking space. She killed the engine.

Erin looked at the station. "You brought me *here*?"

"Yep. I've got an interview I'm late for, so come on."

"But what about my betrayal and being a civilian?"

Patricia shrugged. "You can wait in the truck if you want."

She got out. Erin hurried to do the same, asking, "Are you sure this is okay?"

"Ruiz might have my ass, but he already has it for numerous other reasons. One more won't kill me." Patricia ran her security badge through the reader. When the tiny light turned green, she pushed open the door and held it for Erin. "Just promise me you'll sit still and keep quiet."

Erin nodded and kept her head low. Patricia could tell she was a little excited.

They wound their way toward Homicide. It was after five but the office was still buzzing. Many folks said hello, some stuttering a little when they recognized Erin.

A group of male detectives clustered in the center of the room. Gary Jacobs turned, caught sight of them, and raised his hands.

"Surprise!" he called out.

"Surprise!" The dozen or so other men bellowed. Streamers flew up in the air along with balloons. They all started in on "For She's a Jolly Good Fellow" before Patricia realized the reception was for her.

On her desk sat a large sheet cake. In the center a book had been drawn in icing, along with the word "Congratulations." The cover of her latest book had been blown up and was on a stand next to her desk. Some of the guys had signed it and others were waiting to do so.

Gary approached with a plastic cup of what appeared to be champagne. "To our esteemed author!"

"Hear, hear!" they shouted, toasting her as Hernandez filled more cups.

Patricia felt her skin heat and redden all the way down to her toes.

She didn't realize she was standing still until Gary took her hand and tugged.

He gave Erin a polite smile, handing over his own cup. She looked just as confused as Patricia felt, but they both followed him over to her desk.

Stewart was waiting with a cake knife. He waved it at Patricia. "I'm assuming I'm not the overweight, overindulging, rude detective in this thing." His eyes were big and expectant.

"Of course you aren't." She smiled.

Stewart grinned. "Good, that guy was a real asshole."

They all laughed and he cut the cake. Pieces were handed out and laughs were had throughout the room. The guys signed the poster board book, since they'd all been involved in the story in one way or another. It was a joke and she was just happy that none of them seemed to be upset. In fact, they all seemed pleased for her.

To her surprise, some of the guys gave her gifts. Gary insisted she sit down and he handed one after the other. She opened some really nice, very costly looking ink pens, a new handheld recorder, a couple of leather journals, and some lingerie.

"We wanted to get you that stripper we had for Stewart that one time but Jacobs wouldn't let us," Hernandez said.

"So we got you some fancy panties and bras," Stewart explained, wiggling his eyebrows up and down, "because we all know you'll get some serious pussy after this."

Gary hit him in the arm.

"Hey, ouch. Come on, she will. She wrote a fucking book. Chicks love that shit."

Patricia covered her face with her hands. Through her fingers she saw the guys continue to laugh as they passed around the numerous bras and panties, examining them fully. When she heard Erin laugh she lowered her hands. Erin was laughing so hard she was nearly crying. After the emotional roller coaster she'd been on lately, it didn't surprise Patricia to see her do both at the same time.

"I forgot how funny Stewart was," Erin explained.

Stewart heard her and paused, fork full of cake in midmotion, as if he'd just seen her. "Mac, what the fuck are you doing here?" He wasn't angry, just truly shocked.

Erin laughed harder.

"Am I drunk already?" Stewart looked around. "Jacobs, I thought you said that sparkly was fake."

"It is," Gary called out.

When no one offered further explanation, Stewart shrugged. "I am funny. I'm a real fucking funny guy." He shoveled in the cake as they all laughed some more.

❖

"Sally Trucker" showed up at the station at the scheduled time. Her name was really Paige Daniels. Right away Patricia pegged her as odd. She'd offered to come in, claiming that she was going to be driving back through Valle Luna anyway. She stood about five feet nine inches tall and wore blue jeans that were two inches too short and a teal green tank top. Her salt-and-pepper hair was cut very short. Long earrings hung from her ears, turquoise dream catchers that swayed as she spoke.

She greeted them loudly as Gary led her in. The little party was over. Ruiz had shown up just to bust everyone's chops, insisting they get back to work. He'd approached Patricia only to say, "Hurry up and get these next two guys. Then you can write all the goddamn books you want." He'd eyed Erin then but didn't say a word. All had breathed sighs of relief as he left.

Paige took the chair she was offered at Patricia's desk. Erin sat a few feet away at Gary's, looking through victim photos. Paige fidgeted constantly and had a cough that shook the walls. When she didn't cover her mouth, Patricia offered her a box of Kleenex. She declined and complained about a bitch of a sinus infection she couldn't seem to rid of.

"Had it for going on two weeks now." She coughed again and stretched her arms outward, displaying long hair under one arm. Just the one side. The other had none.

How do you have just one hairy armpit? It baffled Patricia.

Gary pulled his chair up to the desk. "Ms. Daniels."

"Mrs.," she corrected. "Got me a husband back in Tacoma. Only want the one, though. One's enough." She winked at Patricia.

Gary cleared his throat. "We wanted to re-interview you after hearing that you have recently remembered seeing someone on the highway leading out of Valle Luna."

"Yep. I did. I mean I didn't remember it at first, when you all first called. But I remembered it driving back by here on another run. Bam." She smacked her forehead. "Just as plain as day, there it was."

Again she coughed. Gary rolled his chair back. Paige didn't seem to notice.

"When did you see something?" Patricia asked. "Do you remember the date?"

"I checked my log, and yeah, I remember. It was five months ago, on the twelfth of October."

Patricia jotted down the date. The woman kept a log. That was something. At least they wouldn't have to trust her memory. "What did you see?"

"Well, I saw a man on the side of the road. He was walking fast, coming up from behind his car. Then he got in."

"That's it?" Gary asked.

Paige began to swivel in her chair. "Well, I noticed because it was strange. His hazard lights weren't on, no lights were on at all. So I figured it wasn't car trouble. Or maybe he needed to pee. But there was a rest stop not even a mile back. So I remember thinking, *I wonder what he's doing.*"

"What did he look like?" Patricia asked.

"Average build. Kinda plain looking. Dark hair."

"Was he tall?"

She shrugged. "Average."

"Do you remember what the car looked like?"

"Oh, yeah. It was one of those smaller SUVs. And it was gold. Reflected real pretty in my headlights."

"You didn't happen to write down the license plate, did you?" Gary didn't sound hopeful.

"No, but I'm willing to be hypnotized. I know you all do that sometimes. Seen it on TV." Paige stood to adjust the small fan Gary had on his desk. She fanned herself as well. "Valle Luna is so hot. I don't know how you people stand living here."

"It's seventy-five degrees out," Gary said.

"I know. It's hot. I never can wait to get back up to Tacoma. When the guys unload my truck, sometimes I just blast the cooler and stand back there and watch instead of stepping out into the heat."

Patricia smiled at her. "We sure appreciate you coming in to talk to us."

"No problem. Think you'll need to hypnotize me?"

Gary cleared his throat as he wrote. "Not at the present moment. Is there anything else you can remember?"

She looked to the ground in thought. Then she jerked and Patricia did as well.

"Yeah!" She pointed at Patricia. "I remember he was dressed funny. He had on jeans and a long-sleeved shirt in October. It was still in the nineties and I remember thinking how crazy he was. I was wearing shorts and a tank top at the time."

Gary looked up from his notebook. "Was there anything on his clothes? Dark patches?"

Paige was perfectly still for the first time that evening. "You know, come to think of it, his knee was dark. A big dark area. You don't think that was blood, do you?"

No one answered her.

"Mrs. Daniels, thank you very much for your time," Gary said as he stood to shake her hand.

"We really appreciate it," Patricia added.

Paige stood, looking horrified and confused. "That's it? I feel so strange. What if I really saw the killer? Are you sure you don't want me to get hypnotized?"

Patricia walked her to the door. "We'll call you if we need anything else."

Paige left, but only after making sure Patricia had both her cell phone and home numbers.

Gary shook his head as she returned to their desks. "Strange woman."

"I'd say she's taken way too many caffeine pills."

CHAPTER TWENTY-THREE

The porch swing creaked as the screen door slammed shut behind Lizzie. She stood there and stared at Jay, who sat pushing herself in the swing, humming down to the bundle in her hands.

"Whatcha doin'?" Lizzie asked.

Jay continued to push against the porch floor with her bare feet. She was humming "Elvira." She didn't answer and it didn't surprise Lizzie. Jay hadn't spoken to anyone in days.

Lizzie turned up her Coke and downed it. She walked to the swing and held a cold can out for Jay, who shook her head. Lizzie sat down next to her and opened the new one for herself. She always drank a Coke to feel better. Her aunt Dayne swore by its medicinal powers. If she had a tummy ache it was "drink a Coke." If she had a headache it was "drink a Coke."

So she sat there in that swing with her sister and downed a second one, hoping Dayne was right.

"Wanna go watch TV?" she asked.

Jay sat and hummed. Her head looked funny where some pieces of hair were still longer than the others. Dayne had tried to trim it all even, but Jay wouldn't let her near her. She wouldn't let anyone touch her. Only Lizzie.

Lizzie looked at the bundle in Jay's hands. A tiny bird head peeked out of a wad of dish towel. Jay was stroking the little head. Lizzie knew it was dead. The eyes were just holes and the beak was open and unmoving.

Lizzie worried that if Jay didn't start eating, she'd end up looking like that dead bird. Just bones covered by feathers.

"You better not let Aunt Dayne see you with that bird again."

Yesterday Dayne was making their beds and she'd found the bird under Jay's pillow. She hollered and cried, had a good fit right there in their room. Jerry came and took it away. Jay had started to have her own fit then, screaming and hollering. She'd been up sick all night long, head hung over the toilet, all because of the bird. So Lizzie had snuck out and plucked the bundle out of the garbage and brought it back to her. Jay had slept just fine after that.

There was no harm in Jay having that bird. It was dead, so she didn't even have to feed it. Dayne was going on about germs and how it wasn't right to have a dead animal, but Jay was just doing what made her happy. And Lizzie would do anything to make sure she was okay. Even if it meant making sure she had her dead bird to pet. Eventually the bird was just going wither away to nothing and it would start to smell real bad. When that happened Lizzie would go find her a real pretty live one to keep. She'd already climbed a few trees looking for eggs. There were three that she was sure would hatch soon. When they did she'd take one and bring it to Jay to hand feed. That way it would be tame. It would be a bird that would never leave her side.

Lizzie couldn't wait. That would make Jay real happy.

Maybe she'd even start talking again.

"It's gonna be okay, Jay," she said, leaning back in the swing. "It's all gonna be okay."

"Lizzie?"

She looked to her right but Jay was gone, vanished. The swing slowed. She looked out at the yard but saw nothing.

"Lizzie?" The call was louder.

She took off down the porch steps and ran toward the woods.

"Lizzie, help me!"

She ran harder, looking everywhere. "Jay!"

She ran farther, her sister's voice growing distant. Tree after tree blurred by as she ran. Finally she got to the last one. It stood large and full of foliage. She slowed to a walk and called for Jay. A sinister laugh echoed around and dozens of birds flew noisily up out of the tree, leaving the skeletal branches looking empty and dead.

"Lizzie!"

Liz sat up, gasping for breath. Her chest was caving in on her lungs, she was sure of it. She reached for Erin. Her bandaged hand hit nothing but sheets. Her stomach fell again. Erin was gone as well. She missed her. Wanted her. Needed her.

She climbed out of bed and hurried to the bathroom. After switching on the light, she turned on the faucet and filled a cup with water. It stung her throat, but she forced it down. Then she refilled the cup and splashed her face.

She studied her reflection as the water ran off her face. She looked gaunt, as if she were dead herself. Deep in her eyes she saw her sister. She'd cut her hair to remind her every day of Jay. Every time she saw herself, she saw Jay. And now, every night when she closed her eyes, she saw her as well.

Jay was calling for her. Jay needed her.

"Where are you?" Liz asked into the mirror. "Oh God, Jay. Help me find you."

❖

"Try to rest tonight," Patricia said as she dropped Erin off at the hospital to pick up her Toyota.

She watched her drive off just to be sure. Then she followed in her Blazer. When she felt certain Erin was simply going home, she turned in the opposite direction and drove in silence. She lowered her window, wanting the fresh breeze. Her phone buzzed and she plucked it off her belt and flipped it open. She smiled when she saw the text she'd been waiting for. She accelerated onward.

Her mind went back to "Sally Trucker" as she drove past narrow rows of newly built condos. The information from Paige was interesting and she needed to talk it out with someone. Her heart rate sped up as she reached her destination. She parked and quickly left her vehicle. When she knocked on the familiar door and heard a voice call out, her pulse tripled in pace.

The lock clicked. She took in a big breath.

Sinclair stood smiling at her.

"Um, wow, hi." Patricia nearly smacked herself in the forehead at her choice of words, just like Paige had done an hour before.

She let her gaze sweep up and down Sinclair again, taking in the dirty jeans full of holes and the see-through wifebeater tank. She was covered in dried clay and paint. Patricia had never seen anything so sexy in her life.

"Hi." Sinclair smiled and the dimple in her cheek seemed to wink at Patricia. "Come in."

"I didn't mean to interrupt."

"You're not." Sinclair closed the door and turned the lock.

Patricia stared at her muscles and then at her bare feet. "You look busy." Thank God the right word had come out, because her mind seemed stuck on a different vocabulary. Words like *sexy*, *edible*, and *goddamned gorgeous*.

"Come on, I want to show you something." Sinclair looked relaxed and happy. Patricia wondered if that was how she looked after making love.

She followed her down the hallway to a room on the right. The first thing she noticed was all the heavy oak bookshelves lining the walls, crammed with books. She recognized some of the titles. Topics from profiling, to serial murders, to basic neurology. She moved closer and looked at the framed photos standing on some of the shelves. A handful were of Sinclair with an older man in front of a small airplane. Patricia wondered if that was her father. She was going to ask but Sinclair seemed preoccupied, leaning over a worktable with a bright adjustable arm lamp clamped to it. The smell of clay and paint tickled Patricia's nostrils.

Sinclair lifted a small figurine from the table. She held it out for Patricia. "I'm going to put another glaze on it."

Patricia felt her face light up. "Oh, my God. It's Jack."

"I hope you like it."

Patricia held it carefully, amazed at the detail. Somehow Sinclair had captured his spirit along with his appearance, from his one brown ear to the way he cocked his head at her. His tail even stood at attention just as it always did.

"I love it." She couldn't believe how wonderful it was, how talented Sinclair was. "Thank you. It's…You're amazing."

Sinclair lowered her head. Compliments obviously embarrassed her a little. She took the figurine back and set it carefully on the table. "I'll put that glaze on tomorrow."

They stood in silence for a moment.

"It was really was nice of you." First the cake, now the figurine. Patricia felt like an ass. She hadn't given her anything.

"I like to see you smile." Sinclair switched off the arm lamp, leaving the room in near darkness. "And you inspire me."

A spark shot up Patricia's spine as she felt Sinclair reach past her to turn on a smaller lamp. She opened a glass door at the base of a shelf and removed a statue of a woman. As she brought it closer, Patricia stopped breathing.

"I did this after I first saw you." Sinclair placed the figure in Patricia's hand. "Your hair, it was so beautiful. You'd walked to your truck after we had spoken and you let your hair down, let it blow in the breeze."

Patricia's skin was on fire. She ran her fingers lightly over the statue, over the glossy auburn hair. She could almost feel that breeze once again. "It's beautiful." She didn't know what to say, what to think. "I wasn't very nice to you that day. Or even after that."

Sinclair only smiled a little. "It didn't matter. I could see who you were on the inside. And it was just as beautiful." She took the statue back and replaced it on the shelf. "I wasn't going to show you this. I didn't want you to think I was some creep."

"I don't think that. I could never think that."

Sinclair straightened, staring into her eyes. "I just think you're… incredible. And beautiful."

Patricia struggled to breathe. "Thank you."

No one had ever said such things to her. She'd written about these things, these very words. But actually hearing them…it made her head spin.

Sinclair gave her that smile again, only it was a little more shy this time. She looked down at her hands. "I'm a mess. Do you mind if I go take a quick shower?"

"Yes." The word came out before she could even think it.

Sinclair looked surprised. "Sorry?"

Patricia searched for something to say to explain away her impulse, but nothing came. Her blood slammed through her body. "I do mind." Her heart was speaking for her. She couldn't stop it. "I like you just like that."

Sinclair stared. "I'm covered in paint. In clay."

"I know. I know you've been working hard on something you made for me. I know it took you hours, and I know you put your blood, sweat, and tears into that little figurine."

She imagined Sinclair sitting at the table, hunched over, staring into the magnifier on the arm lamp. She imagined her working for hours to mold the perfect replica of Jack, a thin sheen of sweat covering her skin. She took a step toward her and Sinclair's body straightened with a large intake of breath. When the air was released, her chest shook. She looked *alive*, in every way possible. Each of her senses balancing on the edge of desire. Her skin was flushed, her breathing labored, her gaze intense and focused.

At the sight of her, Patricia felt her own senses sharpen, wanting desperately to experience all that was Sinclair. "I want to feel the dry clay on your hands, feel the paint on your fingertips. I want to smell your skin, taste the sweat on your neck. Please don't wash it off."

The air became thick and heavy, hard for Patricia to pull into her lungs. "Audrey," she whispered. It was the very first time she'd said her first name, aloud or to herself. She loved the way it sounded, the way it felt coming from her mouth.

Sinclair moved then. She came to her quickly, eyes ablaze. "Patricia," she said, reaching to touch her face.

A gasp of surprise and desire escaped just before Sinclair covered her mouth in a kiss. Then a moan at how deep and passionate the kiss was. Sinclair pushed into her, thrusting with her tongue. Patricia went limp, overcome with the stronger woman's power. She let Sinclair hold her up, let her kiss hard and deep. She wrapped her arms around her firm shoulders. Her toes curled at the raw feel of Sinclair's muscles.

"I want you," Sinclair said into her ear.

Patricia buried her face in her neck. She smelled and felt the working sweat of her. Warm and slightly metallic. Hot bleachers at a sunny ball game. She kissed her skin, needing to taste it. She bit, the tangy taste of her swimming through her blood.

"Then take me," she whispered, wanting nothing more.

"I'm afraid I'll scare you."

Patricia pulled back to look into her eyes. "Why?"

"Because I want you so bad, I'm aggressive. And—"

"Passionate?"

"I was going to say strong."

"You won't scare me." Patricia ran her fingers through Sinclair's short hair. She loved the look of her, the thick lips, sharp cheekbones, and burning ember eyes. She could stare at her for eternity. "In fact, the only thing that does scare me is the thought of you doing nothing. If you don't touch me…"

Sinclair kissed her. Hard and fierce. Her tongue plunged in and Patricia groaned, meeting it with her own for a long dance. She heard Sinclair groan as well and then she was lifted and carried backward. She clung to Sinclair as her stomach did flip-flops. Her back met the wall and Sinclair lowered her legs and attacked her neck with teeth and tongue. Patricia's knees sagged and she had to hold tight to keep from falling.

"I can't stand for much longer," she confessed, her entire being melting at a white-hot pace.

No one had ever taken her like this before. Not even Adams. No one had spoken such words and then backed them up with such passion. This was what she had dreamt about, written about. It was fiction. She closed her eyes and let out a yelp of pleasure as Sinclair sucked on her skin. No, it was better than fiction.

Using one hand, Sinclair fumbled with her jeans. Patricia tried to help but she was quickly jammed against the wall, hands pinned above her head. Hot cinnamon eyes baked into hers as a finger trailed down her face to her neck and below. The button to her jeans opened, along with the fly.

Sinclair lingered, tickling the skin just above her panties. "I want to look into your eyes as I touch you."

Her hand went lower then, slipping into Patricia's panties. Their eyes held until her fingers curved under and hit flesh.

"Oh, God." Patricia closed her eyes, it felt so good. She was so swollen and ready.

The fingers rubbed over and around, dipping lower to gather her excitement. "Open your eyes," Sinclair whispered. She stopped her hand.

Patricia did so, breath heaving out of her chest.

"Look at me," Sinclair softly insisted. Her hand started moving again, painfully slow.

Patricia moaned, wanting so badly to close her eyes. But every time she let her eyelids droop, Sinclair threatened to stop.

"Does it feel good?" Her fingers slid up and down, squeezing together against her clit.

"God, yes."

"Tell me."

Patricia sank lower, her knees buckling. But Sinclair stepped into her, holding her up by her center. The added pressure sent shock waves through her. And then Sinclair went farther, moving her fingers lower to thrust into her.

"Oh fuck! Oh God, I can't. It's so good." Her eyes wanted to roll back in her head. Sinclair was holding her up with her fingers. Fucking her tight and hard against the wall. "Oh, my God. Oh, my God." She couldn't stop saying it. She felt like she was being fucked alive with wonderfully burning fingers.

"Come," Sinclair said, watching her intently. "I want to watch your face." She worked her harder, longer, fingers curling against her tender and swallowing walls.

Patricia stared into her eyes, saw and felt the intensity. Never before had she felt so desired, so wanted or needed. Sinclair desired her, wanted her, needed her pleasure. And she wanted it too, not only for Sinclair but she wanted it *of* Sinclair.

"Audrey, I..." She tried to explain but she came instead. The orgasm overtook her, completely, slamming into her body and then madly clawing its way out. She lost all control, finally closing her eyes. She didn't even feel it when Sinclair released her hands. She just cried out, waved and convulsed, her hips fucking the fingers up deep inside. Noises came out of her, strange lengthy ones that she didn't recognize. Then, when everything stilled, she opened her eyes and found Sinclair watching her, her cheeks flushed with desire. Sinclair eased her fingers out and lifted her again.

"What are you doing?" Patricia wrapped her arms around Sinclair's shoulders, her legs around her waist.

"I'm taking you to the bedroom."

"Oh." Patricia grinned. Her face felt so relaxed that the smile seemed to just plant itself there, as if it were comfortable, snuggling down into a pillow. "So it will be my turn now?"

Sinclair didn't bother with the lights and suddenly Patricia felt herself being tossed onto the bed. She laughed but then stopped as

Sinclair stood and tore off her tank top. Patricia sat up and eased to the edge of the bed. She reached out for Sinclair's thick belt and tugged her closer. Sinclair sucked in an excited breath as Patricia unbuckled it. But as she started to unbutton her pants, Sinclair stopped her.

"Wait." She grabbed hold of Patricia's hands. She moved quickly to her closet and reemerged holding a box.

"What's that?" Patricia's brain was firing way behind her body.

"Something I ordered with you in mind," Sinclair said as she tore at the cardboard.

Patricia watched closely as the light spilled in from the streetlamp. She could see her own slickness reflecting off Sinclair's fingers as Sinclair tossed the box and unwrapped a clear-looking dildo.

"Ever used one?" Sinclair held it out for Patricia to inspect.

Patricia took it from her, noting its length and girth. She even noticed the glitter sparkles glinting inside. "Many times." She looked up at Sinclair. "In my books."

"Would you like to try it?"

"Right now?"

Sinclair gave her a crooked smile, the dimple working its magic. "Yes." She fingered the fly of her jeans. "I thought I could secure it in here."

The thought made Patricia's body flash with fire. Her clit seemed to twitch with need.

Sinclair dropped a tiny pack of lube on the bed and crawled on after it, slinking over to Patricia like a hungry, hunting cat. "I could lie on my back and you could ride me." She kissed her and her mouth felt so soft and hot.

"Okay," Patricia said, lost in the feel of her.

"Yeah?"

She pushed Sinclair back and rubbed her upper body with her free hand, amazed at her strength and then equally amazed at the softness of her breasts. She bent her head and kissed her nipples, causing Sinclair to hiss.

"You better hurry." Sinclair wrapped her hand in Patricia's hair. "Before I turn you over and take you."

Patricia laughed wickedly, knowing just how she felt. She handed the dildo back and watched as Sinclair eased it into her fly, buttoning her jeans up around it. "We should probably use a condom since I didn't get a chance to clean it." Sinclair pointed. "I have some in the nightstand."

Patricia crawled over and retrieved the small box. She felt nervous at the idea of being fucked by something other than fingers. She'd never been with a man and she'd never let anyone do this before. But she trusted Sinclair. She couldn't explain why, but she felt safe with her. On many different levels.

Sinclair rolled on the condom. Then she opened the packet of lube and rubbed it on. Patricia gazed in wonder as her hand went up and down the shaft, readying it just for her.

"Watching you do that really turns me on," she confessed.

Sinclair stopped, held the packet over the dildo, and squirted more on.

"Yeah? Why don't you take off your clothes and help me?"

Patricia eased off the bed and unbuttoned her shirt. Sinclair watched her, trailing one hand up to caress her own nipples. The lube glistened in the filtered light, encircling her areolas.

Patricia hurried, peeling off her bra and then pushing off her jeans and panties. Sinclair tensed, obviously aroused by the sight.

"Come here," she said.

Patricia slid back onto the bed and Sinclair's hand moved down to the dildo. She held it while Patricia stroked the lube on, up and down.

"Patricia, I want you so bad," she said. "I've never seen anyone so beautiful." Sinclair sat up on her elbows and stopped Patricia's hands. "I mean it."

Patricia didn't know what to say. A hot rush of blood made her cheeks tingle. "Okay."

"When I first saw you, I couldn't believe you were real, much less a cop. Detectives don't look like you. And if one ever did, she'd probably be married." Sinclair smiled. "And then when you spoke…"

Patricia rolled her eyes at the memory of her behavior. "Please. Don't remind me."

Sinclair laughed. "I wanted you even more."

"You did?"

"Yes." She stroked Patricia's arm in a way that sent shivers right through her. "All that fire and passion. All that seriousness and intelligence."

"I was a bitch."

"Whatever you want to call it."

Patricia laughed.

"I liked it." Sinclair's gaze was full of desire. "It was you." She sank back down fully to the bed. "And now I want to give you pleasure. In every way possible." Sinclair's hands meshed with Patricia's on the dildo, thoroughly encasing it with liquid silk. "Will you climb on now?"

Patricia stared down at their hands, then looked up into Sinclair's eyes, glad for the light floating in from the street. "Yes," she said softly.

Inhaling deeply, she straddled Sinclair just below the dildo.

"Take your time." Sinclair placed her hands on Patricia's hips.

Gazing down at her, Patricia took in her flexing torso and the soft movement of her breasts. She held herself higher. Sinclair gripped the base as Patricia eased herself on.

"Oh, oh God." Her voice was tight and throaty, as if the dildo were sinking up into her throat. "Oh, God," she said again, feeling it slide all the way in.

She closed her eyes, the pressure filling her up entirely. Slowly, she began to move, gyrating her hips back and forth.

"How does it feel?" Sinclair wanted to know.

"It burns." She opened her eyes.

"Go slow." Sinclair's fingertips traveled up to Patricia's breasts where they caressed and pinched lightly. "Just relax and it will burn real good."

Patricia's hips kicked involuntarily. She arched her back into Sinclair's hands. "Yes," she hissed. "It's feeling good now."

"Is it?" Sinclair tugged on her nipple.

"Oh, God yes." Her hips quickened even more. She felt so full. Full of molten pleasure. The dildo was shooting magma up into her, filling her entire body with sweet, sweet pleasure. "It burns so good. Really fucking good."

Sinclair took hold of Patricia's hand and brought it to her mouth. Patricia watched helplessly as she placed it on her bottom lip and licked it. Then she took a finger in and began to suck.

Patricia cried out, the feel of her hot, slick mouth too much to take.

Sinclair groaned, pulling her finger in and out, sucking it off. Then she moved her other hand down from Patricia's hip to her pussy. She pressed her thumb tight against her clit. Patricia jerked hard. Sinclair matched her hips to Patricia's rhythm, pushing up into her.

"Fuck, oh fuck." Patricia fucked like she'd never fucked before. The hot pressure, the hot mouth, the hot thumb. "Oh, God. Audrey."

Her eyes flew open and she came so violently she screamed. She rode and she fucked and she screamed. Gripping Sinclair's hands, fingers locked in midair, she bucked harder and harder and harder. The pleasure owned her. Every inch. She was a slave, doing as she was told. Her head was tilted back, the pleasure coming out in small screams. Yet her vagina was squeezing and pushing on the dildo, pressing pleasure out that way as well. She just kept thinking how full she was. So incredibly full.

Sinclair held her safe, letting her ride it out, watching in what could only be wonder. When Patricia finally slowed, her body began to shake. She could hardly breathe and every last muscle twitched.

"You okay?" Sinclair reached up to touch her face. She smiled so sweetly, Patricia melted into her hand.

"I've never been better," she said, almost in disbelief. Seeing Sinclair's eyes so full and shimmering, and feeling her unconditional passion and understanding, Patricia began to cry.

"Shh, it's okay, it's okay." Sinclair drew her down, wrapping warm, strong arms around her, and Patricia cried into her shoulder. She cried for the love she'd never had and always wanted. She cried for Sinclair, who seemed to offer all of it. And when she stopped crying, she stilled and closed her eyes.

She fell asleep feeling the one thing she'd never felt before... fulfilled.

CHAPTER TWENTY-FOUR

Liz couldn't take it anymore. It was early morning and the sun shone like it had no worries. She detested its happiness and seeming eagerness to burn through the morning cloud cover. How could the fucking sun shine like that when she was dead inside?

She stared at Patricia's house. The last time she'd been parked here it had been raining. She wished it would again. She climbed out of her Range Rover and headed for the door. Tyson's words kept replaying in her head. *Go make it right. Go make it right. Life is too short to push the one you love away.*

They'd been up most of the night talking. He'd confided in her in a way he never had before. He'd told her what he really thought. And something else had happened as well. She'd sat and listened. She learned that for years he hadn't approved of her lifestyle and her use and discarding of women. He didn't approve of men who behaved in such ways either. But for a long time he overlooked it, respecting her and his job too much to say anything.

Until Erin.

When Erin came along he relaxed a little, knowing true love had finally found Liz, regardless of the crazy way it had happened. "You can't control love," he'd said as they talked into the early hours. "It just is."

He thought Liz had done the wrong thing, trying to push Erin away just to keep her safe. That excuse wasn't good enough, according to her head of security.

"You don't push the one you love away, for any reason," he told her sternly. "Because if you do, sometimes they will actually go. And then there's no getting them back."

"I thought I was doing the right thing," she said.

"You were afraid."

"Of her getting hurt, yes." She'd had no idea what was going on. With Jay or anything else. All she had known for sure was that it was dangerous and she herself was going to get in way over her head.

"You were afraid of her," he said matter-of-factly. "You don't have to admit it to me, but you need to admit to yourself."

"How do you know so much?" All this time, and she'd had such insightful wisdom at her fingertips.

"I have a couple of fancy papers saying I know some psychology."

"No shit." She never knew this about him. The background check she'd run had included education, but she hadn't been interested. She was impressed enough with his size and articulation. "Tyson, why are you here, working for me?"

"Because being big and black pays a whole lot better when you're a bodyguard. I found that out real quick. But I didn't much care for it, and when I met Teresa I wanted something safer."

"So you found me."

He smiled. "Yes, ma'am. Who knew watching over a bunch of lesbians could be so dangerous?"

She'd laughed with him. It felt good to laugh, and then suddenly she was tired. She'd been up for over twenty-four hours again. He got her a glass of water and half a Xanax, telling her she needed to rest. Then he helped her to the bed, slipped off her boots, and covered her up.

"I'll lock everything up on my way out," he said. "And when you wake up, you go make things right with Ms. Erin."

Liz could only nod. She'd slept with her lover's name on her lips.

Erin.

Liz stared at the house. Patricia's front door seemed larger than it was the last time. It loomed over her, as taunting as the sun. She rang the doorbell and her heart rose to her throat. She was somewhat surprised by its determined beat.

A dog barked from the backyard. She waited to hear it barking from inside the house but it never did. She waited for what felt like an eternity and rang the bell again. Then suddenly her mind flashed with visions of Erin and Patricia in bed together. They were probably curled up and fast asleep from a long night of lovemaking.

Feeling sick, she hurried from the door. How could she have been so stupid? Of course they were together. She'd turned Erin away again and again. What did she expect? And Patricia had always been after Erin.

She nearly ran to her vehicle. When she climbed inside she noticed her hands were shaking. Tyson's words replayed in her head and she looked at herself in the rearview mirror.

"What if I'm too late, Tyson? What then?"

❖

Jack's claws click-clacked down the hallway as Erin stumbled out of bed. He ran into her room, tongue and tail wagging. She buried her face in his neck and could tell by the way he smelled, all warm and earthy, that he'd been outside.

"Did you hear the doorbell?" she asked. He cocked his head. "Of course you didn't, what am I thinking. You can't hear anything."

She made her way down the hallway, stretching as she walked. The slit of sunlight was piercing as she stared through the peephole. No one was there.

"Damn." She turned and headed back down the hallway. Suddenly she wondered where Patricia was. Pushing open her door, she quietly peered inside the master bedroom. The bed was made. Patricia had already come and gone, or she hadn't come at all.

Erin scoffed. Or maybe she came a lot.

She trudged back to her bed and collapsed. Jack accompanied her, digging his way under the covers. She tried to remember all the drinks she'd had the night before but couldn't.

Tonight, though, she thought, she'd go out for some real fun.

CHAPTER TWENTY-FIVE

Look, asshole, I told you I'm not into that." The man he'd picked up rose quickly from the bed, rubbing his neck.

"You haven't tried it." He sat up, his frustration turning to anger. He opened the nightstand drawer. "Take some more E."

"I don't need to try it." His latest, "Mickey," faced the wall and began yanking on his pants. "And I don't want any more E."

"Going to run home to your wife?" He popped the E himself.

Mickey whipped his head around. "Hey, fuck you, man."

He laughed. Mickey continued to dress. He eased up behind him. *Fuck me?* He reached down and pulled the long, thin leather belt from his pants. "No, Mickey, fuck you." He slung the belt over Mickey's head and pulled.

Mickey lost his footing, heels digging in the carpet, fingers digging at the belt.

"You like that? I told you, you would." He swept Mickey's feet out from under him and fixed the buckle tight, making a noose. After pushing Mickey down onto his stomach, he pulled harder, forcing Mickey's head back.

"Yeah, motherfucker. Feel it real good." His dick grew hard as he watched the veins start to pop out from under Mickey's skin.

This was what he loved.

He let go of the belt and tore at Mickey's pants. He had to have him. He had to be in him when his soul left his body. The pants wouldn't budge. He fumbled with the button, cursing. He turned Mickey over a little in order to better reach his fly. He was halfway down the row of buttons when Mickey threw back a hard elbow, knocking him nearly senseless. He fell onto his side and groaned, holding his busted lip. Hot blood poured onto his hand. Mickey crawled onto his knees, madly tearing at the belt. His eyes were wild with fear. When he couldn't get it loose, he stood and ran from the room, pants sliding down his hips.

"Shit." He pushed himself up to his feet and stumbled after him. His tooth felt loose and his mouth was full of rust-tasting blood. He heard Mickey milling around in the kitchen.

When he caught sight of him he was standing by the unused stove, trying to cut the belt with an old pair of scissors. His face was purple, his breathing labored. His hands worked hurriedly as his eyes bulged with every beat of his heart.

"That's my favorite belt." He smiled wickedly, knowing his teeth were blood red. He loved the fear he saw in Mickey's eyes. The only thing better was the dimming of life he often saw in the pupils.

Mickey cut harder, panicked. When he finally cut through, he gasped and hurled the belt to the side. He coughed, one hand holding his neck as if his head might topple off. He looked like he wanted to run but couldn't.

"Where are you going, faggot? We were just getting started." He had him backed against the counter.

Mickey took a few steps, pacing, an animal in a cage. He looked around for some other weapon or maybe a phone. All the things that should be in a kitchen.

"I don't live here," he explained. "I just fuck here." He chuckled again, and spit some slimy blood from his mouth. He should've drugged the bastard better, loaded him up with more drinks. He should've known he wasn't into kink, all he'd done was talk about his kids all evening long.

"What are you going to do now? Call out for your wife, yell for your mama?"

Mickey lunged at him with the scissors.

He laughed. "Go ahead." He narrowed his eyes. "But you'll only get one cut. So you better make it good."

Mickey stepped back, fear shaking his hand. Then suddenly his bloodshot eyes widened and he whipped his arm back and threw the scissors. The heavy metal flew through the air and slammed into his chest. He looked down at the worn black handles and couldn't see the blades. Mickey bolted past him as he pulled the scissors from just below his left nipple. He winced in pain, shocked. He heard the front door slam.

"Shit!"

Dropping the scissors, he ran for the door. He pulled it open and started after him, but it was useless. Mickey was long gone and probably well on his way to tell. He held his chest and reentered the house. The wound was deep but he didn't think it was life threatening. Blood from his hands smeared the walls as he made his way down the hall.

He fumbled through the linen cabinet near the master bedroom and found an old washcloth. Head spinning, he went back into the kitchen and picked up the scissors. He cut a small piece from the cloth and shoved it as hard as he could into the wound. He cried out in pain and white orbs floated in his vision.

His cell phone rang. It was his wife. Breathing deep, he focused and answered.

"Where are you?" She sounded annoyed and bitchy.

"I told you I'm working today." He tried to sound upbeat and patient.

"Liar!"

He cringed and slowly walked back to the bedroom.

"Your boss has been calling here all day looking for you. I just got home and heard the messages. So, where the hell are you?"

He sat on the bed and clutched his hair. "What did the messages say?"

"Where are you?" she continued as if she hadn't heard him. She always spoke to him that way. He hated it.

"I'm working. I'm just not in the office at the moment."

"You son of a bitch," she seethed. "You're out fucking around on me, aren't you?"

"No. Listen, babe, I'm not. I swear. Things are just bad at work. I'm trying to handle it. I love you."

"Bullshit." She was well beyond anger now. "The nice clothes, the fancy boxer briefs, the two-hundred-dollar haircuts...You're cheating. And let me tell you something, mister, when my father finds out, you're a dead man."

"Martha, honey, please. Just calm down."

"Don't even think about coming home. I'm throwing all your shit on the lawn right now. Then I'm going to change the locks."

"Will you just listen to me?" He never raised his voice at her and she fell silent for a moment. "I'm not cheating, I'm working." He spoke meekly, the harmless, devoted husband. That was how he'd always won her over. He smiled all the time, said what everyone wanted to hear. He had it down to a science.

"I know you're not working," she said, her voice laced with venom. "Because your boss fired you."

She hung up on him. He glared at the phone, pressing the button to dial home. The line was busy. He threw the phone and tore at his hair, then threw more shit around the room. His autographs flew off the walls, crashing to the floor. Signed baseballs thumped hard as he threw them. His life's collection, the one his wife wouldn't let him display at home. He hated it now, hated it all.

He marched into the bathroom and looked at himself in the mirror. His heart raced just above his oozing wound. It was all coming to an end. A man had run out on him, probably headed straight for the law. His job was gone, his boss finally realizing what he'd been doing. The bathroom light glinted off the chain hanging from his neck. He fingered the crucifix and knew what he had to do.

He had to bring it all to an end. His way.

And he had to hurry.

❖

"Please tell me he didn't die," Patricia said, running up to Gary. The hospital hallway was stark white and reflective, and she worried she would slide across the floor.

"No, he didn't die," her partner answered, sounding like he had a cold. "He woke up."

Patricia stopped dead. "You're kidding."

"No, I'm not kidding. I still can't believe it myself."

He smoothed down his tie and bounced a little on the balls of his feet. He coughed and cursed "Sally Trucker," then laughed. He was anxious, though crisply dressed as always. It was Saturday and she wondered if he'd gotten up and dressed that way instead of sleeping in and eating a bowl of Cheerios in front of cartoons as she often did.

"When did you find out?" The curtains to the victim's room window were closed. She couldn't see a thing.

"About forty minutes ago. I stopped by to check on him and he just opened his eyes and groaned at me."

"Did he say anything else?" Her heart continued to race. This was big news. The big break they needed. She closed her eyes and prayed for the victim to be aware enough to tell them something important.

"No, the doctors ran in and booted me out. Where have you been?"

Patricia looked away and willed herself not to flush. "I've been going over the case."

She had been. But she left out that she'd done it while lying in Sinclair's arms, after having made love all night and well into the day. She remembered discussing Jay and the fact that Jay was left-handed. The gunshot wound was to the right temple and the gun had been found in her right hand. It didn't sit well with her, and Sinclair had agreed.

"Nat's secretary has been calling the station," Gary told her as his beeper went off. "Wonder what the good doctor wants." All the autopsies were complete and the labs concluded.

Patricia's cell phone rang. It was the coroner's office. "Speak of the devil," she said, picking up.

Nat sounded relieved. "Detective Henderson, hello. Sorry to bother you on a Saturday."

"What's up?"

"Well, at the request of Ms. Elizabeth Adams, I did a second autopsy on Jay Adams. My colleague did the first, but Ms. Adams insisted I do a second myself."

"Really?"

He cleared his throat. "Elizabeth was also kind enough to make a very generous donation to my body research farm."

Patricia tried not to think about the secluded acres of land where Nat placed donated bodies in different areas to study decomposition. Offering him money for his research had been a smart move on Adams's part.

"Anyway," he continued, "I found something interesting. There was no gunshot residue on Jay's hands. And I reevaluated her clothes and there was none there either."

Patricia squeezed her fist. She knew it. And goddamn it, they should've tested for residue but no one had listened. They had wanted a suicide finding.

"What about the first autopsy? Didn't you scrub her hands?"

"Yes, and that would have removed any GSR, but with such a close-range shot, her shirt sleeve certainly would have tested positive."

"She was also left-handed," Patricia added.

"Was she now?" He seemed to think for a long moment. "The powder burns on her temple aren't making sense either. The spray is spread too wide, as if the gun were fired a few inches from her head. Most suicides press the gun up to the head, making direct contact." He sighed. "In taking all this into consideration, I'm going to change the cause of death from suicide to homicide. I thought you should know."

"Thank you, Doctor." Patricia closed her phone. She was so worked up she was nauseous. And yet her voice came out just as calm as could be. "Jay Adams was murdered."

Gary started to reply but a handful of medical staff exited the room of John Doe. He stopped the doctor with the plethora of eyeglasses around his neck.

"How is he?"

"We'll run some tests to find out for certain. To make sure there is no permanent damage. But I'm satisfied that he'll keep improving now."

"Can we see him?" Patricia asked.

The doctor glanced back into the room through the open door where a nurse was adjusting his pillow. "Make it quick."

Gary held on to Patricia's arm, halting her. "Do we know who he is?" he asked the doctor.

"Juan Ricardo Stanford."

Patricia's legs felt weak. "J.R.?"

They hurried into the room. Patricia went right for the bed. She held a bandaged hand and waited for the eyes to open. When they did, she knew for sure.

"J.R.?"

"Henderson," he croaked. "Am I in…hell?"

"Not yet," she said, trying to offer him a comforting smile.

"Feels like it." His eyes rolled left to right, taking in the room slowly.

She wiped away a tear. Seeing him like this was heart wrenching. His head was still wrapped, but his face was mostly free of bandage. He looked so helpless. And somebody had tried to beat the life from him. It terrified her. "J.R., do you know what happened to you?"

He licked his dry lips. His voice was hoarse from the tube that had been down his throat.

"A man." He raised his other bandaged hand to his neck. "He kept strangling me."

"Did you know him?" Gary asked.

"We're trying to find him, J.R.," Patricia explained. "We think he's the serial murderer."

"Said his name…was Jim. But I knew he was lying." His breath whistled as he inhaled and exhaled. "Met him at Boom. Said he was into erotic strangulation and did I want to try it? Told him no, but I went with him because he was strange. Mac had asked me to sniff around. She's going to blame herself," he said. "But it was my fault. I should have been more careful."

"What happened?" Gary asked.

"I don't remember much after I got in his car. He said we had to meet someone."

"Do you know who?"

"No. Don't remember."

"Who was this guy, J.R.? Do you know anything that can help us?"

He licked his lips as he wheezed. "Yeah. Before I got in his car, I memorized his license plate."

❖

Erin danced. She moved her body and willed her mind to float away up into the lights. When it remained firmly within her skull, she walked back to the bar.

"Hit me again, Chastity," she slurred, slapping the counter.

Chastity eyed her wearily. "*No más, señorita*. You've had more than enough."

"Come on, be a pal." Erin smiled but Chastity didn't budge.

"I already called a pal and she should be here any second."

"Who?" Erin felt her face contort in anger.

"Adams."

Erin laughed. "Go ahead, she won't give a fuck."

She stormed back out onto the dance floor. She didn't need anyone to baby-sit her. She was fine. What was wrong with wanting to get a little drunk and have some fun? She needed it, deserved it.

The door to the tiny lesbian bar opened, a cool breeze blowing in with it. Erin stopped and stared, as did all the other women.

"I don't believe this!" Erin marched up to the man standing there. "She sent you? She couldn't even come herself?" She stalked to the bar stool and grabbed her sweater. "Thanks a lot, Chastity." She brushed out the door. When she turned around, he was behind her, car keys in hand.

"I'm only going with you because I know I'm too drunk to drive."

He pressed the button on his keychain, unlocking the doors, and she climbed into his gold SUV. She sat sulking, arms crossed over her chest as he started the engine.

"I want to see her," she demanded.

"I don't think that's a good idea," Reggie said.

"Are you her whipping boy now?" Liz already had Tyson, now Reggie too? First he'd been hired to do the books, but then his accounting job had quickly led to script work. Could anyone tell Liz no?

He smiled. "No, I'm not her whipping boy."

"Well, I'm sorry she made you come and get me." She forced a smile back at him. "I'm fine, just a little tipsy."

"I see that."

She sat back and relaxed as the vehicle's quiet rhythm began to seep into her skin. Her eyes drifted closed and when she opened them again a voice on the radio was shouting with conviction, "Thou shalt not lie with mankind, as with womankind. It is abomination. For whosoever shall commit any of these abominations, even the souls that commit them shall be cut off from among their people."

"Jesus," she whispered as she grabbed her forehead. "What are we listening to?"

It had begun to rain and she watched as the wipers went back and forth. She thought back to the night a long time ago when Liz herself had come to Chastity's to get her. They'd ridden up into the mountains and Liz had confided in her. Erin started to tear up at the memory, but the alcohol had seemed to drain her dry. For the first time ever, no tears fell.

The preacher on the radio continued ranting. "Homosexuality is a sin. The greatest sin man can commit next to murder. Brothers and sisters, listen to me…"

"Can we please turn that shit off?" She was drunk, but not that drunk.

Reggie stared straight ahead. "No."

"Don't tell me you believe this stuff?"

He pulled into a short driveway and put the SUV in Park. They were at a modest older home in the historic district. She'd always wanted to live in this neighborhood, loving the nostalgia and the unique architecture of the homes.

Reggie continued to stare straight ahead. "It's a sin, Erin. An abomination. And you will go to hell along with all the other faggots."

She tried to focus her blurring vision. A chain swung from the rearview mirror. An elaborate gold crucifix was nestled among various wedding bands. Her stomach rose to her throat and her vision swayed with the chain, back and forth, back and forth, making her dizzy.

"Reggie." Her mind fired suddenly, making connections. "You don't really think that."

She fumbled for the door handle. The crucifix. She kept staring at it as if hypnotized. The wedding rings. Her mind fired images of deceased men discarded in the desert, dirty dry hands facing upward to the sky, pale bands of flesh around their left ring fingers. The Highway Murder victims were all missing their wedding bands. The recent victims both had crucifixes drawn on their backs. And Jay had one drawn on her hand.

"I don't think it, I know it." He pulled a gun and aimed it at her face.

The preacher continued, shouting, egging him on. "If a man also lie with mankind, as he lieth with a woman, both of them have committed an abomination. They shall surely be put to death. Their blood shall be upon them."

"Their blood shall be upon them," Reggie cried. His body shook and she could see that his lip was swollen and his skin unusually pale.

Reggie was a killer. And he was going to kill her. If he had found her, then he must've gotten to Liz.

"Where's Liz? Did you hurt her?" She choked on the words, terrified of the possibility.

"I don't need to hurt her. Killing you will do the job for me."

"Where is she?"

"I went to find her, but that big, black, scary bulldog of hers told me she was out searching for me." His eyes narrowed. "Then came the call about you. You were too drunk to drive, a dyke bouncer had said. At Chastity's. I overheard just enough before the bulldog tried to wrangle me up and keep me there."

Erin found the handle and shoved the door open. A gunshot rang out as she fell from the car. Pieces of glass sprinkled down on her head with the rain. She crawled to her feet, but Reggie had already rounded the car.

"You're all going to burn! All of you!" He tilted his head up to the sky, arms held out as if he were welcoming the rain. He laughed and opened his mouth, catching the falling silver drops. He licked his lips and looked as if he'd just taken communion.

"I'm doing the Lord a favor," he declared, pointing the gun at her. "Ridding the earth of evil."

She saw his face set in determination and she knew he was going to fire. He pointed it away from her at the last second, firing into the night instead.

She closed her eyes, feeling the cold rain, knowing the end was near. "I am love," she said. "We are all love."

"What did you say?"

She opened her eyes. "I love Liz. I love her. I even love you, Reggie."

"Shut up. You're a sinner. God's judgment shall rain down upon you."

"You love too, Reggie. I know you do." She had nothing to lose, and with every word she expected to hear and feel the pop of the gun. "Look at you." She pointed. "Your heart is bleeding."

His white shirt was wet and soaked through from the rain. A red stain was spreading out from under his heart.

"If your heart is bleeding, then I know you understand."

He looked down at the stain as if it were betraying him.

"That's what it's all about, Reggie. This life of ours. It's about love."

She saw the glint in his eyes and dove to the ground as he fired. She came up quick, hammering her fist into his balls. He cried out and doubled over in pain. She grabbed his dark hair and slammed her knee up into his face. He fell backward, the gun skidding across the concrete. She picked it up and stumbled away from him. Her head spun and she felt sick to her stomach, like she'd been kicked in the gut and tossed off a tall building. She retched a few times, her body contorted in pain, trying to rid itself of the evil Reggie represented.

Behind her a car door slammed. Calming, she sat back on the wet concrete, gun pointed at Reggie. She couldn't afford to look away.

"Erin!" Suddenly there were hands on her and someone was holding her tightly. "Oh, my God, Erin." Liz's face loomed into view.

Was this real or was she dying? Had one of Reggie's shots actually hit her? "Liz," she whispered, her vision tunneling.

"What happened?" Liz held her so tight and she was trembling. "I love you, I love you so much."

"You fucking bitch."

Liz stiffened and Erin saw Reggie standing over them. He didn't have a gun, but he had a baseball bat. The red stain had run all the way down to his waist. Long trails of blood hung from his lip and nose.

"You fucking dyke bitch. I should've killed every last faggot working for you. For God is almighty…"

He raised the bat and Erin fired. Once, twice, three times. Each bullet ripped into him and he jerked with the impact. She was about to fire a final shot when he collapsed.

Sirens wailed in the distance. Liz pulled her in tighter, crying. Erin sat in silence, dropped her hand, and let the gun fall from her grasp.

CHAPTER TWENTY-SIX

H i."
Erin opened her eyes. The light stung her irises but she knew the voice.

"How do you feel?" Liz was at the bedside, holding her hand.

Erin grimaced. "Hungover." Her head ached as she vaguely recalled being taken to a hospital. Then she remembered giving a statement and answering dozens of questions. She'd been exhausted afterward and she wondered how long she'd been asleep.

Liz smiled but then her face clouded over with seriousness. "I'm so glad you're okay."

Erin realized she was at Liz's house, back in their bed. Everything still seemed so surreal. Especially the whole thing with Reggie. "Am I dreaming?"

Liz stroked the back of her hand. "No."

"The whole thing with Reggie, then?"

Liz nodded.

"Damn. He killed Antwon and Joe?"

Liz held her eyes. "Yes. And a bunch of others. They're pretty sure he was the Highway Murderer."

Erin didn't speak. She didn't know what to say. Pieces of the puzzle had been flying around in her mind for a long time. It was strange to feel some of them settling into place. The crucifix. The wedding rings. The hatred.

"They found a lot of evidence at that house he took you to," Liz said. "He was a big closet case and a religious fanatic. He'd been killing men like him for a long time. And then he started in on my employees, to frame me. To ruin the business."

"He hated himself," Erin said. It all made sense. He killed what he couldn't stand in himself. "It's all so sad."

"Yes, it is."

Erin met her eyes. "He killed Jay, didn't he?"

"They think so."

"Why?"

"To get to me."

"How did he get to her, though?"

Liz's eyes clouded over in pain. "He met her at the studio late one night. I was sneaking her in there. They must've talked without my knowing."

"God." Erin squeezed her hand. "They don't think Jay had any involvement, do they?" *Please, no. Just please let it all be over.*

"No. Reggie kept a journal of his rantings and ravings. He said that he framed Jay by lifting a bloody tissue from the bathroom garbage."

"Jesus."

"I know."

"I'm so sorry." She couldn't believe what she was hearing.

"It's okay. At least we know." Liz squeezed Erin's hand in return. "At least I know where Jay is now. She's at peace and free of pain. You have no idea how good it makes me feel to know that."

Erin hugged her, held her tight. "Yes, yes she is. She's better now."

"I still dream about her, though. I dream that she's lost and I can't find her." Liz cried on her shoulder, her body thin and frail.

Erin held her until she calmed and when they eased apart, Erin gently examined Liz's hands. One finger on her right hand was still splinted and so were two others on her left. But the cuts had healed nicely. "Are you sure *I'm* not dreaming?"

Liz gave a small smile. "I'm sure."

Erin touched her short, dark hair. God, how she loved this woman. She'd been through so much, yet she was still there, still alive and trying. Many would have given up or run away. But not Liz. Erin thought again how grateful she was that Liz was alive. An image of Reggie looming over them with a baseball bat flashed behind her eyes.

"Why were you there? At Reggie's. I mean, did you know?"

Liz patted her hands, her expression one of concern. "The past couple of months I've noticed some changes with the books at the studio. Money started coming up missing. So I started investigating and it all kept pointing to Reggie. I tried to question him but the more I did, the faster he ran. I hired a private investigator and found out that he had the money in some personal offshore accounts."

"So you were there to confront him?"

"Yes. I wanted my money and I was afraid he was going to leave the country. He nearly bankrupted the studio, which I now believe he was trying to sabotage all along. My P.I. found him at this house he was supposed to be renting out. He was using it as a fuck pad instead, something his wife knew nothing about."

"Were you the one who called the cops?" She could remember the sirens.

Liz smiled. "My ankle bracelet did. But Patricia already knew. They'd got his license plate from one of your former colleagues. A J.R. somebody."

"J.R.?"

Liz grew serious. "He was the John Doe they found in the desert with Jay."

Erin covered her mouth in horror. "No! Is he okay?"

Liz nodded. "He's roughed up good, but he's awake and talking."

"Oh, my God, It's all my fault." Erin's head felt heavy and her body ached for J.R. The room started to spin. "I can't believe all this."

"I know." Liz held her softly. "There's something else I want to tell you."

Erin shook her head. "Really, Liz. I can't take any more. I—"

"I want you to come home for good."

Erin blinked, startled. "You do?"

"Yes."

Erin reached up and touched Liz's face. She still looked so wounded and pained. But her eyes had a familiar spark in them. She was surviving, somehow, someway.

"Are you sure?"

"I am."

"I can't take another rejection, Liz. It will kill me."

Liz leaned in and kissed her softly. Her eyes were full of tears. "I know. I'm so sorry."

"Why did you? Why did you push me away?" Erin's voice shook and tears fell onto her cheeks. She wiped at them hurriedly, upset at herself for crying. She was supposed to be stronger than that now. Nothing was supposed to get to her anymore. She inhaled deeply as Liz tried to explain.

"Because I knew this whole thing with Jay was going to go bad. I didn't want you involved. I was protecting you."

Erin stared at her, waiting. She knew there was more, needed to hear more.

Liz sighed. "And I was scared of you."

"Why?"

"Because you make me feel, Erin McKenzie. And for so long I haven't felt at all. You scare the shit out of me sometimes. The way you make me feel inside."

"It's a bad thing?"

"No, it's not a bad thing. It's a good thing. But I'm not used to it. And when Jay came back, I really did start to worry for your safety. And that really scared me. I didn't like those feelings of worry and anxiousness. I didn't want to care so much about anything or anyone. You make me feel, Erin. And I'm just not very good at it."

Erin watched her, knowing she was serious. Liz had changed the past couple of months. Her insides were finally showing on the outside. She wasn't some strong, cocky, self-involved woman. She was fragile and sensitive and kind. She was vulnerable.

Human.

And Erin realized she was too. And that was how they both needed to be. The tears fell freely then, and she let them.

"Well, do you think you'll get better at it?"

Liz looked deep into her eyes. "I'm going to try."

"How hard?"

Liz kissed her, so gentle and soft. "As hard as I can."

"Promise?"

Liz met her lips again. "I promise."

Erin wrapped her arms around her neck. "Okay."

Liz smiled. "I love you."

"I love you too."

"I want to take you away and marry you."

"I would like that very much. But…" Erin placed a finger on Liz's lips. "Not yet. Not right away. We need more practice first."

Liz was silent for a moment. "I came for you, early in the morning. To Patricia's."

"You did?"

"Yes. I wanted to ask you to come home. To tell you that I couldn't live another moment without you."

"Oh." She could vaguely recall checking the door.

"I should've done it sooner, should've never let you go, but Tyson said maybe in the end it was a good thing. That way I had to work out my feelings and get to the root of the problem. So when I ask you back now, it's for all the right reasons. Because I'm ready."

"Tyson told you all that? Wow. He's quite a guy."

"You have no idea." Liz's eyes filled with what could only be love, the edges softening. "I'm giving him a piece of the club. He's been a good employee and an even better friend. He deserves it."

"I think that's nice." Erin stroked the dark circles under her eyes, wishing she could erase them with her fingertips.

"He's going to manage it while I focus on the studio. And on you."

They kissed again, softly. Erin pulled her tighter. She felt so wonderful and alive and promising. Liz was there in her arms feeling and smelling so good. Erin moaned, her body reacting regardless of the fatigue and dizziness.

"Come back to me," Liz whispered. "I love you."

Erin answered with a kiss, this one deeper. She searched with her tongue and Liz responded with her own. It was gentle, tentative. Two lovers finding their way back.

"I'm here," Erin said, breaking away to tug softly on Liz's lower lip. "You have me."

Liz groaned and pressed her back onto the bed. She positioned herself on her side and ran her hand up and down Erin's abdomen.

"I want to feel you," she said, blue eyes ablaze.

Erin caught her hand and kissed the splinted finger. "You'll hurt yourself."

Liz tore the splint away and tossed it over her shoulder. She bent the finger. "I'll hurt worse if I don't." She ran her hand down under Erin's panties.

Erin gasped and turned on her side. "Okay, but only if I get to touch you too."

She ran her hand over Liz's hip and unbuttoned her jeans. Liz didn't object and Erin watched as her pupils widened with desire. She gasped again as she found wet waiting flesh. "Oh, baby," she whispered.

Liz's eyelids fluttered in response. She moved her fingers and Erin jerked, already so swollen and needy. "Yes," Liz whispered back. "Come with me."

They stroked one another, hands slick with arousal. They squeezed and milked, pulling and tugging at one another, their flesh flooding with pleasure. They locked eyes, hands moving furiously.

"I love you," Liz said.

"I love you," Erin whispered.

"Come with me," Liz commanded, eyes fluttering closed.

Erin's body jerked hard, the orgasm invading. "Always," she said, slipping into oblivion. "Always."

CHAPTER TWENTY-SEVEN

"I come bearing gifts," Patricia said with a smile. She held out the pie box as proof.

"Well, in that case…" Sinclair held the door and stepped aside to let Patricia enter. Jack took the cue and ran into the apartment, tail wagging. Sinclair chuckled and eyed the pie.

"Lucky I thought to stop and get it, you might not have let me in otherwise."

Sinclair took the box from her, kicked the door closed and tugged her in for a kiss. "Mmm, you're all the pie I need."

Patricia laughed. "Likewise."

"Unless," Sinclair said playfully, "you brought me another one of your books. I would gladly accept that as your fee for entry."

"I'll remember that." Patricia's skin heated. Sinclair had only recently discovered her lesbian fiction pseudonym and the half dozen or so books. She'd taken a few home and even had Patricia read to her from them in bed. She was by far Patricia's biggest fan.

Sinclair nibbled on her neck, then spun around to place the box on the counter. She opened it and raised a playful eyebrow. "Key lime?"

"Uh-huh."

Sinclair groaned. "You evil woman."

Patricia looked her up and down, loving the threadbare white undershirt she had on, along with the blue cotton sleep pants. She wanted to run her tongue along the V-neck of the shirt and taste the remnants of the soap she'd just washed herself with. Patricia loved her like this, all freshly scrubbed and cozy in her nightclothes. She couldn't wait to get her out of them.

"I feel the same about you," She said.

"Are you saying you want a piece?" Sinclair carried the box farther into the kitchen.

Patricia grinned. "More than anything."

Sinclair laughed. "Okay then." She fished out a cake knife and cut.

Patricia readied plates and forks and stood next to her, biting her shoulder. She loved Tuesdays and Wednesdays. Almost more than she loved Mondays and the weekends. Tuesdays and Wednesdays were the nights she spent at Audrey's. She loved coming into her home, inhaling the scent of her apartment and snuggling down into her soft sheets. She couldn't get enough of her.

Sinclair had said the same about staying at her place.

"How was your day?" Patricia asked.

"Not bad." Sinclair lifted a Key lime coated finger and Patricia eagerly sucked it. "How was yours?" she asked Patricia, barely able to do so.

Patricia held her finger between her teeth. She waited until she saw the cinnamon eyes spark with desire. Then she plucked the finger out and kissed it. "It was good."

"Yeah?"

"Uh-huh. We tied up the De Maro and Gillette cases. And Jay's is also closed."

Sinclair placed the pie on the plates and closed the box. "Who would've thought? Reggie Lengal. Mild-mannered guy with an average income. Caucasian. Middle-aged. Who would've thought he was a closeted gay and religious freak? Did I mention a serial killer too?"

"Are you really going to say I told you so?"

"I don't have to. You had a feeling the cases were related all along."

"A feeling was all I had. I wished I'd had more. You're the one who said it was a gay male and that the other killings were sexually motivated."

They took their plates and sat on the couch. Sinclair fed her a bite of pie. "It's over now. We were both right and our bosses are still slugging it out."

Patricia chewed, loving the soft tartness. "They always will." She forked out a bite and fed Sinclair. "How many men do you think Reggie actually killed?"

Sinclair swallowed. "Honestly? I think he started years ago. He had a sick fetish to go along with his homosexual feelings. He liked erotic strangulation and one time he took it a little too far."

"That was all it took," Patricia said. "Then he couldn't get enough."

"And he used his religious beliefs and guilt to feed his need to kill."

Patricia agreed. They'd found dozens of journals full of Bible scripture, hand-drawn crucifixes, and fantasies about sex and killing. Reggie Lengal had been a sick, sick man. She thought of the victims and their families.

"I feel bad for all those widows. All those women left without husbands. And now they find out their husbands were secretly gay on top of everything else."

"Yes, that has to be hard."

"At least we were able to give them the wedding rings back. For whatever they were worth."

The sat in silence and ate another bite of pie.

"How's your friend Erin doing?" Sinclair asked.

"Good. Liz has been cleared, her charges dropped, and they're working on some issues."

"So things are going good?"

Patricia leaned in and kissed a graham cracker crust crumb from her lip. "Yes."

"I hope it works out," Sinclair said.

"I think it will." They kissed again. "Liz has finally grown up and Erin truly loves her."

"After all they've been through, they deserve happiness," Sinclair said.

"Mmm. I don't think anything else could possibly happen to them."

Sinclair set their plates on the coffee table. She held Patricia's face and kissed her again.

"Let's hope nothing does."

EPILOGUE

Baby, somebody's buzzing at the gate," Erin said as Liz bit on her collarbone. They'd just emerged from the shower, their bodies coated with slick moisture.

"It's probably just the limo driver." Liz held Erin closer, fingers already strumming her clit.

Erin clung to her shoulders. "Don't you think you should go let him in? Our flight leaves soon."

They were finally taking that oft-postponed trip to the Caribbean. Liz had surprised her with the news, promising only love and some much-needed rest.

"I wanted to have you one more time first," Liz groaned. Reluctantly she backed away and pressed on the keypad.

"Drive in and wait," she commanded into the speaker. Then she came back and tackled Erin, pushing her onto the bed. "Now, where was I?" She lowered herself, tongue trailing downward.

Erin clung to her short, wet locks. "Liz," she hissed.

"I fucking love the taste of you." Liz flicked her tongue and Erin arched up into her.

The doorbell rang. Liz continued, flicking faster. Erin bucked up into her.

"Yes, fuck my face, baby," Liz insisted.

Erin clung to her hair, crying out.

The doorbell rang again.

Erin came, thrusting hard, holding Liz's face to her.

"Yes," Liz gasped, sucking the last of the orgasm out of her.

"Liz. Oh, Liz." Erin stilled, chest heaving.

Liz licked her one last time, hard and slow, and grinned. "That was good."

Again the doorbell rang. The dogs had entered the house and were going nuts.

"God damn it!" Liz stood. "Is he deaf?"

She threw on a robe and stormed down the hall. Erin hurried after her, envisioning the many different ways she would insult the idiot driver. "Be nice," she called out.

Liz grinned. "Of course."

She shooed the dogs and threw open the door. Her body went rigid. Erin came up next to her. She gasped.

The woman standing there appeared nervous. She ran a hand over her short, dark hair. Her glacier blue eyes looked just as shocked as Liz's. "Are you...Elizabeth Adams?"

"Yes." Liz cleared her throat. Slowly, as if she hardly dared voice her question, she asked, "Who are you?"

"I'm looking for Jay Adams." The stranger looked down at the papers in her hand. "I found her name, but it led to you."

"Who are you?" Liz asked again. Her voice seemed haunted.

"I'm...I'm her daughter."

About the Author

Born in North Carolina, Ronica Black now lives in the desert Southwest where she pursues writing as well as many other forms of creativity. Drawing, photography, and outdoor sports are a few of her other sources of entertainment. She also relishes being an aunt and she thoroughly enjoys the time spent with family and friends.

Ronica Black also has short story selections in *Erotic Interludes* 2, 3 and 5 from Bold Strokes Books and *Ultimate Lesbian Erotica 2005* from Alyson Books

For more info, visit Ronica's Web site at www.ronicablack.com.

Books Available From Bold Strokes Books

Deeper by Ronica Black. Former homicide detective Erin McKenzie and her fiancée Elizabeth Adams couldn't be happier—until the not-so-distant past comes knocking at the door. (978-1-60282-006-7)

The Lonely Hearts Club by Radclyffe. Take three friends, add two ex-lovers and several new ones, and the result is a recipe for explosive rivalries and incendiary romance. (978-1-60282-005-0)

Venus Besieged by Andrews & Austin. Teague Richfield heads for Sedona and the sensual arms of psychic astrologer Callie Rivers for a much-needed romantic reunion. (978-1-60282-004-3)

Branded Ann by Merry Shannon. Pirate Branded Ann raids a merchant vessel to obtain a treasure map and gets more than she bargained for with the widow Violet. (978-1-60282-003-6)

American Goth by JD Glass. Trapped by an unsuspected inheritance and guided only by the guardian who holds the secret to her future, Samantha Cray fights to fulfill her destiny. (978-1-60282-002-9)

Learning Curve by Rachel Spangler. Ashton Clarke is perfectly content with her life until she meets the intriguing Professor Carrie Fletcher, who isn't looking for a relationship with anyone. (978-1-60282-001-2)

Place of Exile by Rose Beecham. Sheriff's detective Jude Devine struggles with ghosts of her past and an ex-lover who still haunts her dreams. (978-1-933110-98-1)

Fully Involved by Erin Dutton. A love that has smoldered for years ignites when two women and one little boy come together in the aftermath of tragedy. (978-1-933110-99-8)

Heart 2 Heart by Julie Cannon. Suffering from a devastating personal loss, Kyle Bain meets Lane Connor, and the chance for happiness suddenly seems possible. (978-1-60282-000-5)

Queens of Tristaine by Cate Culpepper. When a deadly plague stalks the Amazons of Tristaine, two warrior lovers must return to the place of their nightmares to find a cure. (978-1-933110-97-4)

The Crown of Valencia by Catherine Friend. Ex-lovers can really mess up your life…even, as Kate discovers, if they've traveled back to the eleventh century! (978-1-933110-96-7)

Mine by Georgia Beers. What happens when you've already given your heart and love finds you again? Courtney McAllister is about to find out. (978-1-933110-95-0)

House of Clouds by KI Thompson. A sweeping saga of an impassioned romance between a Northern spy and a Southern sympathizer, set amidst the upheaval of a nation under siege. (978-1-933110-94-3)

Winds of Fortune by Radclyffe. Provincetown local Deo Camara agrees to rehab Dr. Bonita Burgoyne's historic home, but she never said anything about mending her heart. (978-1-933110-93-6)

Focus of Desire by Kim Baldwin. Isabel Sterling is surprised when she wins a photography contest, but no more than photographer Natasha Kashnikova. Their promo tour becomes a ticket to romance. (978-1-933110-92-9)

Blind Leap by Diane and Jacob Anderson-Minshall. A Golden Gate Bridge suicide becomes suspect when a filmmaker's camera shows a different story. Yoshi Yakamota and the Blind Eye Detective Agency uncover evidence that could be worth killing for. (978-1-933110-91-2)

Wall of Silence, 2nd ed. by Gabrielle Goldsby. Life takes a dangerous turn when jaded police detective Foster Everett meets Riley Medeiros, a woman who isn't afraid to discover the truth no matter the cost. (978-1-933110-90-5)

Mistress of the Runes by Andrews & Austin. Passion ignites between two women with ties to ancient secrets, contemporary mysteries, and a shared quest for the meaning of life. (978-1-933110-89-9)

Vulture's Kiss by Justine Saracen. Archeologist Valerie Foret, heir to a terrifying task, returns in a powerful desert adventure set in Egypt and Jerusalem. (978-1-933110-87-5)

Sheridan's Fate by Gun Brooke. A dynamic, erotic romance between physiotherapist Lark Mitchell and businesswoman Sheridan Ward set in the scorching hot days and humid, steamy nights of San Antonio. (978-1-933110-88-2)

Rising Storm by JLee Meyer. The sequel to *First Instinct* takes our heroines on a dangerous journey instead of the honeymoon they'd planned. (978-1-933110-86-8)

Not Single Enough by Grace Lennox. A funny, sexy modern romance about two lonely women who bond over the unexpected and fall in love along the way. (978-1-933110-85-1)

Such a Pretty Face by Gabrielle Goldsby. A sexy, sometimes humorous, sometimes biting contemporary romance that gently exposes the damage to heart and soul when we fail to look beneath the surface for what truly matters. (978-1-933110-84-4)

Second Season by Ali Vali. A romance set in New Orleans amidst betrayal, Hurricane Katrina, and the new beginnings hardship and heartbreak sometimes make possible. (978-1-933110-83-7)

Hearts Aflame by Ronica Black. A poignant, erotic romance between a hard-driving businesswoman and a solitary vet. Packed with adventure and set in the harsh beauty of the Arizona countryside. (978-1-933110-82-0)

Red Light by JD Glass. Tori forges her path as an EMT in the New York City 911 system while discovering what matters most to herself and the woman she loves. (978-1-933110-81-3)

Honor Under Siege by Radclyffe. Secret Service agent Cameron Roberts struggles to protect her lover while searching for a traitor who just may be another woman with a claim on her heart. (978-1-933110-80-6)

Dark Valentine by Jennifer Fulton. Danger and desire fuel a high-stakes cat-and-mouse game when an attorney and an endangered witness team up to thwart a killer. (978-1-933110-79-0)

Sequestered Hearts by Erin Dutton. A popular artist suddenly goes into seclusion, a reluctant reporter wants to know why, and a heart locked away yearns to be set free. (978-1-933110-78-3)

Erotic Interludes 5: Road Games, ed. by Radclyffe and Stacia Seaman. Adventure, "sport," and sex on the road—hot stories of travel adventures and games of seduction. (978-1-933110-77-6)

The Spanish Pearl by Catherine Friend. On a trip to Spain, Kate Vincent is accidentally transported back in time—an epic saga spiced with humor, lust, and danger. (978-1-933110-76-9)

Lady Knight by L-J Baker. Loyalty and honor clash with love and ambition in a medieval world of magic when female knight Riannon meets Lady Eleanor. (978-1-933110-75-2)

Dark Dreamer by Jennifer Fulton. Best-selling horror author Rowe Devlin falls under the spell of psychic Phoebe Temple. A Dark Vista romance. (978-1-933110-74-5)

Come and Get Me by Julie Cannon. Elliott Foster isn't used to pursuing women, but alluring attorney Lauren Collier makes her change her mind. (978-1-933110-73-8)

Blind Curves by Diane and Jacob Anderson-Minshall. Private eye Yoshi Yakamota comes to the aid of her ex-lover Velvet Erickson in the first Blind Eye mystery. (978-1-933110-72-1)

Dynasty of Rogues by Jane Fletcher. It's hate at first sight for Ranger Riki Sadiq and her new patrol corporal, Tanya Coppelli—except for their undeniable attraction. (978-1-933110-71-4)

Running With the Wind by Nell Stark. Sailing instructor Corrie Marsten has signed off on love until she meets Quinn Davies—one woman she can't ignore. (978-1-933110-70-7)